THE RULEBREAKER

PIPER RAYNE

Cover Design: Buerosued

1st Line Editor: Joy Editing

2nd Line Editor: My Brother's Editor

Proofreader: Olivia Winston

ABOUT THE RULEBREAKER

I'm the coach's daughter. Falling for one of my father's players was never the plan.

Especially not Decker Davis.

Chicago Colts third baseman.
Dependable. Steady. The guy everyone trusts.
And the man who's spent years keeping his distance—
especially from me.

We have history. The kind that ten years and a thousand miles can't touch.
So, this time, I promised myself I'd be smarter.
No getting attached. No blurred lines. And definitely, no falling.

He broke every last one within the first week.

Because Decker doesn't just show up for me. He shows up for my daughter.
Because he fits into our lives like he was always meant to be there.
Because he looks at me like I was never something he wanted to lose.

And suddenly, the walls I've spent years building don't feel nearly as solid as they used to.

But if I let him in, I'm not just risking my heart—I'm risking hers too… and I already know what losing him costs.

I won't let my daughter pay that price.

The Rulebreaker

CHAPTER
ONE

Dr. Nora Bell

I open the door to my private waiting area and know right away that I'm going to earn my hourly fee with these two.

They're sitting on opposite sides of the room—heads down, thumbs moving, not a single inch of eye contact between them.

Famous clients aren't my usual lane. But these two were referred to me by my college friend Paisley Petrov. She's hard to say no to. Plus, there's a reason a person goes into a career in psychology—we want to help people.

Still, seeing them in person hits different. The headlines didn't accurately convey the distance between them.

"You can come in now." I step out of the doorway to give them room to move past me.

They stand at the exact same time.

Pocket their phones at the exact same time.

Cross the room at the exact same time.

At the doorway, they hesitate. Both gesture for the other to go first.

They're polite and courteous, and so tightly wound I can feel it in my own chest.

The dark blond with tattoos and shoulders with sharp edges steps through first. The darker-haired one follows with a small nod that says *I'm the nice one, but don't dig too deep into me.*

They each take a seat on the couch as though we're preparing for a boxing match—opposite ends, bodies angled away.

I don't reach for my notebook. It's our first session. People talk less when they feel observed.

I fold my hands over my knee and offer my kindest smile. "So, what brings you two here?"

Neither of them even glance in my direction.

And the longer the silence stretches, the more obvious it becomes—this isn't about what happened last season. It's about something rooted deeper from years earlier.

I keep my expression smooth, but inside, I'm already texting Paisley in my head.

You owe me a big European vacation for this one.

CHAPTER
TWO

Penelope

I double check that I have everything in my bag.

Sunscreen, snacks, water bottle.

As if the one thing Hazel doesn't have in her life might've slipped in there unnoticed.

"Are you missing something?" Leighton's voice is easy and nonchalant, pretending I don't look like a frantic mom searching for her kid's brown bag lunch before a field trip.

"No. Just checking something." I stop rummaging because if a father for Hazel has somehow wedged himself inside my tote, he's not going to pop out saying, "Finally, you found me. I was suffocating between your wallet and dispensable birth control."

"Thank goodness we have such good weather today." She sips her coffee, eyes tracking the kids as they run from station to station across the playground. "I remember hating field days when I was younger. I never excelled at any of the events."

While her gaze bounces between the kids, mine analyzes the parents in attendance. There's no denying I'm alone on the island of single parenthood at this school.

"Do most kids here have two parents?"

Leighton pauses mid-sip and glances my way.

I might as well be wearing a flashing neon sign that says, *Feeling insecure. My daughter comes from a one-parent household.*

Her gaze flicks across the field. "I guess so. I never noticed."

And why would she? She has Hayes—currently running the tug-of-war station as though he popped out of the birth canal with a whistle in his mouth. Most of the stations are being run by one of the parents, while the second half of the pairing is on the sidelines like Leighton and me. My dad was supposed to run a station for us, but he's running late.

"It's a small school." Her hand lands on my shoulder. "I'm sure there are other single parents. We're just not noticing."

"I'm looking. And I'm coming up empty."

Leighton's mouth twists. "Me too. But it's not a big deal. You do not need a man. You've raised Hazel to be an amazing young girl."

I know I have. But school events have a way of poking at the bruise I pretend doesn't exist.

It was easier when it was just the two of us in our little routine and world back in Philly. Now all these flyers come home with big blaring letters that spell out Parents or Guardians. Parents/Guardians volunteer to read. Parents/Guardians show up for the art exhibit. Parents/Guardians sign up for fundraisers.

There is only parent, singular, in our household.

And Hazel is old enough now to notice that most kids get to hold a second hand.

Leighton's voice softens. "Seriously, Penelope. I can see you spiraling."

"It's just…" I scan the sidelines, gauging how many adults are close enough to overhear.

When your dad is the Chicago Colts manager and you're standing next to the starting catcher's wife, people tend to develop a sudden interest in whatever you're saying. Thankfully, today most of them are more invested in watching their kids chase bubbles and sack race each other in the grass.

"It's just… I haven't dated since Hazel was born."

Leighton's brows lift.

Heat creeps up the back of my neck. "It's not like I haven't… you know. But I never wanted anything serious. I never wanted anything that could take time away from Hazel."

I'm not lying. I'm just… sanding down the sharp edges.

Because there's one man I would've let inside our two-person bubble had he been ready to be welcomed in.

"Hazel seems to like Decker a lot." Leighton waggles her eyebrows.

I groan. Of course she says his name.

I'm pretty sure everyone in our little group knows there's history between us. Unfortunately, they also know I have history with his twin brother—which is a whole other story I'd prefer to leave buried under the same rock I've been living under for the last decade.

"Well, that's never going to happen."

"Why not? He's always looking at you."

I bark a humorless laugh. "He is not. And even if he was, that means nothing. He's good with Hazel because he's good with kids. Look how he is with all of yours. He's just… a good guy."

Leighton exhales as though she's trying not to push too hard. Then her expression shifts, attention snagging over my shoulder. A slow smile tugs at her mouth. "It's as if we manifested him."

My stomach drops before I even turn my head.

CHAPTER
THREE

Penelope

Decker walks through the gate, tall and loose-limbed, as always. He doesn't look toward me. Instead, he goes straight to Hayes. They talk, heads bent as if they're discussing something serious.

"Did you ask him to come?" There's a note of teasing to Leighton's voice.

"No." I'm trying to read Decker and Hayes's lips across the yard as though I'm the lead detective in a spy movie.

Hayes points toward one of the stations, directing Decker where to go, but he doesn't get two steps before Hazel and Monroe intercept him. They fling themselves at his legs as if he's the latest Disney star, and he says something that makes them scurry off, giggling.

Hazel darts away to do whatever he asked, then looks back over her shoulder. Her eyes find mine. And she smiles so wide it tugs something inside my chest that I don't want tugged.

This is trouble.

Not because Decker is here. Not even because he's smiling at my kid as though she means something to him.

Because Hazel is happy to see him.

Because I *know* that look.

It's the same look she had when she was a year old and I thought I'd finally gotten rid of all the pacifiers—packaged them for the fairy, had a ceremony, the whole production—until I checked her room before bed and found her sucking on one as if she'd been hiding her favorite thing for weeks.

"Why can't you and Decker..." Leighton keeps her voice low. "You have a past, and I know he has feelings for you."

I don't want to have this conversation here, where the school moms could turn us into an instant rumor. Plus, I need to shut it down, otherwise I'll allow hope to sink in. Her words open a door I'm not brave enough to walk through.

"It's... there's a lot of history. A friendship."

Leighton frowns. "A friendship where you haven't talked in almost a decade?"

"Didn't you just marry your best friend's brother this offseason who you'd had a crush on since high school?"

She chuckles. "Touché."

I shrug. "It's complicated."

Her mouth quirks. "Isn't it always?"

I could entertain Leighton's version, where Decker's been pining for me all this time, where he's stalked my social media the way I've stalked his, where his silence was never from indifference but based on fear. But what good would that do?

Hope is a risk I stopped indulging in the moment Hazel's father made it clear he didn't want any part in her life.

"I think it's time I start dating." The words feel strange on my tongue.

"Yes!" Leighton's brown eyes brighten. "Decker."

Her cheeky smile does something treacherous to me—

makes me want to believe there could be something there, makes me want to turn around and catch him staring.

But he's had years. Years to make a move. Years to change what we are.

And he hasn't.

I shake my head. "Hate to burst that bubble, but Decker and I aren't meant for each other."

Decker heads to the hula hoop station and swaps in for a dad who looks thrilled to pass the job onto someone else. Except the dad doesn't leave. Rather, he stays and chats with Decker, probably about the Colts.

Leighton holds up her hands. "Okay. We'll take Decker off the table. Why now?"

My gaze tracks Hazel as she skips between stations. She's come out of her shell this year, but she still clings to Monroe, still lets Monroe talk for her more than she should.

"For Hazel. For myself. I'm ready to have a partner in my life." My throat tightens. "I know it'll take a while to find someone. There aren't exactly a line of men raising their hands begging to be a dad."

Leighton snorts. "Sure there are. Lots of guys are into hot moms."

I roll my eyes, but I can't help the smile that tugs at my mouth. "You're always so complimentary."

"I'm speaking the truth."

Hazel runs toward the hula hoop station, grabs one, and tries to swivel her hips. The hoop immediately drops to the ground, and her shoulders bend inward.

Decker steps in, gentle and easy, showing her how to start the motion. Then he does it himself, his hips moving with ridiculous confidence, the hoop spinning as though he's a professional circus act.

Leighton makes an impressed noise. "Who would've thought Decker had moves like that?"

Little does she know.

"Of course, Callie did say he can dance."

"His mom taught him." I keep my voice casual.

I don't add that I taught him a little too.

Another mom approaches Leighton, pulling her into a quick conversation about snacks or sign-up sheets or something equally earth-shattering in the elementary school world, and I keep my gaze trained anywhere but on Decker.

Except I stray.

I keep catching myself watching him with Hazel, and a version of my life flashes in my head like a cruel movie trailer designed to torture me. I hate myself for wanting it.

I wouldn't have Hazel if I had Decker. The blink of a relationship that gave me her is the best thing that ever happened to me.

When Hazel was three, she asked me what the word *daddy* meant as though it was a brand name. Like it was something we could grab from the grocery store if we walked down the right aisle.

Should I have a daddy, Mommy?

I remember the way I smiled through the tightness in my throat.

As if the universe is trying to be funny, my dad finally arrives and gives me a wave before beelining straight for Decker. My dad shakes his hand, claps him on the back, then crouches as Hazel sprints into his arms.

Decker gives Hazel a high five, gives Hayes a quick wave, and then—finally—turns, but instead of leaving the school grounds, he walks toward me. My heart rate spikes hard and fast, my body reacting before my brain can remind me he means nothing to us.

Decker stops right in front of the painted line on the pavement, as if it's the proverbial line in the sand he won't cross. "Hey." He runs a hand through his dark hair.

"Hi." I think my attempt to keep a casual smile is failing. It feels awkward and forced.

"Your dad was running late and sent an SOS text to a few of us." His thumb jerks toward the street. "I was the closest."

"You didn't have to come."

He shrugs, but there's a hesitation—one beat too long, as if he wants to say something else.

This is what it's like between us now. We're strangers who happen to share a history instead of two people who used to be able to read each other from across a room.

What happened to him being my person?

To him looking at me?

"I gotta get back." His gaze flicks past me, toward the field. "Workout."

"Yeah. Of course." My voice comes out even and polite. Thank goodness. "Thanks for coming."

He gives me a short chuckle and glances toward my dad. "I'd prefer not to get benched."

My chest tightens painfully. There's the reason he's here.

He's here for my dad.

Not for Hazel.

And definitely not for me.

"I'll see you." Decker is already stepping away, lifting his hand in a small wave.

"Bye."

Leighton returns to my side with an apologetic look. "Sorry. Lincoln's friend's mom, Jade, cornered me."

I nod, but my stomach has already turned into a rotten knot I can't swallow past.

A future with Decker Davis is not on the table.

"Penelope." Leighton waves her hand in front of my face. "What did I miss?"

"It's time for me to start dating," I blurt. "Right? Like... I need to do it for me and for Hazel."

Leighton rocks back a little, then her expression softens. "I'm always going to vote for what's good for you. It just... can be hard to execute."

"So, what?" I yank my phone out of my bag. "Do I download a dating app? Is that the best option these days?"

Her eyebrows crinkle. "I'm not sure. It's been a few years since I was on them." She confiscates my phone. "But how about you let me fix you up? There's a doctor at the hospital. He's sweet, funny... real."

"The dating apps feel safer." I don't totally believe it, but it does mean fewer expectations from the people around me.

Leighton snorts. "Have you ever been on one?"

"No."

She clutches my phone. "Then let's do this the old-fashioned way first. If there's no connection, we'll move to the apps."

I inhale a cleansing breath, summoning my courage. "Okay." She hands me back my phone, and I slide it into my bag, trying to ignore my tightening chest. "I just think it's time to move on."

Leighton's gaze flicks past my shoulder.

I don't look. I'm sure Decker is long gone.

I just wish she didn't have that look on her face—the one that says she's already mourning the happily-ever-after she crafted in her head between Decker and me.

"I work tomorrow." Her voice drops lower. "I'll ask him if he's seeing anyone."

"Perfect." I force a smile, even as my insides twist.

Decker Davis is never going to make a move.

So it's time I put Hazel and our future first.

CHAPTER
FOUR

Decker

"Again, Davis." Mercer hits another ball to my right, cognizant of my recent weak spot.

My jaw locks, and I force my face to remain blank.

A ball hit down the line used to be my ESPN highlight reel play, but lately, I'm lucky if I get a glove on it. That's the part that twists—not the miss itself, but the fact that it no longer shocks him.

"Another off day, Davis?" Mercer teases.

I inhale a deep breath, keeping my temper in check. Me crashing out on a coach during practice isn't going to help. My control is the only thing I still own right now.

"Hit it again." I'm determined to leave here without Mercer thinking I'm not the man for the job anymore.

"Goldie, man, give it a rest. Maybe go take a break. Give Harkins a chance to take a few," Easton says to me.

I look over my shoulder, seeing the guy I'm pretty sure upper management wants in my spot. It hasn't been said out loud, but it doesn't need to be. If I'm not doing my job, they might as well take a chance with a rookie like Harkins who comes with a lot less overhead than me.

"Again, Mercer." My teeth grind as I clench my jaw.

"Sorry, Harkins, you should've taken that deal with the Trojans." Easton laughs and fields a ball from Mercer as clean as if it was routine, but everyone knows Mercer isn't hitting dribblers to us. He's hammering them fast and in every weak spot we possess.

Easton throws it to first and smiles a cocky grin to himself, making the play look effortless. His game is never off. Meanwhile, it looks as if it's my first day in the majors and there's a hole in my glove. I can already hear upper management in my head.

Davis has lost a step.

Davis isn't the same.

Davis is expendable.

Mercer hits me another one, and he's nice enough to hit it so I don't have to break for it. I scoop it up and throw it to first, but my throw is low, and it gets by Donnelly. Sharp heat crawls behind my eyes. The kind that makes my vision narrow. I don't miss throws. That's the whole point of my job.

"Fuck!" I shout, and Mercer rests the bat on his shoulder, waiting for me to finish my little tantrum. The field goes quiet for half a second as some of the guys pretend not to watch.

"Take a break, Davis," Mercer says, and there's no point in arguing.

Cursing on the field isn't unusual for any player other than me. I don't ever let my frustration get the better of me. I'm the steady one. The reliable one. The guy who doesn't unravel. So why does it feel as though I'm coming apart at the seams over the one name I haven't said out loud in three years? Three years. Long enough that I thought I'd buried it. Apparently not deeply enough.

She's the reason so many teams passed on me in the draft,

picked up other players who weren't nearly as good as me. So why am I surprised that when she comes back into my world, my focus is shit? Penelope's not to blame, but my chest tightens as I remember the way it felt to watch my name slide down the board. I remember swallowing my pride, pretending it didn't matter. Pretending she didn't matter.

I got good at that. I'm still doing it.

I go to the dugout, away from prying eyes, and throw my mitt against the wall. The crack echoes off the concrete, and I stand there, chest heaving, hating myself for feeling like I need something to hit. I am not this guy. Except lately, I keep having to remind myself of that.

"Another shit day?" Foster walks out of the locker room and into the dugout.

The sight of my twin brother still hits me sometimes—the strange, quiet miracle that we ended up on the same team, in the same city, as if the universe decided to give us one more shot at getting it right.

"Shouldn't you be in the bullpen?" I throw myself on the bench, acting like a fucking baby instead of the grown adult I am. I might as well just spiral all the way down to the center of the earth.

"I'm on my way." He studies me for a beat, then looks out onto the field. "Harkins getting to you?"

I glance at the field and witness Harkins fall to his chest to catch a ball down the line. He rises to his feet and still gets the throw to Donnelly. Not as clean and quick, but still showing the job could be his.

Foster's cleats tap along the cement, coming closer. There was a time when him coming closer meant an argument was about to ensue, but now he sits beside me. Ever since Callie came into his life, he's changed. That chip on his shoulder, all his anger, it dissolves more every day.

"You have no idea what they're thinking."

We watch Harkins take the reps that should be mine. Reps I'm supposed to own. Reps I've earned.

"Your bat will keep you in, and you're way too fucking good. You have how many Gold Gloves?"

I frown. "Everyone has their day when the game gets too fast, too much. I'm on the downward slope."

He laughs. "You were a late bloomer, remember? That gives you a few extra years."

"I don't think it works like that." Contracts only care about numbers.

"Are you going to address the real problem?" Foster asks, arms crossed, tattoos stretched taut across his forearms.

My stomach drops. I keep my eyes on the field as though it can save me because if I look at him right now, he'll see everything I've been pretending isn't lying just under the surface.

We could be in the *Guinness Book of World Records* for how different two fraternal twins can be. But even with our differences, he has everything I want in life. A woman who looks at him with stars in her eyes. A daughter who reaches for him like a safety blanket. The problem is I want all of that, and I want it with the one woman I can't ever have.

"That they're not even talking about signing me again? Saying they'll see how the season plays out." Talking about my spot on the roster is the easy answer. The safe topic. The one that doesn't blow up everything we've been trying to rebuild.

Foster doesn't say anything for a minute. "You should've let me hit Dad."

"I don't think it's a black mark on my record. Certainly not the reason they aren't re-signing me. Besides, it felt too good." It had been years in the making, the dreams I had of hitting him.

He chuckles. "Another reason you should've let me be the one to hit him."

"He's our father." I can't deny the soft spot I still have for a man who never loved me. He only ever saw value in Foster and Foster's abilities. I hate that I still crave anything from him. Even just a *sorry for leaving you behind.* He doesn't deserve any time in my head.

"Bullshit, he wasn't a proper father to either of us."

All the shit that went down last year with our dad brought my brother and me closer, so I can't hate him, but I also know that while I was raised by our mom, Foster endured our dad's punishing demands that he be perfect on the mound. Somehow, he survived it. And I'm the one falling apart now.

"But this shit? What's happening out there? Sulking because they're not discussing re-signing you isn't going to help. You know you're better than what you're showing out there. So, whatever is in that head of yours, straighten it out."

His words land like a shove. Not cruel, but honesty we never gave each other before.

Foster rises to his feet but stands next to me for a moment, eyes still on me. His pause is loaded, and I'm not sure how long we can both ignore my real problem.

"What?"

"Is it her?" He arches an eyebrow.

My throat tightens. I don't answer because I don't want to start our newfound relationship with a lie. If I say it out loud, it'll be another problem standing between us.

"Penelope?" he clarifies, and just her name leaving his lips tightens that hold inside me.

My fingers curl around the edge of the bench. I keep my face neutral, the way I've learned to whenever she's around. "Give me some credit. I think I can narrow it down to who you're talking about."

A cocky smile crosses his lips. "You didn't answer the question. I know you guys and—"

"No. We were over a long time ago." Three years ago, to be exact. Probably before then if I'm honest with myself.

His eyebrows raise. "You sure?"

I tip my head and stare him dead in the eye because I want this reconciliation with my brother. It's something I've wanted for years but thought was a pipe dream. Only one thing could demolish it, and that's if I decide to go after Penelope Ripley.

"Yeah. It's the contract and playing for a team who might not see my worth." I hate how easy the lie comes out, but God knows I've practiced it long enough.

Foster's gaze stays on me longer than a beat, an uncomfortable tension running between us. He doesn't buy it. Or maybe he's choosing not to push. Either way, my chest feels as tight as though I'm holding my breath underwater.

Because although he's moved on with Callie, more in love with her than I could've imagined, Penelope is a reminder of what destroyed our relationship all those years ago. Although she's entwined in our friend group, me entertaining rekindling a relationship with her would damage what Foster and I are building.

"Okay then. I better get going before they don't want both Davis brothers next year." He walks away from the dugout but pauses right in front of me on the field. "Stop being a fucking jackoff and get your ass out on the field. You're better than Harkins. Show them." He smiles, then jogs toward the bullpen.

I fight a smile because this—whatever this is between us now—is something I didn't know I was still allowed to want. It's proof we didn't miss our chance. That we can still have a future together as brothers.

Until I realize how badly I wish things could be different. Like Penelope Ripley not being the one thing I want that could cost me everything I've just gotten back.

CHAPTER
FIVE

Penelope

I should have homeschooled Hazel.

That's the thought I can't shake while standing outside St. Pat's, clutching my coffee and trying to look like I belong.

I might be standing here with a fresh coffee from the preferred café and wearing similar clothes as the other moms, but none of them have even glanced in my direction. Sure, Hazel and I are new here, but I thought the whole mean girl group was a myth. Or something that ended when the yearbooks were signed senior year. Of course I've never been included in one, mostly because I always keep to myself.

I'd been looking for a new house for Hazel and me, needing to get out of my dad's place before Hazel thought ice cream was a staple breakfast food. Leighton couldn't stop talking about St. Pat's, and it felt like fate when a nearby, not-so-perfect house came up on the market. The house is older than I wanted and needs a lot more work than I have the skills for, but it's close to the school.

Since I really want to help ease Hazel into this transition and allow her to find herself, I figured starting somewhere where she knows some of the kids was a better option than her not knowing anyone.

But I never thought I'd have this hard of a time with the moms.

Then they all turn my way, and I offer a soft smile and start to lift my hand in a friendly wave. But none of them even crack a smile back. God, when did this turn into high school all over again?

It's then I realize they aren't looking at me. They're looking past me.

As discreetly as I can, I glance over my shoulder to see what might be grabbing their attention.

Suppose it should've been obvious. Leighton told me that she was working today.

Hayes jogs across the residential street and slows, pressing something on his watch, before he looks up and gives me the first smile I've gotten in this small school entryway.

"Penelope." He catches his breath as he walks toward me.

"Cutting it close, Hayes," one of the moms says, tapping the watch on her wrist.

Hayes gives her a small nod and tight smile as he stops next to me. "I thought for sure I was going to be late. Got caught up at practice."

"Oh, I thought you were out on a run."

He chuckles. "I was. Have to make sure I don't have two kids crying for me on the school steps."

"You guys can always call me. I'm happy to watch them for you. Hazel would love it."

He nods and smiles. "Thank you. We'll probably take you up on that. But Lincoln has a playdate with two friends today, and you do not want three ten-year-old boys running around your new house, believe me." He pushes up to sit on the concrete ledge. "I'm happy to take Hazel too."

The other moms have somehow opened their little circle into a horseshoe so they can all watch Hayes.

"No, you have a full plate. How about I take Monroe?"

He laughs and rocks his head back. I can understand his appeal. Hayes is attractive and a genuinely nice guy. It's not like I want to date him. One reason of course is that he's taken, and I absolutely love his wife. The other reason I'm in the process of trying to delete out of my brain.

He shakes his head at me. "Look at us, trying to give the other one a break."

The bell rings, which gives us about five minutes before the kids rush out.

Hayes pushes himself off the ledge. "Your time to help us out will come, I'm sure. We'll be in Texas soon and then Atlanta. But you probably know that."

I nod. "Your schedule is posted on the fridge. Hazel likes to follow her grandpa, plus he always brings her stuffies from the cities he visits. She's getting older, so now she's asking for specific things."

He chuckles. "Am I going to be fighting your dad for a Texas longhorn and a right whale stuffed animal?" My shocked expression must give me away. "Leighton and I apologize." He places his hand over his heart. "Our Monroe has never found a list she didn't want to check everything off of."

"I think it's cute they have something to share. And I'd tell my dad to pick up two, but I have a feeling you want to buy them for her."

He's already nodding before I finish. "It's kind of our bonding thing. This time of the year is hard enough, and it helps a little. Leighton and I are trying to schedule some days out just us and one of them." He shrugs. "So, it's hard."

The doors of the school open, and we get interrupted by kids pouring out of the school.

Monroe and Hazel are the first of our crew, both of them running toward us.

Monroe clings to Hayes.

Hazel lingers and hugs me around my middle, but there's no tight squeeze. When I look at her face to try to decipher if it was a bad day, she's staring at Hayes and Monroe.

I watch Hayes lift Monroe, and she wraps her legs around his waist as though it's the most instinctive thing in the world, and something quiet and complicated moves through my chest—because I want that for Hazel so badly it almost looks like anger from the outside.

"Tell me one good thing from today," Hayes says to her.

Monroe stares at the blue sky.

"She got picked to bring someone special on Friday," Hazel interjects, and I run my hand over her long braid. She sounds super excited for her friend.

Monroe's lips tip down. "You can't come."

Hayes's eyes close for a moment, and his mouth twists. "I'm sorry. Maybe I can talk to the teacher. Swap days with someone."

Monroe squirms, and he lets her down. "It's okay." She turns to Hazel. "This is what happens with them."

Hayes and I share a look of confusion, as Monroe's comment is kind of cryptic, as though the two of them have been discussing something.

"Let's swap," Hazel says. "I'll take Friday. My mom can come." She looks at me, and I nod.

Monroe's mouth twists. "It's okay. You don't understand how busy their schedule is."

"Monroe, don't you mean *my* schedule?" Hayes has clearly picked up on the words they and them, as I have.

"All of you… but anyway, Hazel has news too." She motions at Hazel, trying to shift the attention to her friend.

"Do tell," Hayes says, crossing his arms, waiting.

Hazel's gaze falls to the ground, and she shuffles her feet. "I'm entering the end-of-the-year talent show."

My eyes widen, and I try to tamp down my surprise. This is a very out-of-the-box thing for Hazel. She's quiet, reserved, and doesn't like any kind of spotlight on her. "Oh, that's awesome, sweetie."

"There's one problem." Monroe cringes, but when Hazel glances over, she smacks on an encouraging smile. "But she totally has it."

Hazel's shoulders slip as if she's already doubting herself. "I have to hula hoop." Her voice is small and unsure.

My mind travels back to field day a few weeks ago when she struggled to get the hula hoop going and to move her hips properly.

"Oh, why did you choose that?" I regret my question immediately when Hazel's lips tip down even farther.

"Everything else was taken. And you don't have a dog, so…" Monroe shrugs.

"I shouldn't do it. It's a bad idea." Hazel shakes her head.

"No!" Hayes and I say at the same time.

I squat down, placing my coffee at my feet. "It's a great idea. So, you just have to hula hoop?"

"Mrs. McConnell said that I could probably do some tricks and have fun with it."

"Tricks?" I ask, my throat closing the more I think about her up there on that stage and the hula hoop not spinning, let alone her pulling off a trick.

I'm not exactly known for my coordination or ability to pick up new things easily. And if she takes after me, then this might be rougher than we think.

"Yeah, we're gonna look some stuff up. Can she come over, Hayes?" Monroe stares up at him, eyes wide and pleading.

Hayes glances at me, silently asking for my permission. "Um…"

Before I can answer, Lincoln strolls over, two of his friends flanked on either side of him.

"Hazel… the hula hoop, huh?" Lincoln nods as though he's impressed.

Hazel looks at all three boys then gives them a small nod.

"Boys." There's a warning in Hayes's voice that says be nice, otherwise there will be consequences.

"We told her at recess that she needs to find someone to help her," Lincoln says. "And not you. You're not flexible."

Hayes's eyes narrow. "I'm a catcher. I'm the most flexible player on the field."

"We saw Decker Davis at field day. He beat everyone with the hula hoop, longest spin. Too bad you can't get him to teach you, Hazel," a brown-haired boy to Lincoln's left says.

I feel Hayes look at me from the corner of his eye. I keep my face perfectly neutral, the way I've gotten very good at doing whenever that name comes up—which is more often than I'd like in his city, his circle, in the life I've built so carefully around the one person I can't seem to get away from.

"Boys, this is Penelope Ripley, daughter of the manager of the Colts." Hayes motions toward me.

The boys don't seem surprised, so I'm guessing either Lincoln or Monroe told them who Hazel's grandfather is.

"Oh, that's right," the brown-haired boy says, stepping forward. "I'm Bodhi Hensley. My dad is the right wing for the Falcons."

I nod. "Nice to meet you. I heard you went here."

"I'm Micah. My dad is just a lawyer, nothing fun," the other little boy says, waving.

"Don't complain. You at least have one." Lincoln eyes Hazel.

Again, she turns toward me. I give her what I hope looks like a steady smile.

"Okay." Hayes claps his hands together. "Let's get this playdate started."

I give him a thankful look.

"Wait, can Hazel come?" Monroe asks.

"Um…" Hayes looks at me again.

"Please, Mom." Hazel's pleading eyes grab hold of the mom guilt I've been drowning in lately.

"Okay." I bend down and hug her. "I'll get you for dinner, okay?"

She nods, and I hold her a beat longer than necessary, my nose in her hair because most days now, the hugs are more for me than for her.

"Thanks, Hayes."

"Believe me, you made today easier by adding a friend for Monroe." He holds out his hand for Hazel.

Holding Hazel's hand in one and Monroe's in the other, Hayes and the boys lead the way to cross the street with the crossing guard and head to their house.

I watch until they disappear around the corner. The quiet that comes after feels louder than it should. The other moms have already filtered away, leaving me alone with my cold coffee by my feet.

I pull out my phone and type a message to Leighton. I need to ask if she's talked to her doctor friend from work yet. Because I've been putting this off long enough, and seeing Hazel watch Monroe and Hayes today makes my plan feel a lot more urgent.

CHAPTER
SIX

Decker

I shut my door and jog down the last steps of the concrete staircase on the side of the condo building. The security gate creaks as I push it open and let it shut after me. I glance over my shoulder to see another cardboard sign posted on the security gate. The Dugout is written in girly script, and a bunch of small notes are stuck on it with whatever the diamond girls have handy. Gum, mostly.

I don't bother taking it down and throwing it in the trash can. If I do, a new one will be in its place tomorrow.

I stopped counting the notes after the third week. They're just women trying to get through the one door that keeps them out. Meanwhile, Penelope Ripley hasn't needed a door in years.

It's odd to me that the diamond girls put so much effort into contacting us. We're just like any other guy they'd meet at a bar. Sure, we play professional baseball, but I'm pretty sure they don't understand the life nor schedule we live. Then again, I remind myself they're probably not looking for a boyfriend, more like a one-night hookup.

I never thought I'd be that guy. For a long time, I was the other Davis twin—the one nobody was watching, the one no scout or coach was driving twelve hours to mold into something. The one who had to figure it out alone.

From the stories they tell, Hayes and Easton were stars of their high school and college teams. They knew they'd go pro from a young age. My dad had Foster down south to make damn sure he'd go pro, leaving me in the dust to play rec ball. The comparison between us twins carved something out of me back then. Foster beat me in everything, and I let it mean more than it should have.

But his words from the dugout the other day ring true. I've been awarded four Gold Gloves in my career. I've proved my worth, so why am I having the yips now—when it actually matters?

It's no surprise Jagger called me to a meeting. Agents want to meet with their players when they're messing up during a contract year. The press says Foster coming back has changed me, but that's not it. I love my brother and couldn't be happier that we're mending our fences after being torn apart most of our lives. Hell, I'm not even going after the one woman I'll always love in an effort to preserve my relationship with my brother. If that doesn't say something about who I'm choosing, I don't know what does.

The pancake restaurant Jagger is known to meet all his clients at isn't very busy since it's midday during a work week. There's still a guy behind the glass making pancakes into the shapes requested by the guests though. One of the waitresses must recognize me because she points toward the far-right corner of the restaurant where Jagger sits in a booth for two.

His tie is thrown over his shoulder, his reading glasses on, his thumbs moving over his phone screen with the focus of a man brokering a million-dollar deal. He glances at his watch when I approach.

"I'm on time."

He smiles. "Early actually. Which is why I love you, Decker." He turns off his phone and sets it on the table face down.

I slide into the other side of the booth and wait.

He laughs and shakes his head. "It always amazes me."

I nod, annoyance coiling around me like a snake. The laugh. The way I walked in. Something about Foster and me being nothing alike. I've heard it a hundred times. I'm done with everyone comparing me to my brother. Sure, I have the favorable reputation, and maybe that's why I hate it. Foster isn't a bad guy. He made the most of who brought him up, and if anything, I'd say we're swapping personalities more every day.

Jagger stares at me long and hard, but I don't stir or fidget. "I wish I had better news."

A sigh escapes me. "I figured."

"They're not budging."

The waitress comes by, and I'm thankful I can take the time to tamp down my anger at a team I thought I'd proved my worth to long ago.

"Hey, Heidi. The usual please, and I've been told to request a lily this time. If it's not too much for Eric."

The smiling blonde shakes her head. "He's done them before."

Jagger nods and smiles. "Thanks. She's into a flower theme lately. Begging Quinn to redo her room."

Jagger and the waitress talk a little more about his daughter, who always gives him the pancake shape she wants him to ask for.

"You're up." Jagger pulls me from my thoughts about what city I might end up in next year.

"Egg whites, peppers, mushrooms, and avocado. Side of sourdough toast. Thank you." I hand Heidi the menu.

She leaves, and Jagger leans back in the booth.

"I get this isn't the news we were hoping for. I had hoped they'd make some promises or at least give me a little more assurance that you're their guy. But payroll is high. The DICs all went into arbitration this year, and the Colts granted them higher salaries. Thankfully they can't go free agent, but... Harkins isn't going to cost them what you do."

I shake my head.

"You're a smart guy, Deck. You get the way the game is played."

"The DICs are outfielders. And I'm not asking for more, just some security to stay with the team."

He sips his coffee and sets his mug down. "They're good players. We knew Drew was a big name when he was drafted. They aren't even the real problem. Harkins is. So far, Ripley doesn't want to play him. I know he has a soft spot for you." He eyes me over his mug again, bringing up the past I share with both the Ripleys—father *and* daughter. "Keep Harkins off the field, and I'm sure you'll get the contract you want at the end of the year, but it's my job to prepare you—and I want you to go free agent next year if the Colts don't take you."

"Free agency is like a bachelor auction, no thank you."

"Free agency is where the money is, and you're going to be in demand. Actually, Graham Sutter called me this morning, asked a few questions about you. They have a hole at third right now and think you're the guy to fill it."

"New York?"

Jagger nods with dollar signs in his eyes. It's probably giving him a hard-on thinking about the contract. They have the money to pay well for free agency.

"Yeah, but I'm not looking for money. I want stability. I like Chicago. I like my teammates, and I like—"

"Penelope Ripley?"

I shake my head, but my jaw is tight, and Jagger sees it.

He always sees it. That's the thing about having an agent who's known you since you were twenty-two—there's no poker face left.

"We're not anything," I say.

"That's good, because if you pursue her, you can kiss not only Chicago goodbye but your relationship with your brother as well."

"I know that." There's a bite to my tone.

Heidi brings over our meals, and I welcome the distraction again.

"I'm not sure you do. I get that you two had something, and believe me, Quinn would kill me if I love-blocked any of my players, so you do you on what you think is best, but I'm warning you—you pick the girl, and there will be consequences. All that to say, I'll channel my wife for a moment—love is a hard thing to shove in a box and hope the lid stays closed. You're talking to a guy who let the one slip away and luckily won her heart again. It's my job to let you know what you're in danger of jeopardizing is all."

I unwrap my silverware from the paper napkin, set the napkin in my lap, and fork my eggs. "I know. I've been sitting on that box for three years, but lately, the lid's been slipping."

He does the same with his silverware and points his fork at me before he dives into his own meal. "That's why I love you—you're smart, you're conscientious, and you have your eye on the prize."

I drop my gaze to the plate so he can't see what his words did—because for the first time today, something cracked. Not anger. Not frustration. Just the plain, quiet truth that I'm tired of pretending this is manageable.

My longing for Penelope is the one thing I struggle to control, and the more she infiltrates my group and my team, the harder it is to act as if we're just friends. Maybe New York is where I should be.

"I don't even have to give you a set of rules like I did Foster and Hayes. You probably already have your own."

I do, but I don't list them.

"Just stick to the grind. Put the work in, and the results will come. Then you'll have options for next year, and since I'm your agent, we'll make sure whoever wants you will have to pay handsomely for you." He shoots me a toothy smile and digs into his meal.

As I put butter and jelly on my bread, I hope he's right, because I'm sacrificing a lot. Penelope has been mine in every way that mattered since before I knew what that meant, and I'm doing everything in my power to keep her out of the wreckage of a life I'm still trying to hold together.

CHAPTER
SEVEN

Dr. Nora Bell

I've learned to read the room before the door even closes.

Today the room says that they didn't speak in the car, and whoever suggested this topic can go dive off a short pier.

That would be me, for the record.

I settle into my chair and let the silence do its job for a moment. Outside, a city bus hisses past the window. Someone's dog barks twice. It's apparent we're still in the "I don't want to talk about my feelings" stage.

"Last week," I say, keeping my voice level, "we talked about starting at the beginning. I'd like to go back to the divorce. You were nine when your parents divorced, but you two were separated at eleven, correct?"

The word divorce lands in the room like a bulldozer dropped from the top of Willis Tower.

On the far end of the couch, Foster pulls at a loose thread on his sleeve. He's been doing that for three sessions now.

Decker has his eyes trained on the middle distance. He does that when he's deciding how much of himself to share.

"It wasn't a big thing," Foster says, which is the most telling sentence a person can offer me. "People get divorced."

"People do," I agree. "What happened afterward?"

Neither of them answers immediately. But something moves through the room. Not discomfort, but more like the feeling before a storm when the air pressure changes and everything gets very still.

"Dad took me south." Foster's voice is even and sounds like a practiced answer. "He had a connection down there. A coach who thought I had something worth developing."

I turn my attention to Decker. He's barely nodding, as though he still can't stomach hearing this chapter of their story.

"So you were separated," I say. "Not just across town, but across states?"

"Yeah." Foster shifts in his seat.

"How did you stay in contact?"

Decker shifts, an echo of the same movements his twin just made. "We had these—" He stops. Starts again. "Mom got us both these phones. Just for calls. No texting, basically. The plan was terrible, and it cost a fortune."

"Sunday nights," Foster murmurs.

Decker turns toward him. It's the first time their eyes have met this session.

"Sunday nights," Decker confirms. Both of their lips almost tip into a smile.

I let the moment sit. Two boys with a bad cell plan on Sunday nights. There's a whole childhood compressed into those three things.

"What about pictures?" I ask. "Seeing each other's lives?"

Foster makes a sound that isn't quite a laugh. "It predated cheap smartphone plans. You didn't just send pictures whenever you wanted. That wasn't a thing. We weren't old enough for email really. Sometimes I'd send him a baseball card from whatever team was local."

"I still have them." Decker's voice is unsure, as if he's not sure what his brother may think of that.

Foster's hand pauses on his sleeve. He doesn't turn toward Decker. But every therapist knows the difference between someone who didn't hear something and someone who heard it and is trying to process the revelation.

"What about Logan Pruitt's signature?" he asks.

Decker nods. "They're all saved in a box. Not sure how the signature held up on the napkin stained with pizza grease."

Foster huffs. "You're welcome. I had to run back and ask him for a second signature and Dad was already halfway out the door."

Decker's lips tip. "I didn't mean to be—I mean... I was just saying."

"Yeah." Foster quickly shuts down any emotion, the way he always does.

"By the time we were in high school," Decker continues, "there was MySpace. Then Facebook. I'd see his games posted sometimes. Stats." He pauses. "It was amazing to see the player he was becoming."

"And how did you feel about that?" I ask gently.

Something moves across Decker's face. He takes his time with his answer, as though he's picking through a box and deciding what to give me.

"Happy for him." A beat. "And jealous." Foster's head stays down. "And then angry at myself for being jealous because it wasn't his fault." A shorter beat. "And then just angry."

"At Foster?"

"At—" He stops and quickly recalibrates himself. "At the situation."

I let that land without any follow-up questions. We all know what the situation is.

Foster hasn't moved. His hand is completely still on the thread now, which reads louder than any fidgeting he could do.

"Foster," I say, "do you want to respond to that?"

A long moment passes, and I'm about to ask another question when he finally speaks.

"I knew." His voice is quiet, but there's something underneath it. "I didn't know the specifics, but I knew. I used to downplay things on the phone. On Sundays."

Decker's jaw tightens. "I didn't need you to do that."

"I know." Foster raises his gaze then, and there's an edge to his expression I haven't seen before. Something that's been simmering. "But I didn't have a lot of room to figure out what you needed. I was eleven, and I didn't choose where I went. Plus, you had Mom."

The room gets very quiet.

Decker drops his gaze.

"She wanted to be there," Decker says carefully, pinpointing that this is a bigger issue—their mom.

"She was a weekly phone call for me." Foster's voice doesn't rise, which might be worse. "She was down the hall from you. I got to share her on Sundays with you." He turns his attention back to his sleeve. "Dad didn't exactly leave a lot of space or understanding for me to be sad about it. There was always work to do."

There it is. The thing Foster has been carrying that doesn't have Decker's name on it.

I stay very still.

Decker speaks first, and to his credit, he doesn't deflect. "I knew that too, and I felt guilty, but I was a kid and thought you had everything. I didn't think about what you lost too."

"I know it looked good from afar, but you had the better parent," Foster says quieter, as though it costs him.

They're not facing each other. But the couch geometry has shifted again. Their bodies are opening up to one another.

This is why I keep the notebook closed in early sessions. Once you open it, people start narrating for the record. Right now, they're just talking. To me, a little. To each other, without really meaning to.

"How long were you apart?" I ask.

Foster answers. "At first, eight months. We went home for Christmas." A beat. "But then two years and four months before we saw one another again."

And four months. He knows how long down to the month. Counted it and stored it somewhere deep.

"I want to ask you both something, and I want you to actually think about it before you answer." I turn to Foster first. "Why did you come here? Not why Paisley recommended it to you. Why did you come?"

Foster is quiet for a long moment. The thread from his sleeve is balled up in his fist now. "He's my brother." He says it simply. As though it's the only math that calculates.

I turn to Decker.

His jaw moves. His eyes are fixed on his hands. "Because I stopped knowing how to talk to him. And I don't want that to be how it stays. I want a relationship with my brother."

It's the most either of them has offered me in three sessions.

I reach for my notebook slowly, and they both notice.

Neither of them tells me to stop.

We're finally getting somewhere.

CHAPTER EIGHT

Penelope

The house is too quiet when Hazel's at school, so I've been filling it the only way I know how—with boxes and a box cutter and the illusion that if I get everything in order on the outside, the inside will come together too.

I moved us here to be closer to my dad, hoping he could fill the role of a male figure in Hazel's life. My dad has a four-year contract with the Colts, which hopefully means he'll be here the entire time. Longer if we're lucky. Even after a lifetime of watching coaching rule his life, I convinced myself this time would be different—we'd have more time to see him during the season. At least we'll have the offseason when his attention isn't so divided.

I'm busy in the basement of our new house, going through boxes my mom shipped to me when she remarried, moved into his place, then decided to travel for the rest of her life with her wealthy husband.

Using the box cutter, I pierce the tape, then pry open the

flaps. For a half second, I stare. Then my stomach drops, and I wish I had grabbed literally any other box from the pile. I thought I'd gotten rid of this box years ago, but apparently, it's been at my mom's, stuffed in a corner of the crawl space.

My hands slide into the box, and I pull out the scrapbook I made so many years ago.

I have no idea why I want to torture myself, but I release a breath as I open the front flap. The first picture hurts in a way I couldn't prepare for.

Decker Davis and I at the ages of eleven and twelve. Me with a medal around my neck and his arm swung around my shoulders.

My finger runs along the date printed at the bottom. Twenty years later and we couldn't be further apart. Those two kids who had a friendship so deep I thought he'd be part of my life forever are long gone. I should have paid attention to the signs. It's in all the movies—once your heart is too involved, the friendship turns fragile, ultimately shattering to pieces.

I continue to flip page after page. Decker with medals, rings, tournament banners. Me on pedestals, him at the fence line cheering. And then one picture makes me stop. I'm mid-run, not even looking at the camera, and he's staring at me with a look I don't remember.

We were really happy then and smart not to step over the line. We should've remembered our commitment to our friendship all those years later when we were in college.

I reach the end of the scrapbook and spot the letter still in the back pocket.

Don't open it.

Do not open it.

My hand is already reaching for it. That's my entire problem when it comes to Decker—I never listen to common sense.

I lift it out of the pocket, and I cross my legs, leaning back against the wall.

The paper crinkles in my hand after years of being hidden, but the ink and his handwriting are still impeccable.

> Pen,
>
> I know you're laughing right now because I wrote you a letter. I can hear you mumbling, calling me an old man. I'm writing this because if I try to say it out loud, you'll interrupt me three times, then I'll pretend I wasn't being serious, and you'll let me get away with it. And for once, I don't want to ignore the truth.
>
> We've known each other since we were ten and eleven, which is ridiculous if you think about it. Most people don't keep friends that long. But you're not most people. You've been the one person I can count on. Especially when I didn't know how to count on myself.
>
> And somehow, you still know me better than anyone.
>
> You know the difference between me being quiet because I'm tired and me being quiet because I'm spiraling. You know when I'm about to do that thing where I act like I don't care—like everything is fine, when it isn't. You're basically the only person who can look at me and read the truth like the pages in a book without me ever saying a word, which is annoying, honestly. But also the thing I'll miss most.

I can't pretend I'm not excited to go to college. New friends. New teammates. New experiences.

But I also keep thinking about the distance. About how easy it is for people to promise nothing will change, and then they get busy and let things fade. I think about how this next year could turn into phone calls that get shorter and texts that take longer and longer to reply to, and then some day I don't know anything about your life anymore.

I don't want that.

What we are is real. And our friendship has mattered to me more than I've ever said.

So here's what I can promise—I'm one call away. No matter what city I'm in, no matter what time it is. If you need me, I'm here.

And I'm saying this now because I don't want you wondering later if I meant any of this. I'm not going to pull you into something messy right before I leave. You deserve better than that. You deserve someone who's here, not hundreds of miles away, too consumed with his own life and dreams.

But you're still my person. My best friend. And I'm still only a call away.

Thank you for being that for me. For knowing me better than anyone and not using the worst parts of me against me.

Being your friend has never been the hard part.

The hard part has been wanting more and pretending I didn't because your dad was my coach, and our friendship was always most important to me. Timing and circumstance always kept that line in place. I just want you to know it wasn't easy.

Go enjoy your senior year without me.

And I hope someday we'll get lucky with timing and end up in the same city again.

Love,
Deck

I chuckle, but it's hollow. Fifteen years and not much has changed. We're in the same city again, and my dad is still his coach, and I'm sitting on a basement floor reading a letter from a boy who grew into someone I'm still not supposed to want.

After carefully folding the paper back up, I shove the letter into the scrapbook and close the box, wishing I had the guts to throw out the entire thing.

Sitting here won't fix anything, but moving forward might, so I grab my phone. There's a message from Leighton.

He's single. You still want me to give him your number?

CHAPTER
NINE

Decker

I grab my batting helmet and try to remember the last time baseball felt simple.

"You guys are behind," Drew says. "You need to get Easton home to even have a chance to get ahead with this series. And since he's currently at first..." He cringes. "Good luck."

"Fuck off, Drew," Hayes says. "Be happy you're making those big new salaries worth it the way you've hit this month."

I glance over my shoulder, and Hayes shakes his head, telling me not to let the DICs get in my head.

When the DICs joined our team, I was all for the monthly bet between the infield and outfield over who could score the most runs. Healthy competition is good, but the DICs take it too far when we're in a slump.

Or maybe it grates on me more now because their shiny

new salaries might be the reason the Colts' upper office doesn't want to sign me again this year.

"Goldie's contract is hanging by a thread. I'm pretty sure Harkins gets third once your bat stops working too."

"Cut the shit, Drew," Ian says, low and firm. At least one-third of the DICs has enough sense to know when Drew's crossed a line.

"Get traded already," someone else in the dugout mumbles.

"You're like fucking warts that won't go away," Torres says.

Drew gets into it with Torres, who bats after me, and I let them go at it while I step out of the dugout to ready myself.

I circle my neck and loosen my arms. This is where I excel. My bat hasn't been dead this year, and I need to keep it going if I have any shot of staying a Colt next year.

Camden hits a grounder that could have been a double play, but thankfully Easton could give a damn cheetah a race, so he makes it to second. He blows out a breath.

"Hey, you moved him, Cam," I call.

He just shakes his head with a frown.

The poor guy is in a slump. I assume Ripley will give him the rest of this series before he drops him, which only adds more pressure, but that's why we get paid the big salaries, I suppose.

"Can't Stop" by Red Hot Chili Peppers plays through the stadium, and I walk over to the plate. Easton is standing on second, probably trash-talking Porter as I step into the box.

I go through my entire routine, twisting my cleats in the dirt, pushing my weight back, lifting my bat. I visualize myself hitting right to the gap between center and right so Easton can get to third, if not all the way home.

The first ball that comes at me is fast, and I swing and miss.

My mind goes to Drew in the dugout and the fucking

opinions he's probably spouting off. I step out of the box to clear my head.

You've got this, Decker. You've been hitting in situations like this since you were in a rec league and nobody watched. This is nothing new.

I step back in the box, twist my cleats, and lean my weight. Another ball whizzes over the plate, but it's a curve on the inside. One pitch that is not mine. So, I hold off and hear the umpire call a strike.

That's a two-zero count, which is not a best-case scenario. It's actually the worst.

I set up again, and this time, the pitch is practically hanging over the plate. I swing, and the ball jumps off the bat. It carries too far for the second baseman to reach it, and the outfielders sprint in.

"GO, KODIAK!" the dugout shouts as Easton's arms pump, his chains swinging from side to side after coming out of his jersey.

I find first since they decide to throw it home, then keep running to second with the hope that they don't catch East at home and make a quick exchange to get me out at second. My feet feel like cement weighs them down, but I'm sliding into second when the fans cheer, and the dugout goes crazy.

At least I'm able to do one fucking thing right. I let myself enjoy it for exactly three seconds before my mind spirals again.

"RBI!" Easton points toward me. He claps his hands and points again. "That's on you, Goldie." Then he turns to the dugout and says something to Drew. A smartass remark, if I had to guess from the expression on Drew's face.

Easton's really been trying to make sure I don't get down on myself with the way I've been playing at third. Or the way third has been playing me more like it.

I'm not gonna lie. Contributing to the team and getting one more run closer to tying Texas feels good. We're still behind by one, but with Torres and Hayes coming in next, we should be good.

Torres gets up to the plate, and I step off second, taking my lead off.

"Tell me, Davis, is it true what they're saying about Ripley's daughter?"

Texas's second baseman, Evan Porter, has the same ego as Easton. I don't want to talk to him for that reason alone. Plus, it could all be a distraction.

"What are they saying?" Of course, I take his bait because I enjoy punishing myself. It's practically a hobby now.

"That she's fucking hot. Sucks for all you guys. Can't date the coach's daughter, but for us… it's open season."

My fists clench. Evan Porter's hands on Penelope… I don't finish the thought because we're in the middle of a game, but that should tell me everything I need to know about how I still feel about her.

Torres lets two balls go by, and I take my lead off again.

"The temptation must be hard if she's as smokin' as everyone is saying."

I ignore him, thinking that if he says anything worse, I'll tackle him to the ground. I don't need to come off as a Neanderthal who can't handle his temper. And I especially don't need Penelope's name attached to the reason why.

Torres swings and hits the ball to deep center. I look at the third base coach, Paxton, and he gives me the sign to come, so I tag the base before sprinting to third. I slide in right under the tag, standing and leaving my foot on the base as I knock fists with him.

"That might be a record for you." Paxton gives me a quick squeeze on my shoulder.

"I had to get away from Porter. That guy drives me crazy."

He laughs. "Well, take your lead off, and let Hayes get you home."

The first pitch comes in. Usually Hayes doesn't take the

first, but he swings, and the crack of the ball off the bat tells me everything I need to know before I even look up. The dugout explodes. I run, leg muscles burning, and I'm not thinking about contracts or Penelope or any of it. I slide over home plate and jump to my feet to see HOME RUN on the Jumbotron as Hayes jogs toward second.

He not only tied the game but put us ahead by one.

I wait for him, and when he reaches home plate, I hug him and smack him on the back. We head to the dugout, where everyone is fist-bumping both of us.

Everyone except Drew, who is pouting on the bench.

"Relax, buddy. You still have some time to save up for that dinner you'll owe us." Easton winks at him.

I swear, the two of them will come to blows before this season ends.

But it feels good. This feels good. I just need it to transfer to my field play.

As I catch my breath and sit on the bench, waiting to see if Ian can help us get even further ahead, Hayes leans in. "Remind me on the bus back to the hotel, I want to give you a heads-up about something."

My eyebrows draw down. "Tell me now."

He shakes his head and eyes Ripley at the corner of the dugout.

Fuck. It has to do with Penelope. Just when she wasn't consuming my every thought. It's a lie, but I've gotten good at those.

CHAPTER
TEN

Penelope

With a lot of help from kids two decades younger than me on YouTube, I manage to get my phone to play on our television.

Hazel stands in the middle of the family room with the hula hoop around her waist and a half smile filled with dread on her lips. I'm pretty sure she's feeding off my anxiety. We're going to be a disaster together. I've never been more certain of that.

I've pushed all the furniture against the walls to give us enough room. Especially since Leighton, the kids, Callie, and baby Ellis are coming over tonight for dinner and playtime. A ritual we've started when the team is away for long stints.

"We totally have this." I press Play on the video on my phone screen, then I pick up the hula hoop next to hers.

"Mom, maybe I just shouldn't do it." She sighs.

"You just need practice, and I can't wait to try too."

She humors me and lifts her hula hoop to her waist, and I do the same.

The video plays, and a woman who is clearly teaching for younger children comes on wearing brightly colored clothes, her hair in a big ponytail. She's in the middle of a play area that's as colorful as her clothing.

I really hope this video is the one that will help Hazel, because just the thought of asking Decker for his help makes me itch as if I have hives. Which is a perfectly normal response when the person you're asking happens to be someone you have very complicated and completely unresolved feelings for.

The woman named Riya talks about hand position and how to start at your back, swing it around, and sway your hips.

We both try. Neither of us gets very far.

Thankfully, Riya moves on quickly, and we're on to doing other tricks with the hula hoop. This isn't what I thought, given the title of the video: "Everyone can hula hoop, let me show you how."

At least Hazel likes jumping through it like a jump rope. "This is fun, Mommy."

I pick up my phone to find another video but stop when I see her smiling and actually enjoying herself. Maybe we can get this going without her having to actually circle it around her hips. She trips at the exact moment hope springs to life inside me.

Hazel falls forward, and I drop my phone, rushing across the room to grab her. She catches herself, but her knee hits the edge of the coffee table, and her cry rings out through the room.

What a great start.

I pull her into me, falling to my butt and placing her on my lap. I don't rush it. Now that she's older, these moments where she lets me comfort her come less and less. I've learned to stay in them as long as she'll allow me.

I lift her pant leg and see a bruise already forming, but no scrape or blood.

Small blessings.

"What if I can't do it?" she says into my neck, her tears soaking the neckline of my shirt.

I run my hand over her back. "You'll get there. I'll make sure you do."

Even if I have to hire a personal hula hoop instructor.

The doorbell rings, and she bolts up so fast, her head knocks my chin, banging my teeth together. I grunt, but she doesn't hear me because her little feet are already padding toward the door.

"Wait." I get to all fours and use the chair to help me stand.

"It's Monroe!" she shouts, looking out the side window.

"Go ahead and open it," I tell her once I'm closer.

Hazel swings the door open, and Monroe doesn't wait to be invited in.

"Monroe." Leighton has two pizza boxes in her hands. "We're guests. Wait to be invited in."

Monroe doesn't pay her any attention though. She and Hazel rush to the family room, and I hear the clatter of the hula hoops.

"Sorry, we need more lessons in manners apparently." Leighton cringes.

Lincoln and Lake step inside. They each give me a wave and a quick hello before slipping off their shoes and heading to the couch with their phones.

"Why did you bring pizza? I was going to order." I take them from her.

"It's on the way here. Callie is, like, two minutes away."

Just then, an Uber pulls up along the curb, and Callie steps out, before taking out Ellis's car seat. Callie's always beautiful, but she does not look like a mom with a six-month-old.

"I need to talk to Foster. We need a bigger place so I can host, and you all have to come to me." She laughs, hauling the car seat and what I assume is her diaper bag between the two parked cars in front of my house.

Leighton walks down the steps and takes Ellis and the car seat from her.

"But this is nice." Callie smiles at Leighton's back walking up the stairs. "Total honesty, ladies? I need a break, and the guys still have another series before they come home."

We all step into the house, and I shut the door.

Leighton busies herself putting the car seat in the family room and unstrapping Ellis. Lake coos over her, and the two of them talk to her in baby talk about how she's the cutest baby ever to exist.

Lincoln groans.

"Hula hooping?" Callie asks, dropping the diaper bag in the corner of the room. "I used to be so good at this."

"You can have mine." Hazel hands it to her.

Even Monroe struggles to get it going consistently.

Callie puts the hoop around her waist, and it spins three times then it falls to the floor. "So, motherhood took my abs, my sleep, and now apparently my hip mobility too?"

Lincoln laughs. "You're as good as Hazel is."

"Linc!" Leighton glares at the boy, then instructs Lake to sit so she can lay Ellis in her arms. "Do you mind if we borrow your kitchen for a second?"

"Of course not." I nod in its direction and take the pizza boxes from her so she can lead Lincoln away.

"This is a cute place," Callie says. "Are you rehabbing it?"

It's probably a gut job, but I haven't even thought about where to start. "Eventually. I bought it for the location, but I don't want to deal with any renovations right now."

Ellis fusses on Lake's lap, and Callie grabs a pacifier and hands it to her.

It's kind of them to bring Hazel and me into the fold. But then Lake smiles at Callie across the room like she already knows exactly what kind of mother she is, and I feel like an outsider again. Not unwelcome. Just not quite speaking the same language yet.

Lincoln sulks out of the kitchen, and Leighton watches from the doorway to make sure he says sorry to Hazel. He does, then he plops on the couch.

Callie grabs the pizza from my hands. "Girl time." She nods for me to follow her into the kitchen. "Let me know if you need me to take her, Lake."

"I didn't get enough Ellis time," Leighton whines.

We get some drinks, chatting about what's going on with everyone's life.

"Foster FaceTimed me last night. I swear if he makes it through this season without walking off the field, it'll be a miracle."

"He's struggling with being away?" Leighton's nose crinkles.

"Yeah."

"He pitched great the other night." I open the pizza boxes and get out the paper plates.

"It's him not being home with Ellis."

"And you," Leighton says.

Callie nods. "Both of us, but mostly Ellis. Every time he comes home from the road, he props her up on his legs. Then he proceeds to tell her he's sorry he had to leave for work, but he thought of her the entire time. And he tells her about anything funny her uncles did. Then he always professes his love for her." Callie laughs and shakes her head. "Who would have ever thought that once you peel back all the layers, he's this sweet little vulnerable peach?"

We all laugh.

"Next year will be better. Hayes had a hard time last year, but now that we have a year in the books, it's been a little easier. But he still insists on doing everything for all the kids the first day back."

Listening to them discuss the schedules, the way they've built whole lives around men who are away more than they're home during the season tugs at something I don't like to examine very often. There was a time I imagined I'd know what that felt like. I was even anticipating it. But that was a different life. I made my choices, and he made his. There's no point in sitting here and mourning them.

"I'm starving!" Lincoln shouts out from the living room.

Leighton's jaw tightens. "I'm not sure whether Lincoln or I will survive his embarkment into pre-adolescence." She stands and walks over to the archway. "We'll feed them first and then continue our conversation?" She tells them all to come in, takes Ellis from Lake's arms, and tells her, "You're in charge. We'll be in the family room."

Lake groans, but then quickly tells Lincoln to only take one piece until everyone else has one.

I start to fix Hazel a plate, but Leighton gently sets her hand on my forearm. "Lake has it."

The teenager nods and takes the plate for me. "Cheese or pepperoni, Hazel?"

Well, that feels nice.

Leighton laughs. "I'd never survive without her."

Lake rolls her eyes, and the three of us and Ellis go into the family room.

As soon as we sit on the couch though, Leighton and Callie look at me with keen interest.

"So, did he call yet?" Callie's nickname should be Calico, because her grin reminds me of a cat with a canary in its mouth.

The fact that my first thought is *why would Decker call* only proves that my attempt at moving on isn't going especially well.

CHAPTER
ELEVEN

Decker

I climb the stairs onto the team bus burdened by the kind of tired I haven't felt in weeks. I'm trying not to trust the feeling too much. In my experience, the nights that feel like turning points usually aren't.

At least I'm the good kind of tired. The kind that bears more peace than anxiety. That's not to say that my body won't feel wound up before the next game. When did that all start for me? Maybe if I can figure out when, I can dissect the why, unravel it, and get back to being the confident player I've always been.

A few of the players give me a nod as they put in their AirPods and I make my way past.

Drew silently brews midway back, by the window.

"It's still a long month. You might catch us."

He flips me off.

I'm not usually the cocky type, but I feel the need to put

Drew in his place. The only one of us who doesn't is Hayes, which explains why he's our leader.

I find my seat—second row from the back, on the aisle—and drop into it, still on a high from the win. I lean my head back and close my eyes, relieved to have had a good game.

"Hey," Hayes says, and I squint one eye open. He stands at the edge of the aisle.

Easton is right behind him. "You get confused, Haymaker? My thighs are killing me, I gotta sit." He tries to slide between Hayes and me, but Hayes puts his hand on Easton's chest.

Easton glances down and back up with raised eyebrows.

"Do you mind if I grab your seat?" Hayes nods in my direction. "I need to talk to Goldie."

Easton's forehead creases. "So talk to him from your seat."

Hayes stares at him. "It's across the aisle."

"So? Lean over."

"I'm not leaning across a bus aisle for an entire conversation," Hayes says. "Just take my seat for this one trip and sit with Foster."

"What's the holdup?" Foster grumbles from behind Easton.

"Carlisle is trying to switch things around. Says he has to talk to Decker."

"And?" Foster's head is buried in his phone, holding it up and taking pictures of himself with silly expressions. I guess having a kid really does change someone.

I hate that Penelope's face is the first one that comes to mind after that thought.

Easton sighs in defeat.

I slide my legs over, and Hayes crawls past to the window seat.

Easton turns around to face Foster. "You get in first."

Foster crosses his arms and shakes his head. "Nope, I'm on the aisle."

Easton leans closer, as if he could lower his voice enough that we won't hear him. "They're keeping secrets. I want to eavesdrop."

"We can hear you," I say.

"It's not your business," Hayes adds. "And it's just to the airport. Relax, Kodiak."

"Sit down." Foster's voice is firm, nodding toward the window seat.

Torres and a few other players groan behind them. "Let's go!" Torres says.

"Kodiak has hurt feelings," Foster says in a higher pitch sing-song voice.

Easton huffs and throws himself into Hayes's usual seat.

"Now he's pouting. Thanks, Carlisle." Foster slides in next to him and eyes me.

While we were fighting to stay on top in the eighth and ninth, I forgot Hayes told me he wanted to talk to me.

"I'm just saying, we're the four horsemen. We don't keep secrets." Easton stares out the window like a teenager who was uninvited to the party he planned.

"I have secrets with Carlisle." I shrug.

Easton's head whips around. "You do?"

Hayes and Foster both laugh.

"Relax, Kodiak, this is a one-time swap."

"One time." Easton raises his finger and puts in his earbuds.

Nobody responds to that, which is the right call. Giving Easton the last word is the fastest way to end any conversation.

The bus starts moving, and the ambient noise of the usual post-game hum settles over the bus. Guys on their phones. Someone's music leaking out through their headphones.

I wait, curious what is so important that Hayes had to sit next to me. Easton has a point—the four of us don't keep much from one another. We've really come together as the foursome Jagger wanted us to be two years ago when Hayes joined the Colts.

We're on the highway before Hayes turns in his seat to face me as best he can.

"What is it?"

"There's this doctor, Elias."

My eyes widen as my stomach sinks. "Shit, are you sick? Leighton? The kids?"

Is he going to ask me for a kidney or something? I'd give it to him. That's not even a question. And, of course, he'd come to me before Easton and Foster. My clean diet would make me a better candidate.

Hayes shakes his head. "He works with Leighton."

I rock my head and try to keep my mind from going to the worst-case scenario like it usually does. "She's not cheating on you, man. Leighton loves you."

"She better not be, but that's not why I'm telling you. He's single." His voice is low. Just loud enough for me to hear. Whatever this is, he really wants to keep it a secret.

"You do know I'm heterosexual, right?"

He blows out a breath and groans. "I'm not trying to set you up."

"Then why do I give a shit about this doctor, Elias, who works with Leighton?"

His teeth bite down on his lip, and he looks as if he just took a hundred-mile-per-hour ball to the inner thigh. But still I'm coming up empty on why he's telling me all this.

"Leighton gave him Penelope's phone number."

The inflicted wound is fast and effective, a glint of light off the knife, then pain before I can make sense of what's even happened.

"Oh... okay." I glance past him out the window, watching the highway lights streak by, trying to contain my immediate reaction.

"I just thought… I don't know… that you should know."

The bus increases its speed, matching my heartbeat as the image of Penelope in the arms of someone else pummels me.

There's no use in reacting before I can decipher how I actually feel. Right now, I feel something close to anger, something close to grief, and about four other things I'm not going to name because they won't help.

"Leighton suggested it, or Penelope asked for it?" I'm not sure why I'm asking—it doesn't factor into anything other than the fact that she's moving on, and I'm still stalled in neutral.

"She told Leighton she was ready to start dating." He pauses. "Leighton alluded to it having something to do with Hazel." He shrugs. "But I don't really know."

And there's the one reason I can't take issue with any of this. The one reason that makes complete sense and also makes my stomach feel as if a line drive hit me square in the nuts.

I think about Hazel at field day. The way she looked back at Penelope when she was trying to get the hula hoop to spin —because her first instinct was to find her mom. And Penelope was already watching with a proud mom smile, clapping for her.

She's doing the right thing. That's the conclusion I keep arriving at no matter how many times it runs through my mind. Penelope's doing the right thing for her and her daughter, and there's not a version of this where I get to be annoyed about it.

"I'll be honest—there was a point when I was jealous of this guy with Leighton. But he seems like a good guy. He's always making the staff laugh at his stories. You don't have to do anything with the information… I just figured you'd want to know before you heard it from someone else."

I swallow hard, willing my voice to work. "No, yeah. I appreciate it."

He nods and leans back, and we don't say anything else about it. That's what I've always liked about Hayes. He delivers the news then lets you absorb it.

Across the aisle, Easton is already asleep, his head tipped against the window. Foster is reading something on his phone, pretending he didn't overhear anything, but I'm not sure how he couldn't have caught at least some of it.

A doctor. Someone with a better schedule than I have during the season, a permanent parking spot, and no agent calling him about trades and the possibility of setting up his life in another city. Someone who doesn't have his career up for review at the end of every season. I let myself sit with that for exactly as long as it takes the bus to pass under one overpass. Then I tuck it away.

I go over the rules I've had for myself for years. They exist for a reason, and they've kept me standing when circumstances tried to take me down.

Rule Number One—don't take what isn't yours.

Although she's never been mine, if Penelope likes Elias and she becomes his, I won't try to ruin that for her.

I followed Rule Number One when she moved to Chicago. I followed it when she started showing up at every friend group dinner and every game. I followed it when Porter ran his mouth at second base tonight and I wanted to do something about it that would've been broadcast all over ESPN.

And I'm going to keep following it.

"You good?" Hayes asks a bit later.

"Yeah. Good game tonight."

He looks at me a beat longer than the question requires. Then he lets it go with a nod. "Good game too."

I stare at the back of the seat in front of me.

Three more games before we're home. I'm going to focus on keeping my spot on this team and keeping my throws where they're supposed to go and not doing anything that costs me my brother or my contract.

Penelope Ripley is going on a date with a doctor, and I'm not going to try to stop her. It will be the hardest thing I've done all season. Which is funny since I've been booting routine grounders for three weeks.

CHAPTER
TWELVE

Penelope

I knock on the door, and my dad's muffled voice says, "Come in."

Stepping into my dad's office, the first thing I notice is that Hazel's pictures outnumber mine on his desk five to one. The second thing I notice is all the dry erase markers—and just like that, I'm nine years old again.

It's amazing how the smell of dry erase markers can make me feel at home. I grew up in offices like this one. I did homework on couches like the one along the wall while men talked batting averages at the whiteboard.

I have no idea why my dad wants to see me—at his office nonetheless—but I forgot how comfortable I was in his favorite space. I guess that's what happens when your mom gets the house and your dad gets the weekends.

He rises from behind his desk, dropping his reading glasses on the folder in front of him as though it's already been a day. "There she is."

He opens his arms, and I step right into them. The scent of his aftershave makes me close my eyes and inhale deeper. These are the things Hazel is missing, and I feel it every time I'm in his arms. The security of the first man in your life who loves you no matter how much you screw up. I want my daughter to know this feeling of security and acceptance too.

I tested it in college, and I'll never do it again. I know what that feels like.

"Hey, Dad." I go to the couch, sit, and cross my legs.

He stands and rests his hands on either side of his hips, leaning back on his desk. "Do you want anything to drink?"

"No. I'm good."

He nods and changes his stance, crossing his arms. I really hope whatever he's brought me here to talk about has nothing to do with the Davis twins. I've spent three years carefully constructing a life that runs parallel to theirs without intersecting, and the last thing I need is my dad accidentally pulling me into their drama.

"I was called into Shane Whitaker's office. You know the GM?"

I chuckle. "I know him, Dad. I've met him more than a few times."

My dad isn't usually nervous around me. Well, that's not entirely true. He gets nervous when he has to deliver bad news, and right now he has the exact same energy as the time he told me he was moving out of Philadelphia.

My chest tightens, my breaths a little harder to take, but I don't spot any cardboard boxes lying around. "Dad?" He quickly shakes his head, and I sink into the couch, thankful he hasn't been fired. "Good. Then why don't you sit?"

He pushes off the desk and sits on the chair adjacent to me. "You sure you don't want a drink?"

"No, Dad. Now what is it?"

The silence stretches thin enough to be translucent. "Shane

is upset that we don't have a WAG group. Says the Trojans are winning the hearts of this city."

The Trojans are Chicago's other professional baseball team.

"Okay…" I decide he must need to vent to me about the politics of managing a professional baseball team, so I don't ask why this has anything to do with me. "Who's in charge of the Colts' wives and girlfriends' group?"

A sharp laugh escapes him. "Only two of our players are in committed relationships."

"Really? No." That's crazy. Especially since I know the only two.

"We're a young team. Shane and the front office were rebuilding the team when I came along, and that tends to leave us with younger guys. I mean, our outfielders are the youngest in the league."

The DICs is what I hear the guys calling the outfielders because their names are Drew, Ian, and Camden. I'm a sucker for an acronym, plus I'm not really a fan of Drew since he's hit on me no less than ten times.

"Sounds like a Shane problem to me."

"Well, he's passed that problem down to me." My dad frowns.

"Well, you have Leighton and Callie."

He shakes his head. "Leighton only became the guardian to the three kids a year ago, and Callie is still nursing her baby."

I cover his hand where it rests on the arm of the chair and squeeze once. "I'm sorry, Dad. Maybe you can hire someone?"

"That's the thing, slugger…"

I wince at the pet name. He's about to ask me something. Something I most likely will not want to do. I decide to get this over with and ask him point blank. "What do you need?"

His hazel gaze turns toward the table before he locks eyes

with me. "Shane has some ideas. Wants to encourage the players to find partners."

"Does he want to plan a speed dating round during the seventh inning stretch?" I laugh, but my dad doesn't.

"A bachelor auction was the idea he was throwing around."

"Does Shane not realize that the real issue is that his players don't want to settle down?"

He tips his head back and exhales as though the whole situation exhausts him. "He swears his wife has changed him. I don't ever mention to him that it's his fourth marriage. But he swears this one is it. He had an instant feeling she was the one."

"Good luck to them, but we're talking mostly about twenty-something professional athletes who have women practically crawling at their feet. Shane is what? In his fifties?"

"Hey now, watch yourself." He smirks.

"You're not in the same category. Do you know how many posts I have to scroll past of women calling you Daddy Ripley or Daddy Ripped? You really need to not use the bottom of your T-shirt to wipe your face when you're overheated, Dad."

He shivers, but I'm not naïve enough to think my dad doesn't have his fair share of women—at least in the offseason. During the season, he's way too busy to entertain anything unless they want to talk baseball.

"Anyway, he wants me to find someone to handle this, and honestly, you're the only one I trust."

"Me?" I point at myself, my mouth hanging open.

"You're the best person for the job. The organization will pay you."

I uncross my legs, then cross my legs again, buying myself a second because I know where this is going, and I already know I'm not going to say no. "The best person is an actual wife or girlfriend of any of the forty players on the roster."

"You organized that amazing hospital fundraiser with your mom a few years ago. And then what about your mom's wedding last year? You had a lot to do with that."

"Dad, that's so different than this. I'm not really part of the team."

"Yes, you are. You're my daughter. And Hazel said you're close to Leighton and Callie. That the three of you get your families together."

I exhale. "Still…"

He holds his hands up, palms facing me. "I know it's a lot to ask. And I'm happy to go tell Shane he'll have to hire someone from outside the organization, but I'd rather handle this in-house. These are my boys, and they're a good team. They could use some bonding, I'm not gonna lie. The DICs are always competing with my infield. Sure, friendly competition is good, but they're all so young and their egos barely fit through the door. An outsider brings drama I don't want. Plus, if you do this, I'll control the narrative more than Shane. If he hires someone, she reports to him, and I have no idea what he'll make these guys do." He inhales and glances at his desk. "This team can do it. They can win the whole thing, and I just… well… Shane's going to do this no matter what, and I'd rather have some control over it, make sure he's not making my guys go here and there, take their eyes off the prize."

I stare at the ceiling, at a water stain mimicking the shape of Michigan, and let it hold my attention while I figure out what to say. "I don't know if I can do this."

My dad is the only one I'd ever admit that to. What I don't say is the part underneath—that agreeing to this puts me squarely in the middle of a team that includes the one person I've been carefully staying away from.

"An outsider will be enamored with the players. Which is why I'm asking you. You know the calendar. And you're not going to be intimidated by the guys because you grew up in a clubhouse."

It's true. I spent enough time in dugouts and training facilities as a kid that the mystique of professional athletes was thoroughly ruined for me by the age of eighteen.

"We can't be WAGs when there are only two women," I say. "We'd have to think of a different way to make this work. Maybe shift our organization to be more about doing charitable things for the fans, Chicago, and getting this city behind the Colts rather than the Trojans."

"I was thinking the same."

"Chicago has a great fan base. One of the best."

He nods. "True, but Shane feels like we're competing against the Trojans. He wants to own this city."

My shoulders rise, understanding that we share Chicago with the other major league baseball team.

My dad pushes to his feet and reaches behind him for a folder on the edge of his desk. He's prepared, which means he never doubted I'd say yes.

"I'd have free rein?"

He nods. "Yes, but Shane wants a meeting. I have someone lined up to help you. So the four of us will meet and discuss schedules and timing, ideas."

"Who will be helping me?"

"I'm still figuring it out."

My head tilts. "But you said you had them lined up?"

His forehead wrinkles, and he acts as though I'm hearing things. "They haven't agreed yet, but they'll make sure the players attend whatever you cook up."

Which will probably be the hardest part, if you ask me. Thirty-eight single guys will be hard to manage. Not a job I want.

"Fine," I say, not thrilled but willing, nonetheless.

"Thanks, slugger. And I'm here to help you with whatever you need."

I stare at him with a bored expression. He smiles, and it's the same smile he's had since I was seven years old—the one that means he already knows he's won.

"Yeah, that's bullshit," he says. "You want your dad to be the youngest manager to win the series, don't you? Hazel would have bragging rights at school."

I stand and tuck the folder under my arm. "I'll do some brainstorming and get back to you."

"Dinner Saturday?"

"So you can swindle me into another thing? No thanks."

He chuckles. "Saturday's game is in the afternoon. I'll take you and Hazel to that play zone place she likes."

I groan. "Just what every single mom wants to do on a Saturday night—go play Skee-Ball with her dad."

He steps around me and places his hand on the doorknob. "I'm happy to take her by myself so you can go to a club or something."

My forehead wrinkles. "Dad."

"I'm just saying… maybe it's time to get out there. Test the waters." He says it lightly, but he's watching me in that way he has that means he sees more than I've ever told him.

"Says the man who's been single most of his entire adult life."

We laugh as my dad swings the door open and I step out to the hallway. Then freeze in place.

Decker leans against the wall across from me, one foot flat against the baseboard, staring at his phone. His hair is doing that thing it does after practice—pushed back, slightly damp, looking freshly fucked in an effortless way.

He lifts his gaze from his phone, and it lands directly on me. There goes any plan to escape unnoticed.

"Hey."

Does he practice that easy, unaffected tone he always uses around me?

I hate that about him.

"Hey." I hold up the folder in my hand as if it explains everything. "Just dropping in on my dad."

"Hey, Deck." I inwardly roll my eyes at my dad using a shortened version of his name.

I also hate that my dad holds no grudges.

Dad's phone rings, and he kisses my cheek. "Thanks again, slugger. See you Saturday."

He's already moving, already shifting gears as always—one thing ending, the next beginning, with no space between.

"Give me a minute, Deck," he says.

Decker pushes off the wall. His eyes go to the folder then back to my face. "Slugger, huh? Do I need to ask?"

I laugh but try to swallow it down fast. Of course, he'd remember that when my dad calls me slugger, it means he needs something from me. "Just another project."

I shift the folder against my chest and hover in the doorway.

Feet, get moving. Walk away. You've done it before.

"Well, see you." I lift my hand in a small wave.

"Yeah, bye, Penelope."

I wince at him using my full name.

I hate that too.

I head for the end of the hallway and don't look back, because there are only two options I might find if I do. Either he's watching me or he's already in my dad's office—and both will break me.

When I push through the door at the end of the hall, the afternoon light warms my shoulders. I tell myself that the tightness in my chest is just the air in my dad's office. Poor ventilation in an old building and nothing more.

I'm getting better and better at lying to myself.

CHAPTER
THIRTEEN

Decker

I'm still coming down from seeing Penelope here. I don't have a better word for it than that because it always feels like a high when I see her. I've been chasing the dragon named Penelope for the majority of my life. I wish I didn't still feel that thing that shall not be named the second I saw her.

I've been in Ripley's office enough times that I know how to avert my eyes from any pictures of Penelope, so I take the chair in front of his desk, keeping my focus on him. Last year, I made a bumbling fool of myself because he has a picture of her with a younger Hazel, both laughing at something just off camera, and I couldn't stop glancing at it. At one point Ripley asked me a question, and I gave him an answer that had nothing to do with what he'd asked.

He finishes his phone call and leans back in his desk chair. "Glad you got my note."

"Janet came down personally." Which is why I'm sitting

here with uncombed, damp hair. When the manager's assistant comes down and says he wants to see you, you don't take time to fuss about your appearance after your shower. You just go.

"Hope I didn't pull you away from anything."

If he only knew how boring my life is now. I'd rather be in here for whatever he needs than thinking about my poor performance on the field—or worse, his daughter.

"Film got delayed."

He nods as though he already knew that. Not surprising. Ripley knows everything that happens in this facility. It's one of the things that makes him hard to get anything past and easy to trust at the same time.

He steeples his fingers. "Hand still good?"

I flex my left hand. The one I jammed sliding in the final game of the Atlanta series. "Fine."

"Good." He picks up his water bottle and holds it without drinking from it. "I want to talk to you about something."

Dread settles low in my gut. Here it goes. Harkins just won my spot. "Okay."

Apparently, I'm breaking out in a sweat and look like I just came down with the flu because he laughs and shakes his head. "Relax, Deck. I'm on your side. Your bat is carrying us in the lineup. I'm not gonna say you don't need to work on your fielding, but the spot is still yours."

One reason I've always loved Ripley is that he's not one of those coaches who gets a kick out of watching you sweat. He's a straight shooter.

"Thanks."

He leans his forearms on his desk and stares at me. Now my mind is racing with scenarios as to why I'm sitting across from him. And the only thing I come up with is that if this isn't about my position, it must be about his daughter.

"Whitaker wants the Colts to be one with the community.

Since we're made up of mostly single guys, we don't have a WAG group. He sees this as a problem and wants to fix it."

"Is he going to start arranging marriages?"

Our team is relatively young, and we do have a lot of guys who aren't anywhere near even wanting a steady relationship. Our starting shortstop, for one. All three outfielders as well. The closest is Torres, but he and his girlfriend are still doing long distance, and from an outsider's perspective, it's not going well.

"I wouldn't put it past him, but he's asked that we plan more community events, and I need a player who will be accountable for the guys."

Oh fuck. He's asking because he knows I'm a yes man. I'm not stupid enough to say thanks for the great offer, but I'd rather sit this one out. Not during a contract year anyway.

"I need a player to be the point man for the team side. Someone the guys will listen to and who won't treat it like a burden." He twists the cap off the water bottle. "I want that to be you."

I wait a beat to play it off as if I'm considering, when all I can think about is that this is the last thing I want or need this year. "You want me to plan parties?"

"God no. I want you to be the liaison between the team and the coordinator. Show up, rally the guys, make sure nobody skips the events because they think they're optional." He gives me a dry look. "Because it's not optional—for anyone."

Last year, two guys showed up forty minutes late to a charity dinner, and Ripley's face twisted into something none of us wanted to see again. They got traded. He doesn't tolerate disobedience.

"I can do that." It sounds easy enough. I was picturing myself on hold with a catering company, arguing about whether the chicken or the fish is the better option for forty grown men, and hot gluing centerpieces in my limited spare time. Making sure the guys get to the facility and do what they're supposed to do is easy.

"I know you can. That's why I'm asking you."

He nods, satisfied, and reaches for a folder on the corner of his desk. He slides it to me, and I open it. A calendar of our schedule with stars next to the dates events will be planned for rests inside.

I flip to the second page, and my gaze pauses on the name listed as the contact.

Event Coordination: Penelope Ripley.

I keep my eyes on the page for exactly one second longer than I need to before I glance at him.

Ripley is finishing his bottle of water and looking at the whiteboard as though he's debating switching the lineup around. The guy never stops working. Which is what you want in a manager.

"Penelope is running the coordination side?"

That sounded casual, right?

He smashes the plastic water bottle and tosses it in the trash can as if it's a basketball. Sinks it with ease.

"She's got some background in event planning, charities, fundraisers." He glances at me as if I've said something mildly interesting and he didn't hear the hitch in my voice. "She knows the calendar, knows the families. Better than someone on the outside."

"Right."

"You'll work together on the logistics. She handles the vendors and the venues, you handle the players and the communication on our end." He picks up a pen and twirls it around his fingers. "Should be straightforward."

I close the folder.

Straightforward. Yeah. That's not a word I would use, but hey, everyone's different.

"Sounds like it."

I think about Penelope in the hallway minutes ago. The

way she held that folder against her chest like a shield over her heart. The way she looked at me twice, thought better of it, then invented an excuse to get as far away from me as she could.

She must know I'm a part of this. And yet she agreed. I turn that over for a second. I don't know if it means something or if I'm doing that thing where I find meaning in things that have absolutely no meaning at all.

She might not care I'm on this project with her. She's moving on. Dating and looking for the right person to spend the rest of her life with. Maybe it's about time I try to do the same.

Ripley studies me for a moment as if he's surprised I have no other questions.

"Good." He drops the pen on his desk. "We have to meet with Whitaker first. He has some stipulations. The meeting date and time are on the second page."

"Okay."

In a boardroom with the woman I love, her clueless dad, and a man who wants me off the team. Sounds like a good time if I've ever heard one.

"Does Shane know you've chosen me?"

"I told him I'd take care of it." He leans back in his chair again, linking his hands behind his head. "Listen, Deck, I think this is a good opportunity for you. Show the front office the guy you are. Or I guess, remind them of the guy you are. You're a Colt. You bleed red and blue. And I believe you're the guy for third base. We need to show them they need you in the clubhouse and in the game."

I smile. Ripley has believed in me since I was eleven—longer than my own father.

"Thanks, Mark."

"We'll show them how wrong they are if they don't sign you next year."

"Sounds good." I stand and pick up the folder.

Ripley is already turning back toward his laptop. Meeting adjourned.

When I reach the door, he says my name, and I turn around.

His eyes are trained on the monitor now, not on me. "She's working hard to build a life here. Her and Hazel both." A pause that lands a little heavier than it should for a sentence about event planning. "I'd like to see this go well."

I tell myself it's not a warning. It's a man talking about his daughter moving to a new city and settling in.

That's all it is.

"Understood." I nod.

He returns my nod, and I leave, pulling the door shut behind me.

The hallway is empty. I stand there for a moment longer than makes sense, as though I expected something different. Of course it's empty. Why would Penelope have stuck around?

I walk toward the locker room and try to figure out what just happened.

Ripley asked me to run point, and it makes sense. I'm reliable, I'm respected in the locker room, and I won't embarrass the organization. He could have asked Hayes, but Hayes has enough on his plate as honorary captain.

He asked me.

In a contract year where the front office isn't sure I'm worth keeping, that means something. Ripley just handed me a reason to be visible in a way that has nothing to do with my fielding percentage. I should be thinking about that. Not thinking about *her*.

But he made his daughter the event coordinator.

He knows our history. Why would he want to throw us together?

And he mentioned it like an afterthought. Except Ripley doesn't forget details. He manages a roster of forty different personalities through a hundred-sixty-two game season without losing his grip on a single man. He called me by my full name when he stopped me at the door. He's only done that one other time. The year I won my first Gold Glove. He pulled me aside and told me not to let it go to my head. He only uses my full name when he wants to make sure he has my complete attention.

Were his words deliberate? A warning to keep my distance?

Is he nudging us together or just filling a job?

I genuinely don't know.

At some point in the next few days, Penelope or I will send a message that says something like "hey, coordinating the first event, let me know what you need from my end, and it's going to be completely normal and professional and fine."

It's just work.

I look at the folder in my hand.

Right.

Just work.

I reach the locker room and tell myself to believe my delusions, and I almost do. Then I remember the look on her face when she stepped out of her dad's office. How desperate she was to get away from me.

She couldn't pretend either.

I don't know what to do with that. So I do what I always do. I file Penelope Ripley somewhere she can't do any damage. I've done nothing about it for three years, and I'll keep doing nothing about it for however long it takes to get her out of my system. Out of my head. Out of my heart.

CHAPTER
FOURTEEN

Dr. Nora Bell

Most sessions, I can tell how they'll go before the patients even sit down. I read it in the shoulders, the way they hold the door, whether they make eye contact coming in. It's pattern recognition after fifteen years of watching people decide how much they're willing to give.

Today, it's Foster who has his walls up. He's already got that look—jaw set, distant eyes.

And that's fine, because today, I don't plan to focus on him directly. I wanted them both to understand their lives during the time they were apart. Now I'll focus on Decker. He's the kind of patient who gives you everything you ask for and nothing you don't. He's cooperative, but genuinely guarded.

I wait until they've settled on the couch—opposite ends, as always, though they don't look like they want to crawl over the arm of the couch anymore. They're more relaxed in each other's presence.

I rest my hands over my knee, legs crossed.

"We've touched on Foster's path to where he is today," I begin. "The move south. The development years. How baseball became the thing your father handed him, and he ran with." I shift my attention to Decker. "Now, I'd like to hear yours."

Decker's chin raises slightly, and he glances at Foster, as if he's worried to share. "Mine?"

"How you got here. To the majors." I pause. "If you were left behind, being raised by your mom, how did you become talented enough to make it to the bigs?"

"Bigs?" Foster and Decker say in unison, glancing at one another as they laugh like teenage boys in their first sex ed class.

I'll take their laughter at my expense if it means they bond over something.

Decker takes his time. I've learned to give him space. He's stalling because he's deciding where to start.

"After Dad and Foster left, it was just me and Mom for a while. She had to take on a second job, which left me with a lot of time by myself." He says it without any bitterness. Like it's just the geography of his life.

"Didn't Dad pay her support? He'd always make a big deal about it at the end of the month." Foster frowns.

Decker's already shaking his head. "No—with the split, Dad said he'd be responsible for you, and she'd be responsible for me. So, the house payment…"

Foster's face falls, and his jaw tenses.

"I figured you knew that." Decker's forehead is creased.

"No." Foster's chest rises and falls with a deep breath, and he glances out the window.

"I was playing ball in a rec league, but my confidence was kind of shot." He turns to Foster. "Not because you were so good—well, that's only partly true. But it was because Dad left me behind like I wasn't worth his time."

Foster turns away from the window and looks at Decker, nodding.

"And then?" I try to keep us on track.

Decker shifts on the couch. "Mom said she had this friend. They'd known each other in high school. She'd lost touch with him, but he was back in town. She invited him to a game, and he came with his daughter." The energy in the room shifts when he says, "his daughter." Foster's shoulders stiffen, and Decker appears nervous. "I was eleven or twelve. After another horrible game where I struck out and sat on the bench more than I played a position, he told me he coached baseball and had played when he was younger. Asked me if I wanted his help. Mom's smile was so big, I said yes, even though I was ready to stop playing."

Foster's head whips in Decker's direction. "You were gonna quit?"

"It seemed like a waste of time. I was clearly behind everyone, and after you left, all the jokes and…"

"Jokes?" I ask, hesitant to go down this path, but willing to try.

"That all the talent went to Foster in the womb. I was left with the garbage genes."

Foster shakes his head, but Decker won't see it since he's looking in the opposite direction.

"That must have been hard," I say.

Decker shrugs. "It was what it was. But Mark changed all that."

"So he coached you?"

"Yeah, he'd meet me at the field while his daughter ran track. He'd help me while she practiced, then usually he'd take us to dinner. He's the reason I got seen. It helped that he was a coach for a small local college. He had some connections and got me on a travel team a year later. It just kind of took off from there and things started connecting. Helped when I hit puberty."

"That jump is crazy, right?" Foster says. "Still one of my best seasons ever."

Decker chuckles. "Mine too."

I smile, watching them interact and share.

"Since I never heard from Dad much, Mark was the male role model in my life."

"You're still close with him?"

Decker almost smiles. "He's the Colts' manager."

"Mark Ripley?" My eyebrows raise.

Decker nods and glances at his brother.

I turn to Foster. "How does that make you feel, hearing Decker's path?"

Foster is quiet for a beat, and his jaw shifts. "Jealous."

His honesty throws me for a second.

"Of your brother's relationship with Mark Ripley?"

"Of the whole thing." His gaze never strays to Decker.

"You had the same outcome."

Foster's shoulder lifts. "Yeah, sure, but he had someone looking out for him." He pauses. "Dad didn't give a shit about me, other than how well I played baseball. I was his trophy. Something to show off." He says it without any self-pity, which somehow makes it sadder. "Ripley chose Decker. Chose to be there for him."

The room quiets. There's not even the sound of birds chirping outside, as though they too can feel the strained silence inside this room.

I turn back to Decker. A guilty expression crosses his face.

"Decker, do you want to respond to that?"

He runs his hands down his thighs, flexing them on his knees. "I spent a long time being jealous of you." He turns toward Foster. "Not of your athletic ability. Of the fact that he showed up. That he packed a bag and took you some-where because he believed in you." He stops. "Ripley is the reason I got here. But he's not my dad. He's a man who was kind to a helpless kid." He pauses again. "I'm not diminishing what he did for me, but Dad deemed you worthy and me not."

"He was there to cash in on the fame he hoped I'd get," Foster says quietly.

"He showed up." Decker's voice is firm, and I think this might be the first time they've truly grappled with this together. "That's more than I had."

Foster opens his mouth. Closes it. His thumb runs along the seam on the arm of the couch.

"I didn't know it felt like that," Foster finally says. "I thought you had the better deal. Mom, and then someone like Ripley—"

"You thought I was fine?"

A sharp nod from Foster. "I thought you were fine."

Decker sighs. "I thought the same about you. Until later in life."

I've been doing this long enough to know when things are coming together. I inwardly clap my hands. Progress.

"When you made it to the bigs and Foster's struggles became more public?" They both smirk at my use of the word bigs, and I can't help but smile.

"Yeah," Decker mumbles.

I stay quiet. This is the part where a therapist who jumps in does more damage than good. I want them to sit with the connection they just made, the raw honesty they gave one another, and really think about what the other one endured.

It's Foster who breaks the silence, and his voice has lost some of its careful evenness. "He's a good man. Ripley. I didn't know all that. So, you and Penelope knew each other back then?"

Decker tears his eyes away from Foster. The pause before he answers is small, but I catch it. I file it away for another session.

"Yeah, Penelope and Ripley became... family."

Foster's expression says this is all a revelation. That he

had no idea the role Ripley and his daughter played in Decker's life.

The day will come when we'll have to dive into that, but not today.

Today we've covered enough.

Some sessions have breakthroughs. Today was one. Two men, same wound—and for the first time, they looked at each other and recognized it. That's a success, and we'll take it.

CHAPTER
FIFTEEN

Penelope

Of course, I find out from Janet.

Not from my dad. Not a phone call, or a simple heads-up, or I don't know, any of the basic human courtesies that a father might extend to a daughter he just volunteered for a task she doesn't want to do. Nope, just Janet emailing me the player contact sheet with the name Decker Davis listed as the Team Liaison.

What the actual fuck, Dad?

I slam my laptop shut, stand, and grab my keys, wishing I had read it last night instead of half an hour before the meeting.

My heroic Uber driver gets me to Webber Field in record time, giving me enough time to corner my dad before we head into the conference room.

He's in the hallway outside his office when I arrive, talking to one of the pitching coaches whose name I can't remember since fire is racing through my veins. My dad catches my approach from over the guy's shoulder and purses his lips as though he's trying not to laugh.

He says something to the pitching coach, pats him on the shoulder, and walks over to meet me with his hands in his pockets.

"Hey, slugger."

"Don't slugger me. Decker Davis?"

"He's a good player. Four Gold Gloves. Great bat." He shrugs.

"Dad…" I say with a mix of exasperation and exhaustion.

He tips his head. "Walk with me. We don't want to be late."

I have to double my steps to keep up with him. "I'd like you to explain why I had to find out from Janet that—"

"Because I knew if I told you, you'd say no." He says it simply and without apology. That's my dad though—he rarely apologizes for much.

I close my mouth.

He's not wrong. Decker Davis being part of this is the one thing that might have made me say no to my dad.

"He's the right guy for the job," my dad continues, keeping his voice low. "The players respect him. He doesn't make things about himself." He pauses. "But you know all of that."

"That's not the point."

"Then what's the matter, slugger?"

I groan. "Can you please stop calling me slugger?"

He presses the elevator button and stares at me as if I'm seven again. "It's my name for you."

"Only when you want something."

My patience thins with every second that passes, and my dad doesn't acknowledge that he knows why Decker and I should not be planning these events together.

I have spent a considerable amount of time and energy over the past several weeks trying not to think about Decker

Davis. And last night I agreed to go on a date with a doctor I've never met, and now I can barely remember his name because it's being crowded out by he-who-should-remain-nameless.

I don't say any of that though.

"It's going to be awkward," I whisper, even though the hallway is empty.

The elevator arrives. At least I'll be able to corner Dad in the small space and convince him to assign someone else on the ride up.

My dad waves his arm for me to step in, and he follows, pressing the button for the level the front offices are on. He leans against the metal wall, studying me for a moment. He's always had the ability to read me like a playbook.

"I thought all that was behind you two."

The sentence lands so matter-of-factly that I'm thrown for a second. My dad had a front row seat to Decker and I growing up side-by-side and has seen every version of what-ever's been between us. Why would he think everything between us is past tense?

Probably because it should be.

Damn that angel who always sits on my shoulder.

"It is." I cross my arms and nod.

"Good." He nods once, as though that's settled. "Then what's the problem?"

The elevator doors open, and I step out and realize I never actually made my case. Somehow between floors, I talked myself into accepting this instead of getting out of it. My dad didn't even have to do anything. Which is the most annoying part.

I stare after my dad already walking toward the confer-ence room. He glances over his shoulder and nods in the direction we need to go.

I know he's playing a game. But why would he ever want me anywhere near Decker Davis after what happened all those years ago? Then again, my dad isn't one for love and emotion. Maybe he just believes that years spent geographically apart can sever heartstrings. Right now, I wish I'd inherited that particular gene, even if I spent most of my childhood wishing he didn't have it.

I fall into step beside him the way I did in hallways like this when I was seven years old. Muscle memory apparently never goes away. My dad moves through the building the way he always has—stopping for a word here, a nod there, never in a hurry but always on time. I stay quiet, smile when he introduces me, and say my polite hellos and nice-to-meet-yous.

Shane Whitaker has been the Colts' GM for six years. He's in his mid-fifties, the kind of man who clearly played sports at some point in his life and hasn't stopped reminding people. He has that particular GM energy—like he's the most important person in the room even though people loathe him.

Shane stands when we walk in, shakes my dad's hand, then mine. "Penelope, thanks for coming in." He gestures to one of the chairs. "Your dad seems convinced you're the one for the job."

My gaze lands on my dad across the table. "He's never been one to highlight my faults."

Shane laughs, but it doesn't feel genuine. He lifts his wrist to check his watch. "Davis should be here soon. I just saw him on the field. Still struggling, I see." His attention shifts to my dad.

Dad's smile dims, and tension fills the room that wasn't there until Decker's name was brought up.

We wait for a few minutes, making small talk that feels more like a method of torture than anything.

Shane sucks on the straw of his Starbucks drink and leans back in his chair. "You like Chicago?"

I'm about to answer when someone knocks on the open door.

Decker.

He's freshly showered, wearing a pair of shorts that show off how muscular his thighs are and a Colts T-shirt that pulls across his broad shoulders.

Seriously, I wish I had opted for a low-cut blouse and pants that mold to my ass to make him as unnerved as he's making me right now. So unfair.

"Decker, please take a seat." Shane waves him into the room.

Decker glances at me—which would be the closest option—but pivots and walks all the way around the table to sit next to my dad. Good. Now I don't have to spend the next forty minutes pretending I can't smell his soap or aftershave or whatever it is that makes him smell so damn good.

"Sorry I'm a little late, but none of you wanted to be stuck in here with me if I hadn't showered." He slips into the conference room seat with ease, but his shoulders are tense, and his smile isn't his usual welcoming one.

"No problem. I'd never want to take you away from practice." Shane tips his chair back and rests his forearms on the desk. "I want to be straight with you two about why this matters to the Colts. The WAG program isn't just a nice thing we do for the families. It's a retention tool. Players talk. When a guy is deciding between two offers and his wife or girlfriend has had a good experience with the organization, that matters." He pauses. "The Trojans just hired a full-time director of family relations, with three staff members under her. They did a rooftop dinner series last season that got written up in two sports lifestyle magazines."

My dad says nothing, his arms resting on the armrests of his chair, face blank.

Meanwhile, I want to say who the hell cares? Except I'm already doing the math on how a rooftop dinner series gets written up in a magazine and what that kind of visibility means.

"We're not the Trojans," Shane continues, "and we don't need to be. But we need our program to feel intentional. Like this organization takes care of its players and their families and most of all the community." He looks at me directly. "Your dad says you're the one to do that. Do you agree?"

What am I supposed to say to that? "Absolutely."

He nods, seeming satisfied. "And having Decker on the player side is the right call?" He glances at my dad, then back at me.

Dad smiles at Decker, quickly interjecting. "He's the perfect fit. The players listen to him, and he's never let me down." A small pause. "It's good for everyone."

"Thanks, Mark," Decker says.

My dad's praise toward Decker isn't subtle.

I know what a contract year looks like. I grew up watching my dad navigate them—the players who were pushing for new deals, the ones on the edge, the ones the organization was quietly evaluating. When my dad says someone makes the whole organization look good, he's telling me that Decker doing this matters. That he's being watched. That there's something in it for him beyond a sparkly Mr. Congeniality ribbon.

I keep my face very neutral.

"So, tell me your vision." Shane nods at me, and my anxiety kicks up.

"I haven't had time to go through it with Decker yet, but this is what I have." I open my folder of notes. "Since we only have two players who have a wife or girlfriend who is a permanent fixture in their lives, I think we should call ourselves the Dugout Social Club, and the events should be referred to as VIP Nights or Events."

"I like it. I like it a lot." Shane points at me and glances at my dad, giving him an approving smile.

We spend the next fifteen minutes going over the event calendar, the budget, and the overall vision, with Shane putting in his two cents on every topic. Decker stays quiet for most of the meeting except to flag some things that wouldn't work for the players. By the time we stand to leave, I have three pages of notes and a clearer picture of what actually needs to be done.

Decker is quick to leave. He's out the door before Shane has finished his handshake—which means I'm going to have to reach out to Decker directly to plan the first event. I'd hoped for more people around us to buffer our initial contact.

Shane shakes my hand again in the hallway. "I'm glad your dad suggested you. He said you were the best person for it."

"He's biased."

"Probably." He smiles and glances at Decker walking toward the elevator. "He's biased toward a lot of people. Glad to see he's right this time." My dad's smile falls flat, but Shane pats him on the shoulder. "Come to my office after you see her out."

Then he's gone. Although Shane doesn't seem like a bad guy, my gut says not to trust him.

Once he's out of earshot, I cross my arms and spear my dad with a look. "What don't I know?"

He nods for me to walk, and by the time we hit the elevators, it's not the manager of the Colts standing beside me, it's just my dad.

"Penelope." His voice is quiet. "He needs this."

His eyes bore into mine, and something in my chest does that thing it always does when Decker Davis comes up—that complicated, involuntary tug I've never been able to argue away. I swallow down the sarcasm I've been directing at my dad all morning.

I think about what I've heard the commentators say during games when I reluctantly turn them on for Hazel so she can see her grandpa. That this is a big contract year, and Decker isn't showing the team the best version of himself.

That Chicago's salaries are too high, and they need to trim some fat, and Decker might be the first to go.

I should've realized sooner why my dad would do this. He loves Decker like a son, even though he's had to maintain some professional distance since he came to the Colts.

I hate baseball. All the contracts and negotiations feel so unfair sometimes.

And I don't have to say anything to my dad—he knows I'll help in any way I can when it comes to Decker.

So, I guess I'm officially on a mission to make the Dugout Social Club a success and keep Decker Davis on this team, which is either the most selfless thing I've ever done or the stupidest. I genuinely cannot tell which.

CHAPTER
SIXTEEN

Decker

I'm just out of the shower when my phone vibrates on the bathroom counter.

> Penelope: Hey, it's Penelope. For the first DSC, I've been able to secure a park, so it will be Dining in the Park. I'm in the middle of organizing food trucks, and I'll get a clown or something to keep the kids busy. If you can just make sure all the players RSVP with the number of guests they're bringing, that would be great. I'll attach the sheet here.

I don't know whether to laugh or cry that she bothered to tell me it was her texting me. As though I wouldn't have saved her new number the second she was put in a group message last year. I've opened a blank text to her four times since then. Just never pressed Send on my message.

> Do you mind if I call you?

The three dots appear, disappear, appear, and keep going.

Fuck it.

I call her.

It rings three times, and I spend all three of those seconds telling myself to hang up. By the fourth ring, my body feels jittery, and I'm trying to convince myself that I'm Decker fucking Davis and shouldn't be afraid to talk to a woman.

"Hello?" She sounds like she was in the middle of something, which is confusing since she was just texting me.

"It's Decker."

She chuckles, which I hope is a good sign. "I know."

"Well, it took you a while to answer."

Only silence greets me for a beat. "Give a girl time to prepare herself."

Is that a good sign? Like she had to prepare to talk to me. Maybe it's actually a bad sign because the last thing she wants to do is talk to me on the phone versus text.

Fuck, calm down, mind.

"It's not like I showed up on your doorstep." I wish I were close enough to do that.

"At least you can't surprise me like that. How is St. Louis?"

"You know our schedule?"

"My dad and Hazel have this thing… anyway."

Of course, *her dad*. Why would I think she'd follow our schedule for any other reason? Three years and I'm still out here finding ways to make things mean something they don't.

"What thing?" I ask.

"Nothing… anyway, what's up?"

I can't blame her for wanting to keep this conversation professional. "Sorry, I'm just getting ready to head out. I just got out of the shower when I saw your text, and I don't have much time, that's why I called instead of replying via text."

"Oh… kay."

And the awkwardness between us just keeps hanging in the air, like a helium balloon that won't quite deflate.

"So, the date is—"

"On the attached list. It has the location and a link for them to RSVP."

"Do you want me to do anything else? I could call some food trucks or something."

"No, Decker." She laughs. "This is my job, remember?"

I pack up my toiletries and head into the main part of my hotel room, dropping them in my suitcase. Then I pull out my clothes, resting the phone on the edge of the dresser.

"I'm not sure you exactly signed up for it, did you, *slugger*?"

She doesn't say anything, and I realize I probably shouldn't have said that. Slugger is her dad's name for her, which means it's a name from the version of us that existed before everything got complicated. I just reached back twenty years without thinking about it.

I'm not sure how to be around her without falling back into exactly who we always were with each other.

"No, I didn't, but you know I've always been a daddy's girl."

I huff. I wouldn't classify Penelope as a daddy's girl. She just never feels like she can tell him no. Those are two different things.

"Thanks for doing all this for the team."

Lame. So fucking lame. Come on, Decker, you can do better than this.

"And me," I add, and she grows quiet once again.

"Decker?"

I sit on the bed, not thinking about having to pack my suitcase and get to breakfast before we play our last game here.

"Yeah?"

"I'm trying to make this as un-awkward as possible, but

I'm not sure this is going to work. Maybe we just stick to texting."

One thing I've always admired about Penelope is her ability to be straightforward. She doesn't hide behind her emotions. She faces them—whereas I push them as far back as they'll go.

"It's really hard." I allow my vulnerability to show with her for the first time since we've reconnected. "You're not just someone I'm coordinating events with. You're…"

She allows the pregnant pause, and I don't fill it because I'm not sure how to.

"Yeah, well, Hazel is calling me, so I need to go."

"Wait…"

She says nothing, but she doesn't hang up. That has to be a good sign.

"I know you have a lot on your plate. Let me help you. I can plan things too."

Again, there's a long pause, and I watch the seconds tick by on my phone screen.

"You have more on your plate than I do. Just be at the park on time and make sure all your teammates are in attendance. I really have to go, Decker… good luck today. Bye."

This time she hangs up before I can even say goodbye. I sit there for a second.

My hand clenches around the phone, and I toss it in the chair, annoyed with myself for even calling.

I'm such a moron. Like she would say yes, come on over, and then make me dinner like she used to. We'd reconnect over whatever she has in the fridge and discover that pull between us is too strong to fight, and then Hazel would go to bed, and we'd make out on the couch like we were twenty again and none of the years have passed.

Come back down to earth. That is never going to be your life.

A knock lands on the door. I cross the room and open it to find Foster on the other side.

"Jesus, I do not need to see you half naked first thing in the morning." He glances at the towel I have around my waist. "Get dressed, I'm starved."

Foster has never once come to my room, nor have we eaten breakfast together unless he was already there with Hayes or someone else.

My forehead creases. "Why are you here?"

"We need to talk."

CHAPTER
SEVENTEEN

Decker

Foster steps in, and his gaze goes immediately to my rumpled sheets, twisted from tossing and turning all night. "You have someone in here last night?"

"No." I grab my clothes and go into the bathroom to change. "Remind me why you're here again?" I say through the bathroom door, still open a crack. "Callie okay?"

I walk out of the bathroom, and his arms are crossed as he leans against the desk.

"Ellis had a rough night. She's fine, but... why didn't you ever tell me about Penelope in high school?"

I should've known he'd never let that go after therapy. This is what happens when you talk to your estranged brother and he's actually listening now.

"You knew that we knew one another from Philly."

"You said you were friends, which I thought was more like acquaintances. You didn't go to the same school."

I've been packing hotel bags after road games for years

and have never once had to concentrate this hard. "You knew about Ripley being Mom's friend. I told you all this when we were in college."

He pulls out the chair and sits. "You left out a lot of details, Decker."

I zip up my bag, spot my charger by the nightstand, and go over to pull it from the plug, wrapping the cord in a bundle. "It wasn't important."

"Bullshit."

"She was Ripley's daughter. Mom and Ripley were close at the time. Her mom had gotten remarried quickly after he started working with me. She was always going somewhere with her new husband, so Ripley had Penelope a lot of the time. We were just close in age and only had each other while our parents…"

Foster may be just sitting there, but I clock it when he stills. "Were they together?"

I tuck my phone cord in the bag and sit on the edge of the bed, meeting his blue eyes. "Truth? I'm not really sure. I think so, but neither of them have ever confirmed anything. Maybe they never defined it, I don't know." I shrug. "I remember Penelope spending the night a few times when we were younger, and Mark would stay late, the two of them building a bonfire and drinking, or sometimes they'd plan trips to the zoo or the museum. Sometimes it was just Mom with me and Penelope, and other times just Ripley and us. But… I think there was some type of relationship."

He gets up from his chair. "I'm playing for my mom's ex-boyfriend?"

I'm thankful he's stopped asking about Penelope and me because I can't really define what we had. We weren't boyfriend and girlfriend, although we did kiss once, but that was more experimental than anything. And then we promised to be each other's best friends, that we didn't want to ever risk losing the other by crossing a line we couldn't uncross. Years later, we made that mistake and realized we should have listened to our younger selves.

"I'm not sure he was her boyfriend."

"Why wouldn't you ask?"

I shrug again and stand my suitcase on the floor. "It wasn't really my place."

"It sure as fuck was. Come on, Deck."

I'm not sure why this bothers Foster so much.

"Did you ask Dad who all the women he brought home were? Try to put a label on them?"

His eyes narrow. "That's different—*no one* was important to Dad. I didn't need to ask to know the answer."

"I'm not sure Ripley was important to Mom either. I think they just used each other, in truth."

"Ew, don't tell me that. Now I'm thinking of Ripley plowing into Mom…" He presses the heels of his hands to his eye sockets. "Jesus, I can't unsee it."

"Grow up, Foster. Mom has sex."

He shakes his head. "It's the two of them together."

"They weren't a couple. It doesn't matter. I don't think Ripley really does relationships."

Foster shakes his head. "And you and Penelope? Did you play games like 'I'll show you mine if you show me yours'?"

"What the hell are you talking about?"

"Don't deflect."

I don't want to tell him about my relationship with Penelope. I like that it's between us—that there's a version of her and me that exists only between the two of us. One that nobody else has picked apart or weighed in on or accidentally ruined with their opinions.

Whatever our relationship is, it is so much more than love —it's understanding one another in a way no one else ever has. At least for me. Maybe whoever Hazel's father is knows all the little details I know about her too. Maybe she was his person too. Where the hell is he anyway? And why does it bother me this much that I don't know the answer?

"We were friends. Two kids thrown together by their parents."

"You used the word family at therapy," Foster says, settling his hands on his hips.

"Which tells you there was nothing romantic between us back then."

He seems to think about that for a second as though he's deciding whether to believe it or not. He stares at me long and hard, though I'm not sure what he's looking for. "You sure?"

I hold his gaze. "Yes."

His gaze doesn't shift for a long time, as if we're in the middle of a staring contest. Or an interrogation.

"Callie told me I'd feel better if I just asked you." He crosses the room. "Listen, Deck, I need to—"

"It's fine, Foster, let's just go eat. I'm starving." I shut down any more conversation on the Penelope front. "We're past it. Let's just move on."

He stares at me for a moment in a way that makes a pit form in my stomach, afraid he's going to ask me more questions.

"Okay." And just like that, he lets the subject go, which is the most generous thing my brother has ever done for me, and I'm not sure he even knows it.

I take my suitcase, wheeling it out of the room, thankful I'll be back in my own bed tonight.

At least one Davis twin has a woman who only brings out the best in him. That's what matters. Foster deserves happiness and love more than I do. He had Dad growing up, which essentially means no one, and I had Mom, which was everything. The scales were never even. Now they'll be balanced.

CHAPTER
EIGHTEEN

Penelope

Hazel and I are pulling up to the curb of Riverside Park when my phone vibrates with an incoming call.

Elias. Leighton's doctor friend, who has already canceled on me once. We're supposed to meet for lunch tomorrow, but now I have a feeling that's not going to happen.

I thank the Uber driver and usher Hazel out of the car onto the curb. Before I click on the voicemail, I tip my driver and leave him a review.

Grabbing Hazel's hand, I lead her through the security gates of the park. This place was a find I'm not sure I'll ever top. It's secluded enough that we shouldn't get too many passersby. The event is only for season ticket holders and their families—a place to meet the team, bring everyone together outside of baseball, and support local food vendors.

I show my pass to security, and we walk in.

Since we're the first to arrive, Hazel runs over to the bouncy house.

I decide I might as well hear what Elias's excuse is for canceling our date. Watching Hazel through the mesh window, I press the voicemail button.

"Hey, Penelope, I'm so sorry, I need to cancel our lunch tomorrow. The chairman of the hospital wants to do a tour, and I just found out. I swear I am not trying to put you off, and I really hope you'll give me at least one more chance to make this date happen. Third time's a charm, right? Leighton says a lot of good things about you. Please call me when you get some time. Hope to hear from you soon."

I can't really be mad at him, but it's concerning how relieved I feel.

"Mommy, look!" Hazel jumps. "Look how high I can get."

"You're doing great, sweetie."

Can I please go back to that carefree life where the only thing to be worried about was the hula hoop talent show? We're still struggling to get a routine down. Which is hard when you can't even get the hoop to swing around your waist. How is this a kid's toy?

This is the second time Elias has canceled. The first time a surgery ran long, which I understood completely and told him so. What I didn't fully think through when I said yes to Leighton setting us up was that trying to schedule a first date with an OB/GYN is apparently harder than booking a hair appointment with a stylist who just went viral.

The bigger problem is I'm not really disappointed. Sure, I need to move on. I *want* to move on. But it was easier before I got thrown into this whole Dugout Social Club planning thing with Decker.

All I've done is replay that phone conversation in my head. His voice. God, I miss that voice. The way he said slugger as if no time has passed and it's still a running joke between us.

"Hazel!" Monroe shouts from the security entrance, running toward us.

I give a wave to Leighton and Hayes to let them know I have an eye on her.

Lake doesn't look thrilled to be here, but she's brought a friend. Lincoln starts tossing a ball with Hayes almost as soon as they're inside the gates.

Monroe stops outside the bouncy house and bends down to untie her shoes. "Hi, Penelope. Today is going to be so fun! Can you hold this for me?"

"You guys are twins." I hold up the bighorn sheep stuffie she's passed me. "Hayes and my dad were clearly at the same gift shop."

"I know. Did Hazel bring hers?" She asks the question, but runs into the bouncy house before I can answer.

Hazel's stuffed animal collection is getting a little out of hand, but every time my dad brings one or two—depending on how long they're gone—Hazel's face lights up.

"Hey, this is awesome. I can see a future in event planning for you." Leighton hugs me and takes the bighorn sheep stuffed animal from my grasp, shoving it in her bag. "I told her not to bring this. If she loses it, she'll go berserk, and I'm not sure when they'll be in Colorado again."

"You'll be hopping on the first plane to Colorado to put yourself out of that misery."

We both laugh.

"Seriously, Penelope, this is great." She looks around, taking in every detail.

White tents with tables are scattered around for all the families to enjoy the food from the food trucks. Red, blue, and white decorations are everywhere you look, and everything is Colts-related.

"It's a generous budget, I'm not gonna lie. I almost had a hard time spending it. But Shane Whitaker is big on making this whole WAGs-but-not-WAGs club a success."

"Seriously, I can help, you know."

Leighton has offered a few times already. Callie too, but I

have this guilt. Because I don't work outside the home, I feel like I should take it on solo. Plus, my dad is the coach, and he doesn't have a wife. Maybe it's just natural for me to step into that role. How many times did I have to go to galas and things as my dad's date through the years?

"Stop it. You're raising three kids and working full-time as a nurse. I can't imagine how busy your life is."

She sips her coffee, which she must have stopped for on the way here. "I'm used to running on empty." She nudges me with her elbow. "So, the big date is tomorrow, huh? Did Elias tell you where he's taking you?"

"He's not taking me anywhere. He's got some chairman coming for a tour of the wing or something."

Her head rocks back. "Oh, I heard something about that when I was leaving work yesterday, but I was so tired that I didn't ask for any of the details. I'm not surprised Elias got roped into being the one to show off our wing. He has a charismatic personality. Everyone just loves him."

"You talking about me?" Hayes kisses her cheek and wraps his arms around her waist, bringing her flush against him. "It's sweet that you're bragging about me."

Jealousy crawls up my back like a spider—quick and unwelcome. Not because I want Hayes, but I do want someone to reach for me like that in public, as though it's the most natural thing. I wish that was my normal.

"Gross. Can we go to the food trucks?" Lake asks when she approaches.

"Hi, Lake." I give her a friendly wave.

"Hi, Penelope. This is my friend Kami." She turns to Leighton. "Can we?"

"Fine, but you stay in this park. Understood?"

Lake rolls her eyes and stalks off with her friend at her side.

"She looks happy," I say.

"Oh, Penelope, you just wait. These pre-teens are like a

keg of dynamite—there's always a risk of an explosion with one wrong move." Hayes walks to the entrance of the bouncy house. "I'm coming in!" he shouts to all the kids inside and reaches in as though he's going to grab them.

The girls squeal and huddle in a corner, but Hayes gets half his body in there.

"Lame, Haymaker." Easton toes out of his shoes and slides through the opening.

"Good—fun Uncle Easton is here." Hayes straightens and nods to someone behind us.

I'm not going to turn around and look because I have a feeling I already know who it is.

"You're late," Hayes says.

"You're early for once in your life."

Goose bumps race up my spine at Decker's voice.

"Leighton has that effect on me. But I got three kids plus one out the door, and you couldn't get your sorry single ass here on time."

"Don't forget, I'm responsible for Easton." Decker's deep chuckle has me wanting to press my thighs together.

"Stop throwing shade, Goldie!" Easton shouts, proving he's never out of earshot.

Everyone laughs, but the man-child is in the bouncy house playing Marco Polo with the girls.

"Decker!" Lincoln shouts and tosses the football over before anyone is ready.

"Watch out, Pen." Decker's voice is tight.

I glance to my right and see a youth-size football coming right for me. When I go to step back, I run into a firm chest. Two arms extend around me above my head, grabbing the ball right before it can hit me square in the nose.

"I got you." Decker's whisper in my ear has me suppressing a shudder.

"Linc, you gotta wait until he's ready." Hayes jogs away, holding up his hands for Decker to throw him the ball.

Decker hasn't moved away from me yet, and I greedily soak in his body heat, his scent. He's everything I crave late at night. Especially when my vibrator makes an appearance.

"You good?" he asks.

I wordlessly nod like a teenage girl whose biggest crush just said hi to her in the school hallway.

He steps away from me and throws the ball to Hayes. The three of them form a triangle to play catch.

"Whoa, that was… should I tell you how hot that was?" Leighton sips her drink, fanning herself with her other hand.

"No need. I felt him everywhere."

"I can imagine."

"No gossip until I get there!" Callie calls, walking over to us with her own drink in hand.

"Reap!" Hayes shouts, but Foster points toward the carrier and puts his finger over his mouth.

Ellis is strapped to his chest, and the diaper bag is swung over his shoulder.

"Man, you sure have him trained." Leighton chuckles.

"Oh no, I volunteered, but every day off, it's him and Ellis time. He doesn't want me to do anything." She sips her drink. "I'm not complaining."

"I don't either. Hayes does the same."

They look at one another like, *aren't we lucky, we found these gorgeous men who love us and our kids, and we're living out our happily-ever-afters.*

"I wonder what it would be like to wake up and not have to get Hazel ready for school by myself." The words come out before I can stop them.

They both give me that look—the pitying one. Which is why I usually don't tell anyone my feelings about being a single parent.

"Let's talk some more about Decker's move," Leighton says with a grin.

"Decker's here!" Monroe says to Hazel inside the bouncy house. "Let's go!"

They scurry out, and Easton peeks his head out. "You're leaving the fun uncle?" He lets his head hang down. "I could use a breather though."

He slides out, puts his shoes back on, and shouts at Lincoln to throw him the ball. Which of course Lincoln does because he loves Easton.

"That guy is like the Energizer Bunny, I swear," Callie says.

"Truth." Leighton nods.

Foster lasts about fifteen minutes watching the guys turn a game of catch into two teams trying to play keep-away from each other.

Callie must notice something on Foster's face because she reaches into the carrier and takes Ellis. "Go play with your friends."

He smiles and kisses Ellis on the cheek. "This doesn't mean Daddy doesn't love you the mostest," he says to his baby girl. "Thanks, Mommy." He kisses Callie, lingering a little longer than is probably appropriate in public.

"Mommy? Is that some sort of role play?" I chuckle.

"No," Callie deadpans and holds Ellis out, but Leighton takes her.

"I've got this shift." Then Leighton walks away, bouncing the baby in her arms.

Callie and I smile at one another.

Hazel and Monroe are all over Decker, tugging on separate arms.

"You seem to like the view," Callie says softly.

I shake my head.

"One day I hope you'll tell me about your past with Decker."

I turn to her. "I thought you knew... I mean..."

She entwines her arm through mine. "Foster told me his

version. And it's okay, I'm okay with whatever happened. I had a life before Foster too. But there's always another side of the story. And from what little he told me, and from the tension I feel when you and Decker are both in the same room, I'd say your story is unfinished."

I shake my head. "It was over a long time ago. It's just hard being around him again."

"Especially when your daughter is so enamored with him."

That's a problem, but I don't say anything. I just nod because it's true.

"She's worse than Hazel!" Monroe screeches.

Decker's gaze lifts to find me as Monroe pleads her case, whatever it is, and Hazel stands next to her, biting her lip.

I don't even want to know what those two are up to.

CHAPTER
NINETEEN

Decker

I spotted her first.

That's always how it goes. I've accepted it as a condition of my life at this point. Just like a thunderstorm will roll in right when you're inching ahead in a tough game. If Penelope Ripley is in the room, I will find her before I find anyone else. I used to think I could fight it. I don't bother lying to myself anymore.

Lincoln and I fall into an easy back and forth of catch, but for the first five throws, I'm only thinking about the scent of her hair and the feel of her body pressed to mine.

I try to get my head back where it belongs. Focusing on Foster peeling away from Callie and jogging over to join us. On Easton crawling out of the bouncy house with a face so red you'd think he'd sprinted from first to home on what was on a shallow drop in right field. On Lincoln's arm—which is honestly impressive for a kid his age.

I do not think about the way Penelope felt with my arms around her.

Okay, I think about it after every throw, but at least I control myself enough not to divert my gaze to her.

Hazel and Monroe tumble out of the bouncy house.

"Decker!" Monroe shouts.

I catch the ball from Foster, throw it to Easton, and pivot toward the voice. Monroe and Hazel are cutting across the grass toward us. Monroe's at full speed, Hazel half a step behind her with a look I've come to recognize. The one that says Monroe has a plan, and Hazel isn't so sure about it.

I crouch down when they reach me. Monroe throws her arms around my neck, and I pat her back. Hazel hangs back, so I hold out my fist, and she bumps it, which makes her smile. She's shy, and I feel a kinship with her because I'm a quiet and reserved guy too.

"What trouble are you two causing?" I ask.

Monroe pulls back. "Trouble? We're never trouble."

I raise my eyebrows, and she laughs. Monroe definitely keeps Leighton and Hayes on their toes, but I doubt they'd ever want her to change.

"Yeah, okay."

She glances over her shoulder at Hazel, who gives a small shrug that must mean something to Monroe because she swings back to face me with an expression that says they're about to ask me something big.

"So, there's this talent show at school," Monroe says, reaching behind her to take Hazel's hand and pulling her closer to me.

I drop to sit on the grass, and they follow my lead. "Yeah? You guys gonna do some juggling or something?"

"Juggling?" Monroe looks at me as if I just suggested her talent was competitive nose-picking. "No."

"Okay, what are you doing?" I direct the question at Hazel, but she glances at her feet.

She looks so much like Penelope—only a few years younger than when I first met her mom.

"I'm doing a dance, but Hazel is doing…" Monroe glances at her friend, who plucks a blade of grass from the ground and winds it around her finger.

"Hula hoop," Hazel says quietly. Her gaze lifts to mine for a second before the grass pulls her attention away once more.

I keep my expression neutral. She struggled with the hula hoop at field day, so I'm surprised she picked it—but good for her for wanting to conquer something she wasn't good at. "Nice. When is it?"

"Near the end of the school year," Monroe answers.

She usually speaks for the both of them. I wonder what Hazel is like when it's just her and Monroe, or just her and Penelope. I'd like to know that side of Hazel.

Monroe's eyes widen in a way that makes it clear there's more. "But there's a problem."

"Oh?" I play dumb, still confused about why they're bringing this to me.

"Monroe," Hazel mumbles, frowning.

"He needs to know." Monroe scoots closer to her friend so their knees touch, like a show of solidarity or something. "She's getting better," Monroe says in the tone of someone who does not actually think that.

"No, I'm not." Hazel's gaze meets mine and holds for at least two seconds, which feels like a win.

"She just needs help from someone who knows what they're doing, and we saw you at field day, and you were the best one there, so you'll do it, right?" Monroe jumbles the words together in one breath and stares blankly at me as if she's already promised Hazel I would.

I keep my eyes on Hazel. "What about your mom?"

"She's worse than Hazel!" Monroe shouts.

I catch Penelope's eye, then Hazel sighs. I spot Lincoln walking over behind Hazel's shoulder and notice that my teammates have been sequestered to sign items and schmooze with the guests.

I'm in no rush to do that.

"Trying to get him to help?" Lincoln asks, tossing the football in the air and catching it himself.

"You in on this too?" I raise my hands, and he tosses me the ball.

It's strange how at ease all the kids are with me. I didn't grow up around any small children, but they're much easier to be around than adults most of the time. Less complicated.

When Leighton's cousin died, and she took over as guardian, I went along with Hayes to help—but now I'm attached, and it feels like they're all my nieces and nephews. Not so much Hazel because I haven't gotten to know her yet. And because she's Penelope's, which… well… when the daughter of the woman you've always loved gets her own special category.

"Nah," Lincoln says. Monroe glares at him, and he shrugs. "We were talking during recess." He points at Hazel and mouths, "You gotta help her."

Hazel plucks another blade of grass.

My gaze lifts across the field. Penelope is already watching, and I hold her gaze because I have no self-control and also because I've missed being looked at by her more than I've let myself admit.

There's no question whether I'm going to help. The biggest question is whether Penelope will allow me.

"How do you do it so good?" Hazel asks.

The fact that she's the one asking opens that spot in my heart for her a little wider.

"Honestly, it's hard to explain. I remember doing it as a kid, and I guess it became muscle memory somewhere along the way. Like riding a bike."

"I can ride a bike," Hazel says with a note of hope to her voice.

"Then I'm sure you'll be able to get the hang of a hula hoop."

"Mom made me watch some videos, but I can't get it to go around my waist properly. No way I can do any tricks."

It's probably a bad sign how happy I am that Hazel feels comfortable enough to talk to me like this.

Lincoln nods as though he thinks she might be a lost cause.

"I wish we had one here." I purse my lips.

"There are some over by the bouncy house." Monroe gets up and runs away.

Lincoln spots Lake with a funnel cake and ventures over to pester her into sharing, leaving Hazel and me by ourselves.

Hazel watches Monroe run off, then her attention comes back to me. "You don't have to help me. They just think—"

"I want to help," I interject and stand. "Are you scared to be up on stage?"

She thinks about it for a moment, the way she seems to do for everything. Maybe that's why I feel such a kinship with her. "A little. I'm more scared of not being good and everyone laughing."

"Yeah." I want to hug her because she looks so distraught, but I know that's not my place. "I get it."

And I mean it in a way I can't fully explain to a seven-year-old—that the fear of failing in public doesn't diminish as you get older. The stadium just gets bigger.

She seems surprised, as if she expected me to tell her it would all work out, and she doesn't need to worry. It's clear that this is important to her.

Penelope stops Monroe, and they talk for a moment before Monroe runs back to us with a hula hoop in her hands.

I take the hula hoop from Monroe and hand it to Hazel. "Okay, show me what you've got."

She steps into the hula hoop, and I try to concentrate on her and not on Penelope crossing the distance toward us in my peripheral vision. Hazel sets the hoop at her waist with the focused expression of a kid who's been at this for a while with disappointing results. She starts the spin, sways her hips, and the hoop wobbles and drops to her feet.

Her shoulders fall.

Monroe's lips press together, and she stares at me with an expression that says, *you gotta fix this.*

"That's a start." I squat down.

Penelope stops short of us, and something catches in my chest that I wasn't prepared for, because she's standing back and letting me do this. It might be nothing to her, but it feels like everything to me.

Hazel sighs and doesn't reach for the hula hoop on the ground.

"I mean it. Your timing is there. You just need to keep your weight further back and move from your hips instead of your whole body." I take hold of the hoop, and she steps out of it. "Watch."

I run through it slowly, exaggerating the movement so she can see the mechanics. Then I do it at normal speed and keep it going.

"I told you he was the one!" Monroe jumps and claps.

I hand back the hoop.

"From your hips," I tell Hazel. "Not your waist. Start it at the back."

She tries again. The hoop makes it four full seconds this time before it drops. She raises her eyes to meet mine, and her expression nearly wrecks me. She's starting to believe it might be possible.

"Better," I say. "A lot better."

Penelope remains a few feet away, her fingers over her mouth as though she's trying not to show how much she needed that.

"Keep practicing, and it'll come." I start to walk away, not wanting to push things too far, but Monroe steps into my path.

"Wait! She has to do a whole routine. You have to help her with it."

Hazel nods, picking up the hula hoop from the ground.

"Let me talk to your mom," I say to Hazel, patting Monroe on the head. "The two of you go have fun. There'll be time to master the hula hoop."

Hazel drops the hula hoop, and before they run off, Hazel stops in front of Penelope. "Did you see?"

Penelope smooths a hand over Hazel's hair with a big smile on her face. "I did. Great job, honey."

Both of the girls cheer and run off.

I stuff my hands in my pockets and close the small distance to Penelope.

"I've tried everything." Her voice is quiet. "Videos, practice. I bought a second hoop thinking if she watched me struggle enough, she'd feel better about her own attempts." Our eyes lock for a beat. "It's incredibly unnerving. She's going to be up on that stage in front of her whole school, and I can't fix this for her."

Throughout my life, I've known many versions of this woman. The twelve-year-old fielding balls and telling me to widen my stance. The girl who saw when I was stuck in my own head—whether it was about baseball, my family, or school.

But this version I haven't yet had the pleasure of knowing —Penelope as a mom, her expression carrying the same nervous energy she had for me when I stepped into the box with college coaches watching from the bleachers.

"Would you let me try to help her?"

What I'm asking is huge. Not only are we already thrown together for the Dugout Social Club but helping Hazel will inevitably mean time alone with not just Hazel, but Penelope.

"Decker, you have enough going on. You do not need to worry about a kid's talent show."

She crosses her arms, and I hate myself for the quick glance I take at her chest. She's wearing shorts and a V-neck Colts T-shirt I really wish had my name and number on the back.

"I want to help."

She inhales and exhales roughly. "Why?"

I shrug. "Because she reminds me a little of myself at that age. Because she's yours. Because I want to see both of you happy."

"Decker." She says my name as though my words pain her, and I brace myself for her to push back. She has an expression that says she's weighing whatever this will cost her against what Hazel needs. "Fine, okay."

"Really?" I can't hide my surprise.

"Yes. Thank you for doing this for her. But I can't let you do it without doing something in exchange—I'm going to cook for you."

"I can cook for myself."

"Would you rather I give you pointers on your fielding?"

She would too. Being a coach's daughter, she probably has more baseball knowledge than some people in the league.

"Based on how it's going lately, I should take you up on that over cooking."

She waves off my comment. "It's just a little blip in your career. You'll get past it."

I run a hand through my hair. "I'm not so sure, but it's nice that you have faith in me."

"I always did."

I nod, emotion clogging my throat. When I can speak again, I say, "We have a day game tomorrow. Mind if I come over after?"

"Oh, so soon…"

"I don't have to—"

"No. The sooner the better. Hazel was doing better just now, and I don't want her to lose any momentum. Come by after. I'll text you my address."

"Perfect."

Lincoln runs over and tells us we're needed at the picture area, and we both fall into step together, walking side by side. My fingers brush hers. It's barely a graze, but I feel it from my hand to the center of my body. Every rule I've ever made for myself says don't do this. But I've been breaking it since I was eleven years old, and I've never once managed to make it stick.

CHAPTER
TWENTY

Dr. Nora Bell

There's a different energy in the room today.

I noticed it before they sat down. I happened to see them through my window, getting out of the same Uber, walking into my office side by side with no deliberate distance between them. In my line of work, you read body language the way a sailor reads the wind. They weren't just walking together. They're no longer putting in the effort to stay apart.

Three weeks ago, they arrived in separate Ubers seven minutes apart.

Progress doesn't always announce itself. It's usually found in the little details. Rarely do two people come into my office and announce, *you're the best, we're fixed, thanks for the help.*

Both men settle on the couch. Still opposite ends, but the angles of their bodies have shifted. Decker's knee is pointed toward the center. Foster's arm rests along the back cushion closest to his brother, instead of pressed against the opposite armrest, ready to bolt at any moment.

I let the room settle before I begin.

"Last time we talked about the split and your younger years," I say. "Mark Ripley. How he came into Decker's life." Both of their gazes land on me. "I'd like to move the timeline to college."

Foster blows out a breath, which tells me we're about to delve into some deep, murky waters.

"So, this is where you reconnected?"

"Yeah. We went to colleges near each other." Decker answers first, which doesn't surprise me.

Foster's thumb moves along the back of the couch. "It was pure coincidence that we both got scholarships so close together."

I turn to Decker. "And how did that feel? Foster being that close again?"

"Good," Decker says simply. "It was the most we'd seen each other since we were eleven. When our schedules lined up, we'd go to one another's games."

Foster nods, and the tiniest smile forms, as if he's remembering.

"So, the proximity helped?" I ask.

"A lot." He glances at Foster. "It was just the two of us. Without anyone managing us. Not Mom. Not Dad. Not any of the family bullshit."

I note the phrase *without anyone managing us*—meaning every interaction before college had a parent attached to it, shaping it, limiting it.

"Foster," I say, "what was that period like for you?"

He clears his throat. "Good… strange at first. I didn't know how to be around him without it feeling forced. Like we were trying to be brothers because we were supposed to. We'd lost our connection."

"And did that change?"

"Yeah," he answers quieter. "It did."

I allow the silence into the room, letting them reflect on the time of their lives when, I think, they felt like brothers.

Decker looks at his hands. There's something careful in how he's holding himself.

"We'd get food after games," Foster continues. "Drive around. Go to parties." His jaw shifts. "Not to sound conceited, but when you're the hot player getting the attention of coaches and expecting offers... well, people aren't always rooting for you. And it was good to have him because"—Foster looks at Decker—"you didn't put me on a pedestal or make me feel like you were wishing for my downfall. We bonded in a way you don't always get to with your teammates at that stage. It was nice to have someone on my side to talk to."

It's the most Foster has ever let me in, and Decker's smile says he agrees and appreciates Foster saying it out loud.

"And you didn't get that with your father?"

"No." Foster's quick to cut off that line of thinking. "Dad wanted a player. He didn't want a son." He says it the way you say something you've already mostly made peace with. "So having Deck around was... I didn't know I needed it until I had it."

I let his vulnerable confession take up space in the room. For a man who has spent most of his life practicing self-sufficiency, that sentence cost him something. I want Foster to know I heard and appreciate it.

Decker stills, but I see his throat work.

"Me too." Decker's gaze shifts to me, as if he's giving Foster room too. "It was hard being away from home, but in a way, we weren't. We found each other. Even on parents' weekend, Mom and Dad actually went to dinner like we were a normal family."

Foster laughs. "Until the check came."

Decker's head rocks back. "God, them arguing about who

pays. That might be the last time they were ever in a room together."

I let them laugh and share the memory, a small ordinary thing that felt like family. These moments matter as much as the painful ones. Sometimes more because they show people what they're actually fighting for.

"So, how long were things good?"

"Three years," they say in unison, and glance at one another from the corners of their eyes.

"How did it all work then?"

"Ripley would have us over for dinner sometimes. He'd come to my games when he could," Decker says.

Foster makes a sound that isn't quite a laugh. His gaze drifts to the window.

"What is it?" My head tilts.

He shakes his head once, as though he's deciding whether to say it.

"Foster?" I ask.

"It's just—" He turns back, and his gaze meets Decker's. There's an edge there I haven't seen directed at his brother yet today. "He hid it from me. I just found out."

Decker meets his gaze. "What?"

"About Ripley." He pauses, and I can see him selecting the version of this he's willing to say out loud. "About him and Mom."

Decker says nothing, and the stifling tension that usually lives in this room reappears.

"Why did you keep that from me? Let me play for him without knowing about him and Mom?" Foster's voice stays even, which I can tell is only because he's trying so hard to keep it that way.

Decker's jaw tightens, but he doesn't deflect. "It wasn't... I didn't think it was my thing to tell. It was Mom's. And by then it had been over for a long time."

"But *you* knew, and *I* didn't." Foster still doesn't raise his voice, a testament, I think, to how badly he wants to improve his relationship with his brother. "The whole time we were rebuilding something, getting close, and you're sitting on that."

"I didn't know how to tell you. I was twenty years old."

"I was twenty years old too."

"And the truth is…"

"What?" Foster positions himself to face Decker directly, resting his back against the arm of the couch.

"I didn't want you to blow up your entire career," Decker says.

"Oh, so you had to coddle me?"

"It's not coddling." Decker presses the heels of his palms to his eyes. "You know what you would have done, how you would have reacted back then, so let's not pretend you would have handled that news without blowing up your future."

Foster sits for a moment, his thumb tracing the same lines on the couch as when we started this conversation, the clench to his jaw he always has when he doesn't want to admit to something. "Maybe, but…"

I gently step in. "Foster, when you found out—how did it make you feel?"

His gaze never lifts off his brother. "It made me feel stupid. Like I was the last one to know something about my own family. Like I'm the outsider again."

There it is.

The line from childhood all the way to the present. Foster has spent his whole life feeling like an outsider in his own family—being the last to know things that concern him, his father moving him south, his mother's life moving on without him. And now this secret.

"I'm sorry," Decker says. "I thought I was protecting you."

"Sometimes you have to let people choose their own reactions—good or bad, healthy or not," I say.

Decker inhales and exhales but says nothing.

"Okay, let's move on for the moment. Junior year puts you at what, twenty-one?"

Foster and Decker look at each other. A quick look, half a second at most, but I've been doing this long enough to know that some looks between people carry the weight of entire conversations they've never had out loud. This is one of those. I make a note and wait.

"We had a good stretch junior year," Foster says. "Our teams were doing well. We were both playing the best baseball of our lives up to that point. The draft was coming." Something crosses his face. "Things were… good." Foster's thumb goes still on the back of the couch.

"Junior year was when…" Decker fills in the way he always does, trying to make things easier for Foster.

Something in my gut says Foster needs to be the one to admit whatever happened to ruin their relationship. "Foster, what happened junior year?"

He looks at me, at his brother, and exhales. "That's when I started dating Penelope."

It's like the name sucks all the oxygen from the room, and tension leaks in from every crevice to fill the space.

Foster doesn't look at Decker.

Decker doesn't look at Foster.

I do my best to hide my own shock at this revelation.

CHAPTER
TWENTY-ONE

Penelope

I try to calm the anxiety coursing through my body by placing the turmeric after the thyme on my spice rack.

It's just dinner. I'll cook while he gives Hazel a hula hoop lesson. Nothing about that requires me to reorganize the spice rack. Regardless, the spice rack is now in alphabetical order and has never looked better.

The garlic butter chicken with orzo is on low heat. I went back and forth on what to make. Is it a reminder of what we used to be? I'm probably overthinking it—but he used to ask me for this dish well before we were anything romantic. I scoop the cheddar biscuits into dollops on the cookie sheet. Hazel will probably eat more of those than the actual chicken. My eyes land on the pan of brownies still cooling on the corner of the counter.

Seriously, what are you doing, Pen? His favorites? You should toss it all out and order takeout.

I turn the heat down on the pan and tell myself to get it

together. He's not here for me or for anything between us. He's here because he's a good person and doesn't want Hazel to be embarrassed.

The doorbell rings at six fifteen on the dot, and my breath locks in my throat.

Hazel appears in the kitchen doorway. "He's here."

She seems to like Decker, but she's still hesitant, which is why she comes to me first, to make sure I'm with her. My daughter and I are handling this the exact same way, and I'm not sure how concerned I should be about it.

"Let's go be good hosts and let him in."

She slides her hand into mine, and we walk toward the door. My footsteps feel heavy, my chest even heavier, my heart pounding against my ribs. It's as though the weight of our past is physically pushing down on me with every step.

This is ridiculous. Decker is gentle and kind and will keep the same respectful distance he always does. We can get through this.

"Do you want to open it, or me?"

"You," she says, tucking herself at my side, almost behind my legs.

Can we please switch places?

No, because you're the adult, Pen.

My hand trembles on the doorknob, but I turn it and open the door. I immediately wish I could slam it shut and say *bad idea, we need to stay on separate sides of this earth from this day forward.*

"Sorry, I got pulled into a media session." He runs his hand through his wavy dark hair that's still damp at the edges.

I've always loved the way he looks effortlessly gorgeous after a game. Freshly showered, smelling amazing, the anxiety of the game shed like a second skin. Decker is undeniably attractive. There's no mystery why he's been the Colts' diamond girls' latest obsession.

"Oh, it's fine." I open the door wider. "We might just have to eat dinner in the middle of her lesson."

"I'm running on a protein bar, so no complaints from me." He steps over the threshold, taking in the cracked baseboards and dated peeling wallpaper in the small foyer. They're all dead giveaways that this place is in desperate need of work. Decker crouches down to Hazel's level—which he always does—and I pretend not to be a little more smitten with him for it. "Hey, Hazel."

"Hi." She steps forward, her hand going limp in mine.

I resist the urge to tighten my grip and warn her about how hard it is to not love a man like Decker Davis.

"She's been practicing all afternoon," I say.

"You have?" Decker stands, smiling at her.

"Since after school." Hazel lets a tentative smile fill her face.

"Okay then, how about you show me?"

She releases my hand, breaks away from me, and picks up her hula hoop.

Decker follows her, and I watch him cross the threshold into the living room, into our space, and I hate that it feels so right. That the anxious energy I've been carrying all afternoon is gone the second he walks in. Because that means trouble.

He sits on the couch and helps Hazel with her start. At one point he pulls out his phone, and they time her.

I make it two rounds before I excuse myself to finish dinner. The smell of the garlic butter chicken pulls me somewhere I wasn't planning to go. I've made this dish dozens of times, but tonight my mind drifts back to my freshman year of college, when my dad took a coaching job at Hartwell College, right by Kingsley University, where Decker attended. That first dinner when my dad invited him over.

It had been a year, and I almost didn't recognize Decker, watching from the front window as my dad shook his hand in the driveway.

That's not true. I recognized him immediately. How could I not? He was the first boy I'd ever fallen in love with. At that point, the only boy I'd ever loved. But the version of him I'd been carrying in my head for twelve months, through my entire senior year of high school while he was off having his first year of college, wasn't this. He was no longer the boy I remembered.

He'd grown into himself. That was the only way to explain it. The boy I'd memorized had become someone I'd have to learn all over again, and I knew standing at that window that I absolutely wanted to.

I heard my dad open the door. Decker's voice—somehow deeper now—saying thank you and congratulations on the coaching job.

I ran into the kitchen and stirred the garlic butter chicken with orzo my dad had requested on Decker's behalf.

Hartwell was a step up for my dad. A better program, more talent, and the fact that it came with free tuition for me settled the question of where I would attend college. I'd never tell anyone how much I didn't mind having the decision made for me, since coming to Hartwell put me half an hour from Decker.

We hadn't had much contact over the past year, but I'd read that letter so many times I was surprised it hadn't been worn thin and broken apart at the creases.

My dad always told me that Decker needed to keep it all together. He'd seen other kids buckle under the pressure, academic and athletic. I didn't want to be the distraction my dad worried Decker would run into. He deserved to get everything he wanted.

It had been a full year. He'd been gone from my life twelve long months.

"Pen, look who I found!" my dad said.

I turned from the stove as if I was surprised Decker was already there.

"Hey," he said in an easy drawl that made my stomach flutter.

Decker crossed the distance with his arms open, and I stood by the stove, never setting down the spoon. He hugged me, and I only used one arm because it felt safer. My cheek rested against his chest and brought everything back regardless. He wore a different cologne now, but the warmth still came off him the same way.

I inhaled as shallowly as possible in an effort to pretend I was unfazed.

"It's good to see you." His voice was low, as though he wanted to say more and wished my dad wasn't five feet away, standing by the fridge.

"What do you want to drink, Deck?" My dad popped our little bubble.

Decker stepped back, and I turned toward the stove to stir.

"Water's fine. It smells great."

"She's been slaving away all day. Cheddar biscuits are in the oven, caramel brownies chilling in the fridge."

"All my favorites."

I didn't turn around so they couldn't see my face, which was surely the same color as my Hartwell sweatshirt.

"Do you need any help, slugger?" my dad asked.

Decker started to laugh but caught himself, coughing to disguise our inside joke.

"No, I'm good. Just relax."

I'd have preferred them to go to the other room so I could get my bearings, but my dad told Decker to sit at the kitchen table.

I didn't live with my dad. I'd opted for the dorms so I could make friends. I was there just for the meal.

They talked about school, Decker's team, the rivalry between Hartwell and Kingsley.

"Have you and Foster reconnected?" my dad asked.

I'd wondered the same thing. I'd seen a few pictures

they'd been tagged in together on social media. There were so many questions I wanted to ask about how it had gone and where they stood, but they were always smiling in the photos, so I assumed things were good between them.

"We have, and things are great. We hang out occasionally and talk a lot. Crazy how it all went down. And now he's playing for you." There was a lightness in Decker's voice that I had never heard before when he talked about his twin brother.

"Rumors are he's a hothead. I met with him last week, and I'm gonna be honest—I don't mind his edge. He's got that win-at-all-costs mentality."

Decker laughed. "That's Foster. Complete opposite of me."

"I'm not sure about that. I think he just lets it out while you internalize everything."

There were moments in my life when I was jealous of my dad's relationship with Decker. They had become so close, and I wondered sometimes if Dad would have preferred a son. But I wasn't going to magically grow a penis, and I wanted Decker to have a man who took on that fatherly role for him since his own father wasn't in his life. So my jealousy faded quickly.

My dad's phone rang, and he excused himself as I was about to say dinner was ready.

"Pen." The sound of a chair scraping across the kitchen floor came from behind me. "Let me help you."

I was mid-reach into the cabinet for the plates when Decker's chest hit my back. "I'll get them."

But even after I dropped back to my heels and his hands were on the plates, he didn't move. The longer we stood there, the more I wanted to turn around and look him in the eye. Would he still have that look in his eyes? That one that said I was more than a friend. Like there was a wordless conversation we'd been having for years because neither of us had the guts to say it out loud.

He eventually stepped back, and I opened a drawer for a spoon.

"Pen?"

"Yeah?" I kept my attention on the drawer, moving around utensils as though I couldn't find the right one.

"You haven't even looked at me yet."

I swallowed against the dryness in my throat and let my gaze lift.

His hips rested against the opposite counter, arms crossed. Then his lips tipped up, and I gave myself the gift of one quick look, but the minute our eyes caught, relief flooded through me.

Decker was still looking at me as though I was his. My shoulders relaxed.

His smile only deepened, and for the first time in a year, we took each other in.

"You look good, Pen."

Warmth rushed to my cheeks as hope swelled in my chest. "Thanks. You do too. I missed you." The last three words slipped out, but I didn't want to snatch them back. I wanted him to know.

His smile faltered. "I... I have a girlfriend."

My muscles all stiffened as embarrassment swamped me. I stepped back, and my lower back hit the counter. "Oh. What's her name?"

What else was I going to say?

Thankfully, my dad came back into the kitchen right after, filling the room with baseball talk while I stood at the stove. I tried to recover, scooping out the chicken and orzo onto three plates while dread wrapped around me like an octopus, pulling me down into the dark depths of the ocean.

I had no idea what it would be like to watch Decker with another girl. But I had a feeling I was about to find out.

"Is dinner ready, Mommy?" Hazel's voice pulls me out of the memory as she barrels into the kitchen. "Decker's stomach is making noises."

"Tattletale." Decker tickles her side, and she squeals, running away.

She runs to my side, clinging to my legs, and my eyes catch and hold Decker's.

Those familiar eyes say so much more than the words that ever come out of his mouth. I'm still a fool.

CHAPTER
TWENTY-TWO

Decker

Peeper's Alley is mostly dead tonight. The regulars are perched on barstools, watching replay games since no Chicago team is competing tonight.

This evening at Penelope's house floats through my mind as I try to process how normal it felt. Normal. Not awkward but for a heartbeat when I first arrived.

The three of us, her preparing my favorite meal. The way the kitchen felt like somewhere I'd been before even though I've never set foot in her house. The farther the Uber drove from her house, the more lost I felt.

Ruby comes out from around the bar with a beer in her hand for me. "I thought I was going to have to call the missing person hotline."

I follow her into the private room in the back, reserved for those of us who live in the building, although we've had to share it with the Falcons a few times over the years. But they're mostly busy raising children and riding off into sunsets these days.

"Our schedule has been crazy." I sit at the table and turn on the television to ESPN. Anything will do as long as it takes my mind off of earlier. Chase tag? Sure, I'll watch people run and try to get away from their opponents.

"You look like you need something stronger." Ruby stands next to me.

"Beer is good. Thanks, Ruby."

Her hand lands on my shoulder. She's always seemed to have a softer side with me than with the others, and I try not to think it's because she feels sorry for me. "I hate to ask, but girl problems or baseball problems?"

I shrug at first, then since it's just the two of us, I decide to open up a little. "Both."

"You know I'm not a yapper. You can trust me."

I laugh quietly. "I'm okay, Ruby. But thank you."

She squeezes my shoulder. "I'm not gonna try to get water out of a dry well, so if things change, let me know."

"I will."

She walks out of the room, and I'm thankful for the alone time—but as her footsteps fade out of the room, I hear her say, "Nope. Room's closed tonight."

"Come on, Rubes, it's our room."

Easton.

"And the three blind mice can find somewhere else to hang," she says.

"Chipmunks, Ruby. Not mice."

Oh, fuck. The Chipmunks are here too.

"Could've fooled me. Sorry, Decker."

"Decker?" Easton walks in and pulls out the chair next to me, dropping into it. "Why didn't you call me if you're here?"

I'm not sure Easton even realizes how much he hates to be alone. Which explains why three large professional hockey players join us at the table, two of them turning their chairs around to straddle them.

"Deck, man, what's up?" Simon says.

"You sick or something?" Theodore asks and slides his chair back, covering his mouth. "I can't catch anything. I'm finally getting regular ice time."

"Nah, he looks like Conor did, remember?" Alvin elbows Simon, and they nod in agreement with Theodore. Then Alvin rubs his hands together. "Lucky for you, we're here now."

"Lucky?" I arch an eyebrow.

"We're the entire reason Conor Nilsen is married to Eloise." Alvin puffs out his chest, clearly not hearing the sarcasm in my voice.

"That's a bold statement." Easton leans back in his chair.

"It's true," Simon says.

They all raise a hand. "Swear," they say in unison.

"In the Uber with him on the way to the church," Alvin starts.

"We convinced him to stop her wedding." Theodore smiles at his buddies.

Easton and I share a look. We've heard the story a few times, and that's not exactly the version we got, but if they think they did it, who am I to argue?

"Goldie, you do look like shit. Talk to us." Easton's face is filled with genuine concern.

I glance at the three guys to my left. They play another sport, on a different team, but I can't risk them finding out who I'm talking about. Easton knows enough to suspect, though I've never come right out and told him Penelope's invading my every thought, my marrow.

"I'm good, thanks."

Easton leans back in his chair, seeming to accept my answer.

We watch some guy chase another guy across the screen,

flying over poles, jumping and sliding under risers. It does take some strategy. Maybe I should quit baseball and enter chase tag. I was always a good runner.

"Come on. Let's play darts." Easton stands and pulls the darts from the board.

"Good idea!" Theodore joins him by the boards. "Here's what we're going to do." He spreads the darts out around each of us as though he's running a board meeting. "Every round, if you hit your number, no questions. You miss, you answer."

I frown. "Answer what?"

"Whatever question we ask." He shrugs with a cocky glint in his eye.

"I'm not playing a game about my personal life with you three."

"Four," Easton says. "I'm playing too."

"Kodiak." My tone implies I'd appreciate him putting an end to this.

"You can trust us. Right, guys? Let us help you." Easton puts a hand on his chest as though he's about to recite the Pledge of Allegiance or something.

I glance at the door, knowing I should leave—but hell, I wouldn't mind a little advice, even from four bachelors who aren't anywhere close to settling down.

"One game." I push out my chair.

Theodore grins. Alvin downs his beer and joins us. Simon nods, sauntering over to the board as if he knew I'd agree.

We move in front of the dartboard, and Easton puts a hundred-dollar bill on the rail. "A little incentive never hurt anyone."

"You have the worst arm on the team," I say.

"Fuck you. That's Torres."

Alvin goes first and hits a seven, using it as a warm-up nobody asked for. Theodore sets the rules. Singles, doubles, and triples count. Hit your number, and the question skips to the next person. Miss, and you answer.

I go first. Hit the twenty clean.

"Lucky shot," Theodore says.

"I throw things for a living."

"Baseballs to bigger targets," Alvin says. "Completely different." He lines up his dart. "Unlike me, who has to shoot a small black puck into a net with a big body blocking it."

Second round. Easton misses by two inches.

"Kodiak, how did you ever become a baseball player in Alaska? Were bears your teammates?" Theodore asks.

Easton takes the time to explain to them how his dad was a hot prospect in college, but then his parents died, and he had to come back home to raise his eight siblings. His dad became the high school coach, and what didn't come from his dad's genes is just raw talent, according to Easton.

Ruby comes in with refills, shaking her head when I miss on the third round, and she overhears Simon's question.

I thought maybe they'd go easy on me, but he goes right for it.

"Who is she?"

The other three guys turn to look at me with the synchronization of people who have been waiting for me to miss.

"I'm not answering specifics," I say.

They grumble, but I hold firm. They do not need to know I want the coach's daughter.

"Okay." Simon puts up his hand. "New question then— how long have you known her?"

"A long time."

"How long?" Theodore asks. "Specifics."

I look at Easton. "Isn't that two questions?"

"Technically, you're not answering the question."

I blow out a breath. "Since I was eleven."

Alvin whistles. "Eleven? That's a lifetime."

"It's not a lifetime."

"It's a long fucking time," Easton says, lining up his next throw.

Fourth round. Theodore misses and has to explain why he's been banned from two bars in the city—the answers involve a live aquarium at one and a deer's head mounted on the wall at another.

Fifth round. I miss again and groan.

"Does she know you're sitting in a bar on a Tuesday looking like someone kicked your dog, asking us for advice?" Alvin asks.

"No, asshole."

"Why doesn't she know?" Simon asks.

"There's no—" I stop. They're all looking at me. Even Easton has the decency to look slightly apologetic about the situation he's created. "It's complicated."

"It's always complicated," Simon says. "That's not an answer."

"She's aware of our history." It feels obvious but apparently isn't. "That's two questions answered."

I line up my next throw. Hit the eighteen. It's a small mercy.

The sixth round passes without incident. Theodore wins the sub round and doesn't have to answer why he called his coach the wrong name for an entire season—which Alvin brings up anyway just to annoy him. I welcome the distraction.

Seventh round. I miss by a margin that seems to match my play on the field lately.

Easton doesn't even turn away from the dartboard. "How long have you been playing like you don't want her?"

"Three years." I give my half-truth because I'm tired, and the beer is doing its job. I've apparently decided tonight is the night I'm done keeping it all inside.

The room goes quiet for a second.

"Three years?" Alvin repeats.

"Give or take." They don't need to know about all the years before that.

"And before the three years?" Simon asks.

"A long time."

"How long is a long time?" Theodore takes a pull from his beer.

"Her dad was my coach." My answer is the left of the truth because I'm not telling them it's Penelope Ripley, but they get the gist of the reason why there's a line in the sand.

Simon sets his darts on the rail. "Her dad was your coach?"

"Yes."

"And you've been in love with her since before that?" Something in Simon's tone tells me he already understands the situation I'm in.

I don't answer.

"That's a yes," Alvin tells Simon.

"I know it's a yes," Simon says and rolls his eyes.

Theodore picks his darts back up. "Okay, here's my question. And I'm asking this as someone with zero personal investment in the outcome." He points a dart at me. "What are you waiting for?"

I open my mouth to answer, but nothing comes out.

Easton crosses his arms and looks at me. We've never had an actual conversation about Penelope and me. Mostly because Foster is tangled up in our history, and it feels like a betrayal to talk to Easton about it.

"I'm out." I set my darts on the rail.

Easton nods, knowing he'll corner me later to really press the issue. Theodore shakes his head. Alvin and Simon go back to the dartboard.

I finish my beer and say good night, leaving Easton to manage the Chipmunks—which he doesn't need help with. He's older than they are. There's a good chance they treat him like their bachelor god, all-knowing.

Outside, the air is cool. I stand on the sidewalk for a minute and blow out a breath.

"Late night?"

I turn to find Foster walking up the sidewalk.

"Diapers," he says, holding up the bag. "She's cute as hell, but damn, she shits a lot."

He studies me for a second with that quiet attention of his that makes me feel as though he sees right through me. Does he somehow know where I've been tonight? And if he did, would he see it as a betrayal?

"You need to get out of your head." He peels The Dugout sign off the door and walks it over to the trash. "I really wish they'd respect that Callie and my kid live here now."

"There are still two single players in the building." I hold the gate open for him.

"Are you sure there isn't just one?" he asks, eyebrow quirked.

"I don't know what you're talking about."

"Sure, you don't." He stops just inside, his stare unnerving. "I'm serious though. You've got to stop being scared."

"What?"

His expression says stop pretending. I think he might know more than he's letting on. "You're playing scared, and that's never going to help get you where you want to be."

He doesn't wait for an answer. He walks up the stairs to his condo, presses in his code, and disappears inside without ever looking over his shoulder.

And I'm still standing here, terrified that if I tell him the truth, that's all I'd see—his back.

CHAPTER
TWENTY-THREE

Penelope

This is why we can't have nice things.

I checked the forecast this morning. Partly cloudy with a slight chance of showers in the evening, which I interpreted to mean we'd be fine.

We are not fine.

The sky has been darkening since ten. It's now noon, and I'm pretty sure the curling iron I used to make my bob look cute was for absolutely nothing.

The North River cleanup has been going well up until this point. Volunteers, including most of the Chicago Colts, spread across a half mile of riverbank with orange vests and trash grabbers, which seem to be everyone's favorite. Too bad they're being used more for who can grab someone's nipple rather than the Styrofoam cups littered around.

My dad is somewhere upstream, Drew at his side and picking up every piece of trash before my dad can reach it. Such a kiss-ass. Hazel is with Monroe and Lake near the family area, which is close enough that I can see them and far enough that it's nice to have a little adult time.

I just wasn't planning to have it with the adult walking beside me.

We fell into step at some point, and the group moved on, and we didn't move with it. So I've been left with Decker, who's scoping out every inch of grass to make sure not one piece of garbage is left. Even though Hayes and Leighton are behind us to pick up what we don't.

I glance at the dark cloud that feels as if it's hanging over us. "I should probably go get Hazel."

He looks at the pavilion where Lake and the girls are handing out garbage bags and bottles of water.

"Lake is a good babysitter. She's okay."

I make a noise, and he laughs.

"You gotta let her have *some* freedom."

I turn and tilt my head. "Says the man without a child."

He shrugs. "Touché. That I don't."

"You're getting up there, old man. You don't want to get so old people confuse you for a grandpa instead of a dad." I regret the sentence as soon as I hear it. What I meant to be a teasing joke comes off differently than I intended.

"Well, maybe if someone didn't leave me without a word three years ago, I'd be pushing a stroller right now."

I suck in a sharp breath. "It was complicated." I pick up a cigarette pack from the ground and put it in the bucket.

"How? I thought…"

I glance behind us to see that Lincoln is now with Leighton and Hayes, although Hayes and Lincoln are doing more sword fighting with their grippers than picking up trash. Leighton laughs and lets Lincoln hide behind her. I can't deny the envy I feel when I see them all together.

I sigh. "Can't we just leave it all in the past?"

"You know I can't."

The pain in his voice leaves my feet cemented to the

ground as he wanders a few feet ahead and picks up a piece of paper, then busies himself cleaning the area around him.

"Decker, what's the point in rehashing the past? We're making this work. This friendship. Maybe one day we can dive into the past, but right now... we each have a lot on our plates."

He doesn't look over when he answers. "Sure."

This is Decker who doesn't like to fight, never wants to push the envelope, never make anyone feel as if he's pressuring them. And I appreciate that side of him right now.

"What do you want to talk about then?" he asks, coming back over to me and standing a little too close. So close that I can smell his cologne.

"I don't know. Want to discuss what other Dugout Social Club activities to plan?"

"I'm gonna be honest, I don't." He glances over his shoulder, but I still hear Leighton squealing with laughter, so I'm pretty sure they're occupied. "I'd rather hear about you and what you've been up to."

"Me? You know what I've been up to. I've been raising a daughter."

"And where were you before you moved here?"

I side-eye him. "You never looked me up?"

"I did one time, then I stopped. It was too hard."

"Yeah, me too. Except you're a little harder to keep off my radar."

He nods.

How many times did I watch his games or interviews? Too many to count. Then I would see pictures of him and different women. There was one in particular a few years ago. A long-haired brunette that I remember from when we were younger. She was the older sister of his best friend. I'd never ask him about it because I clearly had my own relationships. Hazel is proof of that.

"Can I ask why you came to Chicago? I mean, you knew I

was here, and Foster got traded. But you willingly came here knowing you'd have to be around us."

I'd half expected Decker to show up on my doorstep or pull me aside the first time he realized I had moved here. But the fact that he didn't told me he'd moved on.

I look for Hazel, seeing her and Monroe playing with Lake. "We needed to be around family. My mom remarried... again. She sold the house, moved in with her new husband, and now they travel everywhere all the time. Plus..."

I don't really want to give him the last reason, which was probably the biggest one. Hazel had friends back in Philly, I had friends, but it was becoming apparent that Hazel was looking for something we couldn't have there. I wasn't ready to date at the time, but she needs a father figure in her life. It's the only reason that makes sense why I would put myself in the situation we're in.

"Sure, my dad would come for weeks during the offseason and stuff, but honestly, it needs to be more consistent." I shrug, and he doesn't say anything. "Maybe I have it wrong, but she was starting to ask questions, notice that our family looks different than some of her friends. I started panicking, plus I think it's good for her to have a male influence in her life. Someone who loves her as much as my dad does. And since I didn't want to date, there wasn't one coming into my life—"

"But isn't that what you're doing now?"

My head whips in his direction.

He raises both hands. "Sorry, none of my business." But his eyes never stray from mine.

"Hayes told you?"

He nods. "He didn't want me to be blindsided."

"And why would you be blindsided? What does he know?" I feel anger brewing inside me, wishing I could be indifferent to us.

"Give me a break, Penelope. Everyone knows something's

up as soon as you and I are in the same room together. And relax, he doesn't know the specifics. My assumption is that Callie is the only one who really knows anything. Foster told her."

I swallow hard. "Well, if you have to know, it's time. I'm not looking for a father for her…" Lies, but not complete lies. "I want someone to share my life with… I want more kids. I want Hazel to have siblings, and I'm tired of doing it all by myself. And since there's no DoorDash for husbands, I have to put myself through the pain and torture of modern dating."

He says nothing, and the longer silence goes on, the hotter my temper gets. He always ignores what's between us, even if ignoring it is what's best. But I'm not in the mood to fight him either.

One raindrop hits the top of my head, then one gets me in the eye. That's the only warning we get before the skies open.

Leighton screams behind me, and I turn around. Hayes swoops her up and runs toward the pavilion with Lincoln running at their side.

Decker's hand slides into mine, then we're running. I'm trying to keep up with his long strides while ignoring the warmth of his hand wrapped around mine.

He leads us under a building overhang, pushing my back to the brick wall. My hair is drenched and sticking to my face, my clothes soaked. Decker shakes the water from his hair and looks at the riverbank. There aren't any more orange vests.

"Hazel." I look around him, searching for her.

"She's fine." Decker points toward the pavilion where her and Monroe are secure with Lake and some other families.

I glance at Decker. He's looking at the river, hands in the front pocket of his hoodie, rain still dripping from his hair. He seems completely unbothered by the fact that we're standing so close under an overhang that feels like the size of a postage stamp.

"You warm enough?" He sheds his hoodie. "It's wet but will warm you a little."

"You'll freeze."

He wraps it around my shoulders, and I slide my arms through. "I'm warm-blooded, remember?"

My eyes lift to his, those brown eyes I stared into so many times and thought I saw my future. But sadly, those dreams never came true.

"Penelope." His voice is rough like gravel as he pushes away the wet strands of my hair from my face.

Our eyes stay locked. Why can't someone cut this tension between us, this thread between us? Set me free from him. But with the rain dropping into puddles on the ground around us, I'm brought right back to a memory of when I thought maybe it really was our time.

CHAPTER
TWENTY-FOUR

Penelope

It rained the night my car wouldn't start. I was stranded at the drugstore, and my dad was away at a conference in New York.

I was a sophomore, and Decker was a junior in college. We'd remained cordial when we were thrown together by circumstance, but other than that, we weren't anything.

He still had a girlfriend, and to my dismay, my dad had told him to bring her to dinner once. It was horribly awkward. The next time my dad asked, Decker said that she was too busy to join us.

She was nice enough. Aurora—who told us she was named after the princess and made it clear that she fully expected to be treated like one. I'd watched Decker hold out her chair and pour her water, and I ate my chicken and said very little.

She didn't seem to care for me. Never made eye contact

and hardly spoke. Looking back, I wonder if maybe she felt the tension between us.

My friendship with Decker hadn't died so much as faded, which was somehow worse. Dead things allow you to grieve. You just keep searching for things that fade away.

I tried turning the key again, but my car wouldn't turn over. I'd gotten to the drugstore right before they closed after getting my period and realizing I didn't have enough tampons to make it through the next day.

I called my friends, but most of them didn't have cars since it was a pain to park on campus. I scrolled through my contacts, and my thumb hovered over the screen.

Decker Davis.

My head hit the headrest. I shouldn't call him. He probably wouldn't even answer, but then the store sign turned off, and my desperation had me tapping on his name.

He answered on the first ring. I hadn't even finished deciding what I was going to say.

"Penelope?"

I still hated when he called me by my full name. Since our friendship was pretty much nonexistent, he always called me Penelope now. I supposed I should get used to it.

"Hey, um… I'm at the drugstore. The one downtown in Hartwell and… well…"

"What's wrong?" His tone was impatient but in the good way. Like he was worried about me. That made me feel better than it should have.

"My car won't start and—"

"I'll be there in forty."

"What?" I heard Aurora in the background. "Where are you going?"

He must have covered the receiver because I couldn't make out whatever he said. A minute later, he came back on the line. "Lock your doors. I'm on my way."

"If you're busy—"

"I'm not. Just don't talk to anyone. Okay?"

"It's Hartwell. I'm fine."

"Just do it, Pen."

Something in my chest unknotted at him using my shortened name. Something I hadn't realized was knotted. He hadn't called me Pen in months. I guess I was keeping track until right then.

"Thanks. I'm sorry for blowing up your night."

"You didn't. I'll be there as soon as I can."

"This is complete bull—" Aurora shouted in the background before the line cut out.

He pulled in next to me exactly thirty-five minutes after we hung up, which meant he hadn't wasted time getting out of Kingsley, and he'd definitely sped to get to me. Some naïve part of me felt as though it meant something. That our connection wasn't as nonexistent as he pretended it to be.

He did all the things—popped the hood, checked the cables, tried to start it three times as if I hadn't already. The car still wouldn't turn over.

Then he pulled out his phone. "We're going to have to call for a tow."

Between looking through the glove box and finding his roadside assistance card, he called and handled it all as we sat in his car with the heater running.

It started with one raindrop, quickly followed by more.

We sat in the front seat and listened to the rhythm of the rain on the roof while we waited for roadside assistance to arrive, which would be an hour according to the miserable person who'd answered the call. I didn't have roadside assistance, but Decker did, of course. Always the responsible one, even back in college.

The windows fogged slowly. I remember feeling as if we were the only two people in the world, cocooned from reality outside the intimate space.

It was dark outside, and I was painfully aware of how close we were, while pretending I wasn't.

We talked. About schoolwork, classes, baseball, how he was going to enter the draft that year and finish his degree online. There was something different about talking in a fogged-up car in the rain at midnight. Maybe because we hadn't been alone together in so long. But I felt the fabric of our friendship quietly braiding back together.

In total honesty, I felt something much more than that in that car. But I was so scared it was just my crush on him.

At some point, he turned to say something, and I turned at the same time, and we found ourselves closer than we should've been. His eyes dropped to my mouth for one second, two, and by the third, I'd stopped breathing entirely.

"Pen." My name was a whisper on the warm air of the interior.

We both leaned in. At least I think we both did. I've replayed that night so many times that the memory has worn grooves in my mind, and I genuinely don't know for sure anymore what's the truth.

My heart floated out of my chest, and I knew that whatever was about to happen would ruin me, but at the same time, I didn't care.

His phone buzzed in the center console, and he startled and pulled away.

Decker picked it up, looked at it, and my heart squeezed painfully as he answered it.

I was so stupid. He wasn't mine, and I knew it.

"Hey." He turned to face the window, his hand wiping away the fog. "We're just waiting for the tow… Yeah, I know… It's okay. Yeah, I'll stop by after… Bye."

I turned to my fogged window and didn't say anything, drawing little flowers onto the glass with my finger. He put the phone down and the car went quiet.

"Sorry."

"For what?" My voice came out normal. Looking back, I have no idea how I managed it.

He didn't answer. Truck headlights poured in through the windows, and the moment was over.

Probably a good thing.

I blink, pulling myself from the memory, and yank his hoodie tighter around me. I try to think of some way I can keep it.

His hand touches a wet strand of my hair, and he tucks it behind my ear, his fingers lingering. I can't turn away from his eyes, and he steps another inch closer.

"Pen…"

He says it the same way he did in that fogged-up car a lifetime ago.

My brain plays war with my thoughts. Push him away. Kiss him. Consequences. This is trouble. Who cares? Take what you want now. Worry about the rest later.

The rain hasn't let up. If anything, it's found a second gear.

He steps forward an inch, and my back pushes flush against the wall.

I don't breathe.

Decker closes the distance, and I tip up my chin. His fingers are warm against my temple, and the rain is loud on the overhang. This is the fogged-up car all over again, only there's no girlfriend holding him back this time—

"Man, it's really coming down out there." A man steps under the overhang, and Decker circles away from me, resting his back against the brick wall next to me, chest heaving with his breath. "Excuse me."

We part so he can get to the door of his building.

He gives Decker a glance, then me. I hope he's not registering that we were a little too close, but after he puts his keycard in the lock, he turns to Decker. "Hope you guys win it all this year."

Then he's gone, and my head falls back against the wall. What was I about to do?

"She's doing better," he says, staring at his phone, acting as though nothing just happened. "Hazel. With the hoop. She's getting the timing down."

How can he flip a switch and go back to normal like that? If he can, I'm going to show him I can too. I'm an excellent actress when I need to be. I've had years of practice, specifically with him.

"She practices every night."

He smiles. "She told me she wants to do a neck roll at the end. I told her we'd see."

"She didn't tell me that."

He shrugs. "She's still thinking about it. I feel like she'll decide closer to the performance."

I laugh before I can stop myself, and he turns to look at me, the way he always has, as though my laugh is something he can locate in a room without trying. I've always hated how much I loved that.

The rain finally slows, and I find myself not wanting this moment to end. Wanting to draw it out.

"Mom!"

Hazel's voice carries across the bank, high and clear, and I step back to find her twenty feet away at the edge of the pavilion, waving both arms as though she's flagging down a rescue plane.

Monroe is behind her and doing the same thing, except screaming Decker's name.

I raise my hand so Hazel can see me. "I should get back to her."

"Yeah."

I pull off his hoodie and hand it to him.

We walk out from under the overhang and head across the field.

It just goes to show—nothing good happens when I'm alone with Decker Davis.

CHAPTER
TWENTY-FIVE

Decker

Leighton and Hayes's backyard on a Sunday after a home game win is the best place to spend the evening.

The grill is going, someone's connected the speaker to their phone, and the result is a playlist that swings between country and nineties hip-hop with no apparent logic. My bet is on Easton. Lincoln is teaching Hazel some kind of card game on the back steps while Monroe narrates her entire afternoon to anyone willing to listen. Currently it's Foster, but he keeps glancing at Callie with an expression that says, *step in*. She just smiles and shrugs. I think they get off on antagonizing each other sometimes.

We're all here except one person. I clocked it the minute I walked onto the patio, but I'm not going to ask.

We're off tomorrow, so I have a beer in hand and am leaning back in the chair, listening to Easton and Hayes argue about a play in the fifth. Hayes argues that it was the right call, and Easton thinks we should've gone for third instead of first. I don't really care because I had a good game for the first time in weeks. No mistakes. Still, I feel Harkins breathing down my neck, waiting for me to mess up.

Hayes finishes on the grill and announces that the food is ready, so everyone scrambles inside to fix a plate.

I'm about to follow when Hayes pats me on the back. "She's not coming until later."

I look at him, trying to keep my expression neutral.

"Penelope," he says, as if I needed the clarification. "She had a thing."

My gaze moves through the glass French doors to Foster fixing Callie a plate while she holds Ellis.

I take a sip of beer, pretending to be indifferent. "Okay."

"Don't you want to know where she is?"

Hell yes, but what's the use in handing my teammate a window into the most complicated corner of my life and asking him to help me make sense of it? Hayes wouldn't feel right keeping any of it from Foster, nor would I expect him to.

"No."

"Oh." He pulls back in surprise. "So, you're telling me it doesn't matter that she's out on a date?"

"With the doctor?"

His grin says he really wants to make fun of me. But Hayes doesn't kick people when they're down. "Thought you didn't care?" He pats me on the back and goes inside.

I take another sip of beer and stare at the grill, thinking about the river cleanup two days ago. The overhang. Her hair wet against her perfect face. The half inch of space between us. How I was less than a second away from kissing her.

If I had kissed her, I would've broken Rule Number Two—don't make promises you can't keep. Because kissing Penelope wouldn't be casual. She knows that. I know that. A kiss would've been a promise, and I'm not in a position to give it or to keep it.

I think about what she said before the rain started—how

she wants more kids, that she's tired of doing it alone, that there's no DoorDash for husbands. She said it as though she was confessing something to me specifically, like maybe I was supposed to say something back. I didn't though. I just stood there in the rain like the man I've trained myself to be.

She's building a life. She's been building it this whole time, and I've been standing on the edge of building my own, hiding behind my rules.

And quickly, I'm brought back to when I made that rule.

Junior year of college.

The bar was named Sullivan's, and it felt right when I returned to Kingsley to give a commencement speech five years ago and found it closed down. Some things should stay in the past. Sullivan's had the sense to know it. I just wish I did.

It was one of those nights that starts as three people getting food and turns into twelve people at a bar. Aurora was there, which meant I was divided the way I always was when she was sharing space with my friends. She preferred for us to be alone and had a hard time adjusting when we hung out with others.

"A prince? Decker?" Foster and a few of his teammates met us at Sullivan's, which was becoming a common occurrence. "Okkkaaay." Foster gave me a look over the rim of his beer glass before returning his attention to Aurora.

"My mom says I'm destined to have a fairy tale, and Decker's the guy. I mean, how lucky am I to land a guy who will most likely get drafted?"

Foster wasn't impressed and had told me so many times that these were not the days to waste on a long-term relationship. But we were different people. I liked sharing my life with Aurora. The problem was the longer we dated, the clingier she became. She wasn't a bad person. She was twenty-one and in love with a guy who was in love with someone else and couldn't admit it. I've had years to feel guilty about that.

"Let me clarify this for you, Princess Aurora." Foster squeezed my neck. "The Davises aren't from a kingdom. There's no happily-ever-after fairy tale in our past."

Aurora smiled, but it didn't reach her eyes. "I don't care about that."

"Good, because our childhood messed us both up." He patted me on the chest. "I'm going for another drink. You want one?" He tipped his glass to me, then to Aurora. We both declined, and he left.

"You guys are so opposite of each other. Are you sure one of you wasn't switched at birth?"

Her comment irritated me. Sure, we were opposite in looks and personality, but he was my brother.

"We're fraternal, remember? Siblings who shared a womb, not an identical replica of the other."

"I know, Decker, you don't have to treat me like I'm stupid." She got up from the table, and I watched until she disappeared behind the bathroom door.

A few seconds later, Foster slid into the spot at the pub-height table next to me. "I'm not sure about her, Deck. I don't think she's the one."

"You don't think anyone is the one." I finished the rest of my beer.

"Because we're twenty-one and about to enter the draft at the end of the season. This is our time." He gripped my shoulder and shook me. "Imagine what it'll be like when we get into the league."

"Do you think of anything else?"

"Sure. My baseball career. Which you should be thinking about too." He nods toward the bathroom. "She's a distraction. Always getting upset about something—or nothing, more like it. You don't need the stress."

He wasn't wrong, but I'd spent a large part of my time in

college with Aurora, and she was different when it was just the two of us.

"It's like I'm talking to myself. It's fine, man. I'm not saying you won't find someone someday." He took a pull from his beer.

"True. Maybe someone will even come along and knock Foster Davis on his ass someday too."

We laughed, and I looked up toward the door. Penelope was walking in with a few of her friends. I'm guessing my eyes stayed on her a beat too long because Foster followed my line of vision.

"Is that the coach's daughter?" Foster asked.

I wasn't surprised he knew who she was since Mark was coaching him, but I was surprised he didn't know her name.

"Haven't you met her?" I asked.

"A few times at team things, but I never caught her name."

"Penelope."

Aurora came out of the bathroom and slid onto the stool next to me. "What are we looking at? Oh." She clearly spotted Penelope showing her ID to the bouncer. "Isn't she, like, eighteen?"

"She's twenty." The words slipped from my mouth probably a little too fast.

"Oh yeah, I forgot you guys are, like, best friends." Aurora said it with an edge, and I blew out a breath, knowing this was going to be the rest of my night.

A few of the Hartwell guys who'd come with Foster pulled Penelope and her friends into the group, razzing her that they were going to tell her dad, joking around. She laughed along with them until she stopped at our table.

"Decker," she said, sounding surprised, which was funny since she was in my part of town. "Hey."

Penelope hugged me, and I held on a second longer than I should have, aware of Aurora on the barstool behind me, but somehow even more aware that Penelope smelled like the same shampoo she'd used since she was fifteen.

This was the one problem that hung between Aurora and me. I wasn't completely over Penelope, and I didn't know how to process that. Especially since she'd never actually been mine.

"You look good," I said, because it was the truth.

Aurora slid off the barstool and put her hand on my arm in the specific way she did in public, a display of possession rather than affection. "Hey, Penny."

"Penelope," she clarified, the way she always did on the rare occasion they were in the same room.

Foster gave me a nod to introduce him. He had surely seen her before, but it would be like Foster not to have paid much attention, especially if it was during a game or practice.

"Penelope, this is my brother, Foster. As you know, he plays for Hartwell."

Penelope put out her hand. "Hi again."

"Again?" Foster asked.

Penelope laughed. "Yes. I've met you, like, five times. Usually I'm with my dad though, and you're distracted."

Foster stepped closer. "I'm not distracted tonight." He held out his hand. "Let me buy you a drink."

Penelope laughed but took his hand, accepting the invitation.

"We'll be back," Foster said over his shoulder, and I watched them all the way to the bar.

The night wore on, and I stopped drinking at some point while Aurora continued. An hour after I was ready to call it a night, I couldn't find it in myself to leave while Penelope and Foster were in the corner together, seemingly in their own little world.

Aurora was talking to someone. Foster was talking to Penelope. I was standing close enough to hear their conversation while pretending I wasn't eavesdropping.

He was good that night. Funny, attentive, asking her questions about school with the kind of interest that seemed genuine because it mostly was. When Foster decided to be charming, he was difficult to pull your attention from. I knew that better than anyone.

At some point, the bar got louder and the group shifted, and I lost them for twenty minutes.

When I found them again, they were near the back, still talking. Penelope was laughing with her whole face at something he'd said, the way she did when something actually got her.

I felt the shift. The specific feeling of watching something happen that you set in motion, and no matter how hard you try to hit the brakes, there's too much momentum to make it stop.

Aurora appeared at my elbow. "Your brother seems smitten."

"He's never smitten."

Throughout our college years, Foster hadn't dated anyone seriously. Hookups here and there. A friends-with-benefits situation for a month or two once. That was the extent of it. Foster didn't like strings, and any girl who tried to tie him up was shown the exit.

"I'm glad I have the hotter twin." She kissed my cheek, and I let her because it was easier than examining the thing happening in my chest while I watched Foster lean against the wall beside Penelope and say something low enough that only she could hear it.

The bar was emptying out by the time Foster and Penelope came back to our table. Aurora was almost asleep on her stool, and I was being a terrible boyfriend.

"Deck, I'm surprised you're still here," my brother said. "We're heading out."

"Oh. Together?"

Foster laughed and put his arm around Penelope. My heart pounded as if it wanted to jump out and rip his hand off of her. "Yeah, Trent is our DD, and he's going to give her a ride."

"Good, can we go?" Aurora perked up. "Goldilocks has a ride."

"What about your friends?" I asked Penelope, ignoring Aurora.

"What are you, her father? Relax. I've got her." Foster patted my chest and turned them toward the door.

Foster misread my question as concern when really it was jealousy. I didn't want the two of them to walk out that door because whatever happened next was going to change everything. I just knew it, though I don't know how.

"I'll see you." Penelope smiled at Aurora and me.

"Yeah, see you." Panic welled up in my chest.

I can't do this. I can't let this happen. Can't let them leave together.

I stepped forward, my hand reaching for Penelope's arm, but at the same moment, Aurora groaned, turned in my direction, and threw up all over my shoes.

I watched my brother walk out the door with the woman I'd been secretly in love with for most of my life.

Foster said something, and she laughed, and the door closed behind them. I stood there with Aurora's mess on my shoes and watched fate turn the tides against me.

Pulling myself from the memory, I step inside to grab a plate of food.

The early evening stretches into nighttime. The music switches to something slower, and Monroe and Hazel show us all a square dance they learned in school. Hayes films it on his phone, and I sit on the back steps, watching my close group of friends. Sure, I have my mom, but this is the closest I've come to feeling like I have a real family.

I get up to use the bathroom, and on my way through the

house, the doorbell rings. Everyone is outside, so I walk over and open it without thinking about who it might be.

Penelope's still in what she wore to dinner. Her hair is curled the way she does it when she takes her time. "Oh… hey."

I step out of the doorframe and take in her dress and heels, her makeup, and the fact that she dressed up for the doctor. She put in her best effort, and I want to ask her how it went as a way to punish myself for sticking to my rules.

"There you are." Leighton comes inside carrying some dishes. "Just in time for s'mores."

Penelope gives me a small smile and moves past me into the kitchen, leaving me alone in the doorway.

As she should.

CHAPTER
TWENTY-SIX

Penelope

Leighton's kitchen is the kind I've always hoped to have. It's warm, and it smells like whatever was on the grill, and there's always something on the counter that someone is in the middle of making. The fridge is lined with calendars, drawings, and schedules, and little piles of belongings clutter the counter here and there.

Callie is perched on a stool with a plate of two s'mores in front of her.

Leighton drops a dishwasher pod in the dishwasher and starts it, then sits on the stool next to Callie to eat the s'mores Hayes just brought in for her.

I feel way overdressed in my dress and heels and full face of makeup, having put in every effort for the man I spent the entire evening across from while I thought of another one.

The s'mores look delicious as Callie bites into one, but going outside to make my own would mean seeing Decker again.

As if she can read my mind, Leighton says, "I'll ask Hayes to make you one."

But the back door opens before she can get up off the stool.

Easton comes in with a plate. "For the ladies." He slides it onto the counter. Four imperfect s'mores rest on the plate.

"Did the kids make these?" Callie asks, finishing hers.

Easton puts his hand on his heart. "Are you suggesting I'm not a gentleman?"

"You? No way. I'm sure if some hot single women were at this table, you'd be turning on the charm no doubt." Callie gives him a cheesy smile.

"There is one hot single woman at the counter." Leighton eyes me as she goes to the fridge and grabs an open bottle of white wine and two glasses.

"Is she though?" Easton's head tilts.

I feel as if I just choked on a s'more. The man barely knows me and has already identified the central problem of my adult life.

Leighton pours the wine, glancing in my direction. "Penelope *is* single. She was just on a date."

Easton laughs, and he's not fully out the door when he says, "Goldie, man, your lady went on a date. You need to get your head out of your ass."

The guys all tell him there are kids nearby, but who are we kidding? All those kids have probably heard way worse than ass by now.

By the time I turn around, Callie and Leighton's attention is on me.

"What?" I pull the wineglass toward me. They both give me a look that says *come on, spill*. I motion to Callie's face. "You have chocolate on the corner of your mouth."

Leighton hands Callie a napkin, and she wipes it away, swallowing the last of her second s'more.

"Seriously, I eat all the time. It's great, but what will happen to me after I stop breastfeeding Ellis?" Callie asks.

"You'll be fine." I remember when I stopped breastfeeding, and my appetite finally settled to something bearable. It was more the boredom that got me once Hazel was napping twice a day and going to bed early. She was an easy baby.

"Okay, we're not talking about that. Spill. How was your date with Elias?" Leighton sips her wine.

"Oh yeah, who cares about me eating like I'm in a competition every day? Please tell us about your hot date with the doctor, Pen."

Callie's shortening of my name pulls a smile from me. It makes me feel as though I've found real friendships here— but there's a problem. They're all linked to Decker, and if I admit how hard it is to be around him, how much I'd love for us to have an honest try, I risk losing them. They're with Decker's teammates.

"He was nice."

Callie makes a sound and picks up another s'more. "My gynecologist is nice. That doesn't sound promising."

Leighton's smile drops.

"He was funny and kind and good-looking. He asked me about Hazel and didn't seem put off by me being a mom. But..."

Leighton nods. "Just not for you?"

I shake my head and reach for a s'more.

"Anything else?" Callie asks.

"Like?"

"Like you were comparing him to someone else the whole time?" Her eyebrows rise.

I figure if they're going to be my friends, if we're building something real here, I might as well just tell them the truth.

"I compared him to Decker the whole time." I drop chest-first onto the cool stone counter. "I'm pathetic."

Leighton glances at the back door, then back at me. "You are not."

"Yeah, Leighton was pining over my brother for years." Callie shakes her head.

Leighton gives her a look that says shut up. "And she hate-fucked Foster and got pregnant."

I hold up my hands and chuckle. "Okay, ladies. This is not a competition, and whatever it was that kept you two from your guys, you cleared it up fast enough."

Callie quirks her lips. "If you consider decades fast."

Leighton picks up a chunk of graham cracker and tosses it at Callie. The two of them laugh. Then the room sobers, and I prepare for another round of *Confessions from Penelope*.

"You thought of Decker the whole time?" Leighton frowns.

I break a graham cracker in half. "Pretty much. Elias was telling me about a delivery that went sideways. It was a great story, and I was nodding along, but in my head, I was thinking about how Decker would've told it differently. Decker would've imitated the voice. And then I hated myself for it and tried to pay better attention."

"Did it work?" Callie asks.

"For about one minute."

Leighton makes a sound I think is her trying very hard not to laugh.

"It's not funny," I tell her.

"It's a little funny."

"It's a disaster, is what it is." I put the cracker down without eating it. "Elias is a perfectly good man. He's handsome, he's kind, and he brings babies into the world for heaven's sake. And what do I do? I spend our entire first date mentally comparing him to a baseball player who has never once chosen me."

"To be fair," Callie starts, then stops.

Leighton looks from me to her. "What am I missing?"

"It's not my story to tell." Callie raises both hands. "But you should tell Leighton your history. She can feel the tension between you two. Then again, I'm pretty sure the people down under can feel it."

I toss a piece of chocolate at her, and she picks it up and eats it.

I look at Leighton, who has the expression of someone trying to look casual and failing completely. "How much do you know?"

"That you two have history. That it's complicated. That Foster is somehow involved." She refills her glass with wine. "The rest I've been filling in myself, which means I probably have half of it wrong."

"Whodunits aren't Leighton's forte," Callie says.

Leighton turns to look at her. "Don't you have a baby to feed?"

They laugh for a moment, and the years of friendship look so good on them. Then they grow serious and turn toward me.

"Okay." I take a breath. "Decker and I grew up together. My dad coached him when he was eleven, and we became close. Really close. He was my best friend for years. There were feelings, but we never acted on them because of my dad, timing, and I'm not really sure what else now that I look back on it."

"And then?" Leighton leans forward.

"And then he went to college a year before me, and we lost touch. When my dad took a coaching job near his school, we reconnected, but things were never really the same. He had a girlfriend." I glance quickly at Callie. "Foster played for my dad, and Decker introduced us at a bar one night, and well…"

Leighton blinks. "You dated Foster?" It comes out as a whisper.

"Junior year. Not for very long." I reach for my wine and glance at Callie again because this involves her fiancé.

She waves me off. "Go ahead. I don't care."

Callie looks out the back window, and I follow her gaze to where Foster holds Ellis against his chest, rocking back and forth, laughing with his friends.

Who would've ever thought Foster would be the first Davis twin to settle down and have a family? No one from Kingsley or Hartwell, that's for sure.

"It wasn't—Foster wasn't ready to be someone's boyfriend. He was focused on the draft, and I understood that, but I was twenty and operating under that stupid belief that I could change him."

They both nod.

I don't know their dating history, but I can tell they've been there. Hasn't every woman? There's always one guy you think will change for you, and you just get your heart broken trying.

"And Decker?" Leighton asks.

"Decker and I—" I can't compress a lifetime into one kitchen conversation waiting to be interrupted by a kid. I tell them a little more of the college story, enough to draw the shape of it without filling it all in, then I jump to my move here, and how I'm planning Dugout Social Club events with him, and he's teaching my daughter to hula hoop, and apparently I can't go on a single date without his face showing up in my head.

"Okay," Leighton says slowly. "I had about forty percent of that right."

"Which forty percent?" I sip my wine.

"The part where you're both completely gone for each other and doing absolutely nothing about it."

Callie snorts and covers her mouth.

"I'm doing something about it," I say. "I went on a date."

"With someone who is not Decker." Callie's forehead wrinkles.

"Because Decker isn't an option." I hear how it sounds as soon as I say it. "Or rather, he hasn't made himself one."

Leighton tilts her head. "What does that mean exactly?"

"It means—it means we shared a moment at the river cleanup. And there have been other moments. And every time one of them happens, something interrupts it, or one of us steps back, and it just—" I flatten my hand on the counter and flex it. "Dissolves."

"So go after him," Leighton says simply.

"I can't."

"Why not? You're both adults. You both clearly—"

"Because he has to come to me." I say it firmly enough that both of them pause. "And I know how that sounds. I know it sounds like I'm sitting around waiting for a man—and that's not... I'm not waiting because I think that's the woman's role."

"Then why?" Callie's voice is soft, and she's looking at me with the expression of someone who might already know the answer.

"Because Decker has things to work through that have nothing to do with me. His relationship with his brother. His contract year. And most of all, whatever he's been carrying for years that keeps him on the edge of things instead of in them." I trace the lines in the stone of their countertop. "He just keeps stepping back. That's not who I want. I want the version of him who can't be without me. Hazel deserves more than someone who's almost all in. I deserve more. We have to be enough for him to get there himself—or it won't work."

Leighton puts her hand on mine. "I get it."

Callie slowly takes apart a s'more. "For what it's worth," she says, breaking off a piece of chocolate and handing it to me, "I think he's getting there."

"You don't know that."

"I can see it. The way he looks at you. The way he is with Hazel. One day he's going to wake up and get his head out of his ass."

I take the chocolate and eat it, deciding not to ask her what she means. It hurts to hope and feel as though I'll be disappointed again.

Through the window, I can see the backyard—the string lights, the group of people who have somehow become mine in the space of a few months. Hazel's laugh carries through the glass as Decker shows her something with a playing card.

I've been waiting for Decker Davis to make a move since I was twelve.

I'm not so sure how much longer I can wait.

CHAPTER
TWENTY-SEVEN

Decker

My Uber pulls up at the park Penelope and I agreed to meet at, and the first thing I see is Hazel waiting on the sidewalk while Penelope and some man get a cooler out of the trunk of an SUV.

It's one hell of a big cooler.

I'm out the door before my Uber driver comes to a full stop, leaving him a rating and a tip as I hustle toward Penelope.

"Decker!" Hazel waves at me when she sees me coming.

"Hey, Hazel. How are you?" I walk over and take the side of the cooler that Penelope is carrying. "I've got this."

She heaves out a tired breath. "I might have overdone it."

"She's been cooking all morning." Hazel outs her mom, and Penelope gives her a look. We get the cooler onto the sidewalk, and Hazel sits on it. "She made these peanut butter goodies." Hazel's eyes fall to the back of her head as though she can't wait to have one.

"Don't make my mouth water, I'll start drooling and embarrass myself."

Hazel laughs, and Penelope's eyebrows rise as though she's telling me to stop embarrassing myself.

"What?" I pull my wallet out to tip the driver for helping Penelope with the cooler.

"Cheesy and…" She hip-checks me. "I have it." She pulls a twenty out of her pocket as though she had it ready and hands it to the driver.

"Thanks." He gives her a quick smile and leaves.

I let it go although I would've preferred to pay, especially if she's been cooking and preparing a lunch for us all morning.

"Now we have to get the cooler onto the grass." I take both sides and lift.

"I can help." Penelope pulls a large bag I'm guessing contains the blanket and other things over her shoulder.

"Hazel, lead the way," I say.

She jumps off the sidewalk with the hula hoop around her arm, heading toward the grassy area where there are a few other families.

Penelope falls into step beside me.

"I could've picked you up to help with this, then we could've headed to the park."

She side-eyes me. "That seems a little close to a date."

"You are dating now, aren't you?"

She doesn't respond, and I regret my words. That's the problem with us—things leak out because we're trying to gate-keep every one of our thoughts.

"I wouldn't say one date is dating."

Hazel continues ahead, and though my arms are getting a little tired, I don't want to rush her. I like having time with just her mom, even if it's only a few stolen moments.

"Want to talk about how it was?"

She huffs out a laugh. "Nope."

I let it go. It really is none of my business, even though I'm dying to know if she hit it off with the doctor.

"Hazel, you gotta pick a spot, honey. Decker is going to strain a bicep, and Grandpa will blame us for taking out his best third baseman."

Hazel stops and looks around as if she's searching for the perfect place. Then she points to the right, and we head in that direction, closer to the playground. Smart girl.

"That's up for debate," I say about my position at third base. I've been playing well, but so far no one in the Colts organization has approached me about a new contract. Every game feels as though I've got a knife at my throat, and if I boot a ball, I've sealed my fate.

"Oh, stop it, you know you are. And if the Colts are idiots and let you go, well, they're idiots like I said."

I smile that she believes in me that much.

"Here!" Hazel stops at a spot by a tree on the edge of the playground area. It's pretty crowded around here.

I put the cooler down and lower my hat a little more.

"Oh, I forgot we're with a celebrity. We could have just gone to my house." Penelope pulls a blanket from the bag.

"It's fine. I do go out in public."

"I know, but I know how it is. My dad went with us to the children's museum and got stuck in the archeology dig area with five dads circling him, telling him how to manage the team."

I grab one side of the blanket to help her straighten it.

"Hazel, do you mind taking that side?" I ask, and her small hands tug on the other side of the blanket. It feels as if we're a family. It's nice. But it's just a fantasy.

Once the blanket is down, I place the cooler on one end to stop the wind from taking it.

"Do you want to help me find some rocks to secure the other sides of the blanket?" I ask Hazel.

"Yeah."

"We'll be back," I say to Penelope. "I'd rather be here than holed up in a small backyard. It's life, but I apologize ahead of time if we get interrupted."

She smiles but says nothing.

Hazel slides her hand into mine, and I clock Penelope's gaze fall to them, her face neutral and not telling me what's going on in her head.

"Let's go," Hazel says.

I walk her to the lake's edge, and we search for rocks, her picking them up and asking if they're big enough, me searching for the perfect ones. When we stop for a second, I hand her smaller rocks and show her how you can make them skip over the water.

"Whoa!" She takes one from my palm, and I squat behind her, positioning the rock between her fingers. Then I put my hand over hers and try to help her. But it doesn't skip.

"Let's do it again."

We try a few more times. Then she finally gets one that skips three times before sinking to the bottom of the lake.

She throws herself at my legs. "I did it!"

Her small arms tighten around my legs, and I glance back at Penelope, who strips her gaze away from us the minute our eyes meet.

"Way to go!" I pat Hazel's back, wishing she was comfortable enough for me to pick her up and swing her around. But we're not there yet, and I'd hate to ruin the progress we've already made because I'm too eager.

"I'm gonna go tell Mommy!" She runs off, and I watch her fall to her knees, her hands flailing, telling Penelope all about skipping rocks.

As I walk over, Penelope says, "Wow, hula hooper extraordinaire and also premier rock skipper on the résumé? What can't Decker Davis do?"

"Nothing." Hazel smiles big and picks up her hula hoop. "Let's go." She tugs me by the hand.

"Hold on, Haze, let's eat lunch. Then you and Decker can do your hula hoop."

Hazel abandons the hula hoop and gets on her knees, opening the cooler. She takes out different containers, one at a time, telling me what's inside. "Turkey sandwiches… brie." She cringes. "Mommy said some people like it. It smells funny."

I laugh, but she keeps going.

"Pasta salad made with small bowties… my favorite." She preens. "Strawberries, blueberries, a cheese and meat tray, some more sandwiches, and the best thing is these." She holds a clear container, showing me the sweet treats inside. "Peanut butter goodies." She falls back. Either Monroe is having an effect on her, or this is how she is when she feels comfortable.

I'd be a liar if I said it didn't give me a bit of an ego boost.

Penelope's hand smooths down Hazel's hair. I've noticed she does that a lot. "Okay, thanks, our little waitress." She takes the peanut butter goodies from her. "These are for later."

"You went to too much trouble. We could've gone to eat after." I shift to get comfortable.

Penelope shakes her head. "We made a deal. You help Hazel, and I cook."

"I didn't want you to."

"But *I* want to."

Our eyes meet and hold as if we're both remembering another time. She's always been a good cook, and I made no secret about enjoying her cooking. Now that we're older, I wouldn't mind cooking with her, but we don't have that kind of relationship.

After we eat, the lesson goes well. I'm starting to think Hazel is going to pull this off. She's got the basic rotation down, and we've been working on the neck roll she wants to do at the end, which is ambitious but not impossible. She's so focused and determined, she's easy to coach.

She also has Penelope's stubbornness, which helps. She never wants to quit.

Now Hazel is on the playground across the open grass, working through the obstacle course with more seriousness than the kids surrounding her. I watch her calculate the monkey bars from the ground before she commits to the first rung.

"She's really great," I say.

Penelope looks up from the container of strawberries. "She is. Thanks."

She pops a strawberry into her mouth, and I have to force myself not to lean over and place my lips on hers. I want to kiss her and taste the sweetness of the berries on her tongue.

"She's going to be good at this," I say.

"The hula hoop?"

"All of it. She approaches things the way any good athlete does. She watches first. Figures out the problem before she tries to solve it."

Penelope is quiet for a moment. "Probably got it from my dad."

"And her mom."

She glances at me then back at the container. "Not sure about that. I ran in a circle, remember?"

"How many medals did you earn?"

She laughs. "Please, that was a long time ago."

"Okay then, let's talk about your four-course picnic here."

"It's not much. I stress-cook."

"You were stressed?" The question is loaded, and I know it might take us down a road we probably shouldn't veer down.

"You must know I would be. Every time we're..." She holds out the strawberry container. "Want one?"

I notice the way she edits her reactions around me, the

same way I edit mine around her. Two people who spent years being completely transparent with each other now performing carefully curated versions of themselves.

Hazel drops from the monkey bars and moves to the climbing structure, where she finds a high platform and sits on it, surveying the other kids.

"Can I ask you something?"

Penelope side-eyes me. "Hmm… I'm not sure."

"Hazel's dad." I watch her face carefully. Not for reaction, just to make sure she's okay with the question. "Is he involved?"

CHAPTER
TWENTY-EIGHT

Decker

Penelope's quiet for a moment. She sets her fork down and looks across the grass to where Hazel is sitting on the platform, legs swinging, a small smile on her face.

"No," she says. I don't think I'm going to get more from her, but she continues a few seconds later. "He found out I was pregnant, and he chose not to be involved… and that's it."

"Oh, I'm sor—"

"I'm not. If he doesn't want her, I don't want him anywhere near her." She sighs. "I've tried to make sure the absence doesn't feel like a hole in her life, but as she gets older, there are more and more questions."

"That's hard."

She exhales. "When she watches Monroe with Hayes, I see it on her face. The longing to have that in her life. I think I'm running out of time before I have to tell her that her dad chose not to be involved in her life. I'm hoping my dad can fill that role a little bit, and I try to be both, although it feels impossible."

"Distract her with a dog." I'm mostly joking, so I don't volunteer and say I'll be her dad. Because to take on the role of her dad means taking on the role of someone important to Penelope. That fucking Rule Number Two floats across my mind again—don't make promises you can't keep.

"Um… no." Penelope turns to me.

"We were in your backyard doing the hula hoop, and there was a dog barking a few houses down. She said if she had a dog, she'd teach it tricks, and then they could do the talent show together." I smile at the memory. "She said you'd say the house needs too much work before you could get a dog."

Penelope opens her mouth and closes it. "That's—I probably would say that."

"She's not wrong about the house needing work."

She gives me a warning glare. "Don't start."

"I'm not starting anything. Just… I know a guy. He does renovation work for some of the guys on the team. He's good, and he won't take advantage."

She looks at me with the expression she gets when she's deciding whether to accept help. I've learned to wait it out. Penelope takes help on her own terms and on her own timeline and pushing only elongates the process.

Finally, she settles on, "Maybe."

I'd love to help her around the house myself, but at some point, we have to stop being in each other's orbit if we're going to move on.

Hazel has descended from the platform and ventures over to the swings.

"She's going to be fine," I say. "She'll survive without a dad. I did."

Penelope looks at me. Something in her expression shifts.

"I know… it's the guilt though. What kind of man wouldn't want her?"

Anger fills my chest. "Not one worth knowing. He's an asshole who doesn't deserve to be in her life. He's the one missing out."

Tears fill her eyes. "Thanks."

"It's the truth. She's got a grandfather who adores and loves her—sure, he might use her as a buffer from the press sometimes, but that's okay."

She laughs.

"She's got Monroe, a best friend who would go to war for her." I pause. "And she's got a mom who would put herself in the most uncomfortable situation she can imagine just to make sure she can hula hoop in the talent show."

She wipes her eyes and turns to me, knowing it's the truth.

I take her hand. "She's not missing anything."

Penelope looks at my hand over hers on the blanket between us. Then she meets my gaze, and neither of us says anything because there isn't anything to say beyond what I know we're both feeling right now.

"Thank you." She looks at the playground, and I follow suit.

Hazel spots us and waves both arms. We wave back at the same time, and she turns around looking satisfied, as if she just needed to confirm we were still here.

I keep hold of Penelope's hand.

She doesn't pull away.

I've been in love with this woman since I was eleven years old, and I'm sitting on a blanket holding her hand while her daughter waves at us from a slide. I keep saying I can manage this. It might be time I stop lying to myself.

CHAPTER
TWENTY-NINE

Penelope

Hazel spots Monroe before we reach our seats in Webber Stadium. Monroe climbs out of her chair, holding up her latest stuffed animal to show her friend. Hazel holds up her matching Boston Terrier.

I usher Hazel down to our seats. Usually, she and Monroe sit together the entire time. Since we got here late, we probably missed Decker and Easton coming to the fence line to talk to all the kids, which I had to hear about from my daughter the entire ride.

I finally sit down next to Leighton and Callie. Lake is talking with Callie's parents.

"Can I raid your closet once I lose these last ten pounds of baby weight?" Callie asks, dipping her chip into the nacho sauce.

"I agree, where do you shop? I need to go there." Leighton gives me the once-over and smiles.

"That cute little skirt…" Callie glares at me. "I'm never going to get there again."

"Yes, you are." Leighton pats her knee.

"She's never had a baby." Callie looks at me. "Tell me the truth, Penelope."

"You've probably got about a year," I answer truthfully. "But who cares? You look amazing."

"I'll be pregnant again by then if Foster has his way."

Leighton's head whips around, and I inch out to meet her gaze.

"What did you say, Callie?" her mom asks from down the row. Ellis is strapped to her chest with her little headphones on.

"Nothing, Mom."

"I think she said more babies, right?" Mrs. Carlisle's eyes glisten with excitement.

"I don't listen to them anymore," Lake says in a typical annoyed teenage girl voice. "I don't know why I have to come to every game. I love Hayes, but come on, I have a life too."

I smile to myself, remembering those days, although I never minded coming to my dad's games. Then again, the guys were usually close in age to me, so it had its upside.

We're already up one run, which is good. Hazel and Monroe play with their Boston terriers as if they're fighting while Lincoln chats with Callie's dad.

The guys take the field, and on the way, the Jumbotron zeros in on Decker jogging to third base.

The announcer's voice rings throughout the stadium. "Ladies and gentlemen, can I please have your attention on the Jumbotron? The Colts organization would like to formally apologize to anyone who just spilled their beer. Yes, that's our third baseman, Decker Davis, the new face of Noir Cologne, and frankly, we're not sure the stadium is big enough for this billboard. Noir Cologne. Available everywhere. Decker Davis, unfortunately, is not."

"Oh my," Mrs. Carlisle says.

"Relax, Jennifer, he's the same age as your son," Mr. Carlisle says.

"Seriously? That's our Decker?" Callie leans forward and squints.

"How do they make him look so sexy in jeans and a white tank?" Leighton pretends to fan herself.

"It's the bare feet," a woman in the row behind us says. "There's something sexy about bare feet."

"Not all bare feet," Mrs. Carlisle says. "Wait forty years, and you won't be saying that."

"Are you suggesting my feet aren't sexy?" Mr. Carlisle asks.

"This is so embarrassing," Lake says, covering her face and lowering in her seat.

"Never, you have beautiful feet," Mrs. Carlisle says. "They're just more distinguished."

Mr. Carlisle leans over and looks at Lake. "Her nice way of saying she doesn't like my feet."

"Close your mouth," Leighton whispers in my ear, and I straighten.

"It's the way his hand is on his lip, the other one pressed down at his side so his muscles are all flexing," the woman behind us keeps going.

"And his hair. That shaggy kind of unkempt look," her friend chimes in.

"I can think of another word besides unkempt," the woman says.

Meanwhile all I can think about is how I want to climb off these bleachers, scale the fence, run over to him on third base, and offer myself up to him.

"You getting hot over here?" Callie says softly.

"I'm fine." I set down my water. "It's a good billboard. He looks good."

"Good?" Callie arches an eyebrow.

"Yeah… good."

They both look at me.

"I hate you both." I roll my eyes at them playfully and cross my arms.

Below us, Decker fields a sharp grounder and throws to first, and the crowd cheers. I watch him jog back to his position with the same unhurried movement he has when he's in his element. The ad flashes on the screen once more. Apparently, I have zero self-control because I can't take my eyes off it.

"Every day we're just a little closer," Callie says. "Oh, complete transparency, I… um… have a bet with Foster."

"What?" I frown.

"I can't tell you the stipulations because that would be cheating, but I think I might win. And I can't wait to rub it in Foster's face." She continues eating her chips.

I decide not to ask questions I probably don't want the answers to.

In the top of the eighth, the lights go out, and Callie gets on her feet, cheering. "Ellis, baby, Daddy's up."

The Jumbotron flashes ALL ABOARD! in bold, blinding letters as "Crazy Train" by Ozzy Osbourne plays. A train engine bursts from the shadows on the screen, wheels sparking as it barrels down tracks of pure lightning.

"Don't tell Foster, she's asleep. Somehow," Mrs. Carlisle says.

I watch Foster knock his glove with all the infield players, including Decker, and Decker pats him on the back. Look at the progress those two have made. Anything between Decker and me would only derail that.

Foster abandons two Minnesota players on the basepath to end the inning.

Decker is the starting batter in the bottom of the eighth, and we need at least one run to tie the game.

"Can't Stop" by Red Hot Chili Peppers plays, and Hazel and Monroe jump to their feet.

"Decker!" Hazel turns around. "Decker, Mommy!"

I smile and nod. "I see."

They both raise their hands, cheering him on. He looks over at the stands and waves to the little girls, which makes the camera for the Jumbotron scan over to us. Everyone claps, and the announcer says something about his cheering squad.

Decker gets into position, feet first, shifting his weight. His stance has changed over the years—probably from working with a lot of instructors. He's hitting the best he has in years, so I try to figure out what's different.

This is the problem with my dad being a coach—it's hard to just sit and enjoy the game without getting all in my head.

The first ball comes in, and it's so inside, Decker twists his body, but thankfully, the ball doesn't hit him.

"Bully!" Monroe shouts, and a few people turn around.

"Monroe!" Leighton leans forward and whispers something in her ear.

Decker steps out of the box and takes a practice swing. I have no idea why my throat feels like a boulder is lodged in it since he looks so at ease in the box. He gets himself prepared again, and the pitch comes in. Outside, and he doesn't swing, but it's called a strike.

The third pitch looks like it's going to float over the plate, but at the last minute, it tails, and Decker reacts, twisting. It nails him in the back.

"He's gonna need someone to tend to that bruise." Callie's eyebrows waggle.

"I volunteer as tribute!" a woman says one row down and over.

Get in line, lady.

Decker jogs to first, shaking his head.

Torres grounds out but gets Decker to second. Decker steals

third since the pitcher is off. Hayes, having one of his best seasons, nails a ball deep left and Decker comes home. Hayes gets to third on his hit. Ian gets Hayes home but then is out when he tries to steal second. We're up by one going into the ninth.

Foster comes back out on the mound when the next inning starts. We need to keep them down so this will be over, and we'll win.

He throws some warm-up pitches to Hayes.

"You got this," Callie says more to herself than anything.

The first batter comes to the plate, and Foster throws it right at the batter, so it hits his shoulder.

"Oh boy," Callie says.

The batter says something to Foster, but he only shrugs and gets back into position. If only he could keep his smirk off his lips.

He looks at Decker and points, then nods.

"At least it was for brotherly love. Big step for the Davis brothers." Callie looks at me, and I nod because it is. Usually, it would be one of them hitting the other. "I'm really proud of him."

It only reconfirms that I'd be messing it all up if I allowed anything to happen between Foster and me.

Foster still strikes out two, and Hayes throws out the runner at third, ending the inning with a Colts win.

"Let's go to Peeper's. There's no game tomorrow," Leighton says.

"Sorry, Mom and Dad are taking Ellis for the night, and I plan on showing how impressed I am with my fiancé's emotional progress." Callie grins.

"In hitting a batter because Decker got hit?" Leighton asks.

"And I have to go to Decker's to go over the seating arrangements for the VIP Night." I cringe.

"Oh, I'll take Hazel then." Leighton waggles her eyebrows.

"No… I'll keep my little buffer, thank you."

Leighton shakes her head. "I think I want in on the bet you have with Foster, Callie. Sooner or later, one of you is going to break."

I stand, and we file out of the seats to go meet the guys. "You both underestimate my willpower."

Leighton and Callie laugh. "Hey, Pen, look at the billboard again."

I glance over and see that it's displaying Decker's ad for Noir Cologne again.

"How's that willpower now?" Callie asks, laughing as she goes to her mom to take Ellis.

"That ad campaign is something else." Leighton shakes her head. "Although if it was Hayes, I'd probably become a keyboard warrior, making sure everyone knew he was mine."

We laugh and wait for Hazel and Monroe so we can walk them down to the family room.

At the top of the stairs, I take one last look before trying to push the ad out of my mind. All the while, Leighton is laughing.

CHAPTER
THIRTY

Penelope

I prepare myself to be one of the last people to leave since my dad is always in the media room after the players.

Hayes comes out and scoops up Leighton and the kids, promising pizza and ice cream. Hazel and Monroe hug goodbye, and it feels like a gut punch when Hazel looks longingly at her friend as they leave, but I need her tonight. There's no way I'm going into Decker's personal space without a sure-fire way of knowing I will not end up in his bed.

Of course, that would mean he can set aside the past and actually make a move. Then again, do I even want him to make a move? The war in my head never goes away.

Foster comes into the family room next, going right to Callie. "Ellis is already gone?"

"You look at me like I'm a consolation prize," Callie says.

"You're the golden ticket, baby." He dips her as if he just returned from war and kisses her so hard and passionately,

I'm thankful that Hazel is distracted at the dry erase board, trying to master drawing a tree.

"Okay, I guess I was wrong. Take me home."

"Every night for the rest of my life." Foster puts his arm around her shoulders, guiding her out.

"Smooth line."

"I'm reading this book." They both laugh but stop right before they pass me. Foster looks at me, and surprisingly, it isn't weird at all. When I look at Foster, I only think about him with Callie. "He'll be out in a second. He was right behind me."

"Okay. Have a good night, you two."

Callie puts her hand on his chest. "Oh… we will."

Foster kisses her temple. "I'm so fucking happy we live next door. I wouldn't have the willpower to wait an entire Uber drive."

They leave, and I can't say I'm not jealous.

Easton dips his head in. "See you, Pen and Hazel. I'm the lone wolf once again."

I wave and tell him good game.

I'm unsure how often Decker goes out with Easton, and I try not to think about it too much. He has a life and has every right to be at those clubs, picking up women. Which means Hazel and I will keep it brief at his house so he can carry on with his night.

A minute later, Decker walks into the room with damp hair, wearing a pair of jeans and a T-shirt that's snug around his shoulders.

"Decker!" Hazel turns around the minute he walks in.

Does she smell his cologne too?

"Hazel, what did you think? Good game?" He gets down on his haunches to talk to her.

"Great game. How is your back? Monroe yelled at the pitcher and said he was a bully." She giggles, covering her mouth with her hand.

"Not gonna lie, it's sore. Probably have a big bruise. So, what do you want to eat?" Decker asks. "We can order it to my place."

"I thought you were going to be my dad," I say. "Foster said he was coming right out."

Decker looks over his shoulder, seeming a little confused. "He's still in media."

"Oh, I..." There's no way Foster would assume I was waiting for Decker, would he? Unless Decker told him that we were leaving with him tonight. Though I'm not sure he'd ever have that conversation with Foster. "Do you mind waiting? Hazel likes to tell him good game."

"Not at all." He straightens, then sits down and extends his legs out on the ottoman. "Guess what I scored from the dugout, Hazel?" He pulls out two pieces of gum for her.

She squeals and runs over, plucking one out of his hand.

"Sorry, do you mind?" He cringes and looks at me.

I shake my head, trying to pretend that I'm not slipping a little further into the fantasy of him being a part of our lives.

Hazel unwraps one piece of gum and chews it.

Decker pops the other piece of gum into his mouth. "Can you blow a bubble?"

She shakes her head.

"Okay, chew it until there are no hard pieces."

Hazel does, her jaw working so hard I fear it might lock.

"Good and soft?" Decker arches a dark eyebrow.

She nods, continuing to chew.

"Now, slide your tongue through it just a little. Just the tip, then push a little further, stretching it. It might be hard at first, but it'll come."

I try not to take his words as innuendo with my daughter standing here in front of me, but it's hard.

Hazel tries to do what he says, and her tongue pokes through the gum.

Decker laughs. "Okay, watch me." He opens his mouth as wide as he can while he works his tongue through the gum.

Am I being tortured right now?

I cross my legs and try to turn away, but willpower is in short supply lately, so I end up watching him expertly use his tongue to get the gum into a thin film. Then he lets air in bit by bit. The gum turns into a bubble and pops.

Who knew you could be insanely jealous of a piece of gum?

"Now you try." He watches her, and she fails three more times before she gets the tiniest bubble that pops immediately. "You're getting there. Awesome job, Hazel. The more you do it, the easier it will get. But you picked that up so fast."

She concentrates on the goal, and we watch her for a minute before ultimately giving her some space to master it on her own.

Decker still blows another bubble, and I'm stuck slyly watching his tongue. Maybe I'm going through early menopause because a hot flash has me wanting to fan my body.

Dad walks in, his hand overflowing with gum. "Who wants Portillo's?"

"Grandpa!" Hazel runs over to him and gives him a hug. "Watch." She tries again, and this time the bubble is a little bigger.

"Whoa, you can blow bubbles now?"

She points at Decker. "Decker taught me."

My dad's gaze lifts and shifts to me.

"Good thing I have all these for us to practice tonight." He holds out his hand, and Hazel's eyes widen.

"She's with me tonight," I say.

"Please, I'm missing everything. She knows how to blow bubbles now? And how is your hula hoop thing going?"

"Great. I can do it around my neck." Hazel is proud as punch, and it makes me so happy to see her confidence grow.

Dad's face lights up. Let's be honest, Hazel could say she ate one pea on her plate, and my dad would give her a high five. "See, I'm missing everything. How about a sleepover?"

I step over to them. "Oh no, not tonight."

Dad picks up Hazel, and I just know he's going to walk out of this room with her before I can stop him.

"Please, Mommy," Hazel begs.

"We're supposed to go to Decker's to do seating arrangements for the VIP Night." I stand tall as if that's going to make a difference to my dad.

"No seven-year-old wants to talk about seating arrangements. Right?"

Hazel nods. "I want Portillo's."

"I'll take you," I say, stepping closer.

My dad glances at Decker, who isn't saying anything, behind me. "Come on, slugger, you're going to deny me time with my granddaughter?"

"Oh… slugger," Decker mumbles behind me.

My shoulders deflate. The truth is, Hazel hasn't had much time with my dad lately. During the season, it's hard. He plays the guilt card, and I'll fold every time.

"Fine. I'll be by to pick her up in the morning."

Dad lifts his one hand, and Hazel slaps it.

I shake my head at them.

A shoulder rubs along mine, and I glance to my right to see Decker there.

I groan and go give her a hug and a kiss on the cheek. And then my dad. "Congrats on the game."

There's something wicked in his smile. "Thanks. You two have fun tonight, and no rush in the morning. I'm taking her to the pancake place."

"Yay!"

"Bye, Deck." My dad waves as Hazel skips toward the door.

"Bye, Decker. Thanks for the gum."

"Keep practicing," Decker says, but my dad is already halfway out the door.

"Pretty soon he'll be the one searching every gift shop for your stuffed animals," Dad says, and I can't tell if he sounds upset or not.

"I guess that just leaves us."

I circle around and hold my hands together in front of me. "I'll be super fast so you can go join Easton."

Decker tips his head. "Why would I do that?"

"I know he went out, and I'm sure you prefer to be out with him. I don't think this will take long."

He picks up his bag from the floor. "Not sure if you know this, but Easton doesn't share."

"Excuse me?" I swing my purse over my shoulder and fall into step with him.

"Easton is having a woman over tonight, and I'm pretty sure he doesn't want me joining him."

My face heats. "Oh, I assumed he was going to a club."

Decker laughs, and we leave the family room to enter the hallway. "Sorry to disappoint you, but I'm free the entire night."

I take a chance and look over at him. "It's not a disappointment."

He smiles in a way that makes my stomach flip. "You just made my day."

I shake my head. "You went three for four today and made that play in the fourth that prevented any runs from getting in."

"Come on, Pen, you know…"

"What?"

He pushes open the door, and we're on the streets of Chicago. Fans are still sprinkled around the area, going in and out of the bars.

"It doesn't even compare to an evening with you."

Tonight is going to challenge me in ways I'm not prepared for.

CHAPTER
THIRTY-ONE

Penelope

The walk to Decker's condo is quiet even with the fans lingering at the nearby bars and restaurants.

Even though the city moves around us, it feels as if it's just the two of us. My brain is clocking everything about our proximity. His hand so close, every fifth step his pinkie finger brushes mine. His breathing is relaxed. His strides are a little shorter, so he stays on pace with me. Mostly, my brain zeros in on his scent, which oddly is the same as I remember back in college after a game.

A group of patrons spills out of a bar on the corner, still in Colts gear, and Decker quickly positions himself to block them from running right into me.

They all say excuse me, but one of them clocks Decker and opens his mouth. Decker nods, and the guy looks at the two of us walking close together and continues on with his group.

We continue down the street, coming closer to his building. I have no idea why my heart is racing. Well, that's not true. I do, but there's nothing I can do about it.

There's a line outside of Peeper's, mostly women, and the minute one of them sees Decker, the group starts talking and pointing. I can't blame them—this is the reason they're here, to meet a Colts player, since three of them live in the condos above the bar.

I inch closer to Decker, seeing some of the people break away from the line, ready to approach us. He must sense my discomfort, because his hand casually falls into mine. His palm is warm, his calluses prominent. His touch makes me feel safe, but people are still approaching. I fear at some point, we're going to be torn apart.

Decker lifts his hand to the crowd. "Have a good evening, everyone."

He leads me to the security gate, not tearing down the sign that says The Dugout with more notes and phone numbers than I've ever seen on it before.

I deny the petty side of me that wants to tear it down and drop it the ground, claiming that Decker is taken because he's not. At least not by me.

A guy approaches, and Decker shuffles me through the security door first. "Deck, man, a picture?"

"Sorry, I don't have time. Thanks for coming out." He allows the door to shut and the guy mumbles, calling him an asshole.

"You could have taken the picture. I would have waited."

"I came to the realization a long time ago that they don't own me."

He never was one to be enamored with the fame that comes from playing a professional sport. He truly just loves the game.

"Now he's going to tell people you were an asshole when he met you."

Decker waits for me at the bottom of the stairs. "I don't really care."

"You should. You know that how the city views you is important, and you're in a contract year."

He still hasn't released my hand, so he walks up a few stairs, turning to look at me. "You keeping tabs on my contract?"

"My dad is your manager."

His eyebrows raise, and I let him guide me up the steps. "Somehow I don't think that's the reason you know it's my contract year."

I say nothing.

We walk up the steps, and I stop on the landing for the first condo.

Decker shakes his head. "Unless you want to participate in a threesome, that's not the door to go through."

Ah, Easton lives here.

"Well, I'm not into the two-women thing, but maybe two guys could be fun."

He tilts his head and the corners of his lips tip. "What if one of those guys isn't a very good sharer?"

We get to the second door, and he stops, his hand moving to the security keypad.

"Then he shouldn't agree to a threesome. And in truth, I'd rather have the sole attention of one man."

He looks at me, and our gazes lock and hold. It's dangerous and stupid to have this teasing conversation minutes before we go into his condo, alone. No Hazel, no friends, just the two of us sharing his space.

He opens his condo door, and I step inside and come to a stop. "Either you have a cleaning lady, or you cleaned."

Decker isn't much for having a clean space. His bedroom was always a mess in high school. College was worse without his mom picking up after him. Even his hotel room three years ago was littered with clothes hanging over the edge of his suitcase, empty water bottles, and wrappers on the night-stand and dresser. It's such the opposite to how he handles himself.

"Hey, maybe I've changed."

I look at him, and he chuckles.

"I may have cleaned more than usual." He looks a little embarrassed by his admission. It's endearing.

The kitchen counter is completely clear. The throw blanket has been folded and spread across the corner of the couch.

"Is that a candle?" I walk over to the end table in the living room and pick it up to smell it. There's a familiarity to it, but I can't pinpoint the scent. I lift the candle, but it just says Good Sunset.

"I may like candles now." He shrugs.

I set it down and continue to scan the area. It's masculine but homey. Not a lot of picture frames on his walls, but there's one of him holding Ellis. I pick it up to examine it.

He sets his keys on the entry table, and he moves into the kitchen. It distracts me from the emotion clogging my throat.

"Callie gave it to me for my birthday," he says, resting his hip against the island, watching me take in his space. "Water, wine, beer?"

I put the picture back and meet him in the kitchen. "I better stick to water."

He closes the fridge with two bottles in his hand. "Afraid your willpower will wane?"

Are we really going to talk but not talk about it?

"Well, you know that Noir Cologne ad and all. I'm not sure I'll be able to contain myself if I have any alcohol."

His cheeks redden. "Ah, that was embarrassing."

"Why? The woman behind us thought you had sexy feet."

He huffs, and his head falls back. "You can't even see them."

I slide onto the stool across from him, placing my bag on

the other stool. "I think it's the whole look. I mean… it's sexy, Decker."

"It's a cologne ad. They're all sexy."

I smile, unable to not enjoy seeing him so uncomfortable because people now see him as a sex symbol. I clicked on social media during the seventh inning stretch, and his new cologne ad was everywhere.

"What?" he asks.

"It's just… I think I've known you so long, it's weird." I sip my water, thinking about how turned on I was by that ad. God help me if he did a commercial with it too.

"So, you didn't find me sexy in it?" Those deep-brown eyes stare into mine.

I wish I could be one of those women who can play hard to get. Who can play it coy. "I didn't say that." It's the most truth I can handle at the moment.

A small smile forms on his lips, and he unscrews his water cap. "I'll take it."

"Okay." I clear my throat, digging into my bag to take out the pad of paper and the roster. I work better visually and need to see it written down, not just on my laptop.

"Let's go to the couch." He grabs my water and walks into the living room before I can answer.

"Or we can just stay here."

"My legs are tired. I promise we'll stay on separate ends of the couch." He smirks.

I love Flirtatious Decker, but doesn't he know I'm hanging on by the thinnest thread right now?

Sure, Penelope, walk right into the fire. Why the hell not?

CHAPTER
THIRTY-TWO

Penelope

I join Decker on the couch. We really have no choice but to be close to one another so we can work off the same paper. His thigh is pressed to mine, his head leaned in close to mine, and the scent of his cologne surrounds me. It's the sweetest form of torture to be so near to him yet have to maintain some kind of distance emotionally.

Working through the VIP seating with Decker goes how most things do with him, which is to say efficiently.

"Keep Drew away from Easton." He takes the pen out of my hand, leans over, and scratches off Drew's name before putting him on the opposite side of the room from Decker and Easton. "Believe me, as far as we can make it."

"They're teammates." I pick up the pen after he drops it, and I scribble some other names. "I figured we'll put a couple players with a few season ticket holders and sponsors at each table."

"Not all teammates get along. Look at Foster and me." He leans back and finishes his water bottle.

I forgot how small I always feel sitting next to him. It's not like I'm petite, but he's six-three, and his body is big and muscular.

"I meant to ask you, Foster hitting that batter after you got hit…"

He shrugs his shoulder and arm as if remembering the hit. I want to ask him how bad it is. Is the bruise already black and blue? Does he want me to look at it or ice it for him? But just having him next to me is bad enough. A shirtless Decker might make me lose all my willpower.

"Yeah, that wouldn't have happened last year." There's an amused expression on his face, and I love seeing it attached to Foster's name.

I didn't ruin them. They won't go a lifetime without talking because of me. That knowledge loosens something in my chest.

I move to sit in the corner of the couch, bringing a pillow into my lap since I'm wearing a skirt. "You two seem good again."

He scrunches his empty water bottle and tosses it on the end table next to him. "We are."

There's something in his tone, but I don't address it since it feels like we may be crossing into territory we shouldn't. "That's great, Decker."

"Yeah." He stretches his legs out on the coffee table. I'd do about anything to straddle him right now. Just picturing it makes my nipples tighten. "It is great. I just… I forgot what it felt like. Before everything went down." He rubs his hands together. "We started going to therapy together. It's been… I don't know. I didn't think I was the kind of person who needed to sit in a room and talk about things."

"And now?"

"Now I think had we not gone, we'd never be here." He peeks over at me. "There's a lot we still haven't hashed out though."

I'm guessing that's code for me.

"Decker," I say, then stop because I don't want to address it. At the same time, I'm so sick of it hanging over us.

"I know." He breathes out a sigh as if he's finishing my thought.

I stand and toss the pillow on the couch. "I should go."

I collect my papers and head to the kitchen, packing my bag so I can get out of here before things get too heavy. He follows and stops in front of me with six inches between us, but he might as well be flush against me for the way my treacherous body reacts. I don't step back like I should.

Decker pushes my hair back from my face slowly, and I stay still as a statue, holding my breath. His thumb brushes my cheekbone, and my eyes fall closed with the gentleness of his touch.

Something in me breaks. I forgot what it felt like to be touched this way. To feel as though I can let the armor I don every day slip away. This man undoes me.

"I'm tired of fighting this." His voice is a whisper, as if someone might hear us.

I open my eyes and meet his gaze, all the fight having left me. "Then don't."

He stares at me, his attention falling to my lips. I wait for the disappointment. For him to step away and say he can't. The longer his hand stays on my cheek, the more strained the tension between us becomes. His thumb moves to my lips, outlining their shape. I stay in place, not giving him anything. This is his decision, not mine.

A pained expression crosses his eyes, and I prepare myself for his rejection.

Then his fingers tighten around the back of my neck, and he pulls me toward him until his lips meet mine.

His kiss is soft at first, careful, as if he's asking for permission. I grab the front of his shirt to make sure he knows I'm in total agreement. I haven't forgotten all the reasons this is a bad idea, but I'm with him—I'm done fighting it. Something shifts inside him, and our kiss turns into the one that encapsulates how long he's waited to kiss me again.

His mouth turns demanding, his hands more explorative, his tongue desperate for the taste of me. I melt into him, gripping his shirt so hard my knuckles ache, but now that I have him again, I never want him to let me go.

I have no idea how long we kiss, but when we come up for air, he rests his forehead on mine, staring into my eyes.

"God, Pen."

My eyes drift close at him shortening my name again. The first time since we've been reacquainted.

I inch up to kiss him again, but three hard knocks land on the door. "Ignore it."

He's still catching his breath, and I wait for him to release me, tell me this is a bad idea. But he presses his lips to mine again, our mouths still ravenous for one another. I wrap my arms around his neck, inching up on my tiptoes. His hands fall to the small of my back, pressing me into his body.

Another three knocks echo on the door. "Deck, man!"

Easton.

We pull apart, and he steps back. He opens his mouth to say something, but I'm not sure he needs to because it's all there in his eyes for me to see. We're out of the moment and guilt has seeped in.

Who am I kidding? We'll never get over this hump. Did I really think we could just move on like that?

He says nothing, turns, and walks over to open the door. "What?"

I catch a quick glimpse of Easton wearing a pair of shorts, no shirt, and just his chains hanging around his neck. He tries to peek in, but Decker shuts the door quickly, so he doesn't catch sight of me.

"I need a condom," he says.

"Seriously?" Decker sounds less than impressed.

"You want me on my knees? Do you have one? *Some* if you've got more than one."

Decker slams the door shut and stalks into his bedroom. I hear a drawer open and shut, then he reappears with a strip of condoms in his hand. A sick feeling settles in my stomach at the reminder that he doesn't keep them in his bedside drawer because I might stop by. He opens the door and tosses them to Easton.

"Thanks, man, I owe you."

Decker says nothing. He just shuts the door and leans his back against it, staring at me with a pained expression. "Pen…"

"It's okay." I smooth my hair and reach for my bag, then pull out my phone as if I have somewhere to be. "We finished the seating arrangements. I'll send it to Janet in the morning."

"That's not what I—"

"I know." I look at him, so he understands that I mean it. I get it. I do, but it doesn't make it hurt any less. I walk toward the door, and he steps forward, but I weave by him. "It's probably best that we stop seeing one another. I'll text you with the details on the Dugout Social Club stuff, and maybe you can help Hazel at Hayes and Leighton's place. I'll leave food in the fridge as payment."

"Penelope, I don't want your food." The words he's not saying are clear—*I want you, but I can't have you.*

I inwardly wince at my full name coming off his tongue again.

"It's safer this way, Decker." I stare right into his eyes so he can see he isn't breaking me.

I place my hand on the doorknob.

The fact that he isn't saying anything tells me everything I need to know. He's far from ready to have me in his life.

I slip the door open and slide through, shutting it after me.

I don't wait for him to fight for us. I don't wait for him to come after me. I jog down the stairs and walk down the street, weaving through the Colts fans still celebrating the win.

I'm done waiting.

CHAPTER
THIRTY-THREE

Decker

The minute Penelope leaves, my body overflows with adrenaline to run after her. Chase her and tell her I'm sorry, that I want her so badly it aches, but she has to understand what I'd be sacrificing. That I chose her once before, and it ruined any relationship I had with my brother.

Besides, she's the one who left me alone in a hotel room three years ago when I thought maybe our time had finally come.

Then I think about who's above me—Foster. It's one thing for Penelope to be in our friend group, it'd be another to remind him of my betrayal every time he had to see us together. There's no way that a constant reminder of my unforgivable act that ruined our relationship we're just now rebuilding would be conducive to us healing things.

Can't she understand it's the hardest choice I've ever had to make?

I did more damage by bringing her here, and not just

because of the kiss. Because now I can visualize her here, in my space. Her water bottle still sits on the counter. A piece of paper with her handwriting that must have fallen off the coffee table lies on the area rug. The space feels like an empty void while the scent of her still lingers.

I throw myself on the couch, tucking the pillow to my chest. My gaze snags on the candle she picked up. I only own it because the scent reminds me of her.

It's safer this way.

I agree with my conscience. I invented the word safer. I built an entire architecture around safer, and it's worked until now. She's gone again, and I'm sitting in the same place I always end up—alone with all the things I should have said and didn't.

How many times have I been here before?

This feeling is so similar to the one I had back then.

Foster and Penelope lasted five months, which was mind-blowing to me.

Long enough that I learned to manage it. Long enough that I got good at being in the same room with the two of them and never giving one hint of my true feelings for her. Long enough that I started to believe I wanted them both to be happy, and if they were happy together, then I was fine with it.

I was not fine with it.

Aurora broke up with me two months into their relationship after the four of us went out to eat, and I was my usual pissy self. She called me out on my shit. She saw through my fake smile and pointed out every time I looked at their entwined hands or Foster's hand on Penelope's shoulder. But as far as I knew, neither Foster nor Penelope had figured me out, which is funny since they knew me better than anyone.

There were times I was with Foster when I would wonder how strong his feelings for Penelope were, but at the same time, I never got the impression that he cheated or crossed a line with any other girl. Once baseball season started though, as usual, we saw less and less of one another. We both had absurdly busy schedules.

When it ended, Foster called me. He didn't say much. Just that it was done, that Penelope deserved better than what he could give her, and that he was going to focus on the draft.

I said the right things, things I probably didn't even mean. I wasn't sorry. Instead, in the back of my head, I wondered what Foster would do if I asked her out. Sure, I'd have to wait the appropriate amount of time. Then I reprimanded myself, reminding my heart that Penelope was now off the list if I wanted to continue a relationship with my brother.

After I hung up with Foster, I sat in my apartment for an hour, staring at schoolwork I wasn't doing, convincing myself to leave her alone.

I didn't call her.

I made it four days. Not like I was marking off a calendar or anything. Okay, I was.

On the fifth day, I called her to see how she was doing.

She told me calmly that Foster had broken up with her. Gave me her version of it, which didn't put Foster in a good light. Apparently, they were down to seeing one another once a week for a meal that Foster usually rushed through. I could tell she was holding back on some details, trying to respect that he was my brother. But I was also her friend, or kind of friend, although we never shared intimate details about our lives with each other anymore.

I should have hung up.

I didn't hang up.

And I let our friendship morph into something closer to what we had shared in high school. I allowed myself the small pleasure of being her person.

Three weeks into a grueling baseball season, I spent every available second on the phone with Penelope. Lying to teammates about who I was calling or texting and why I couldn't go grab something eat.

We arranged for her to come to my apartment one night. I convinced myself that we were just friends. That I could be both of their friends. Eventually, after the season was over, I'd tell Foster that we were friends, and he'd have moved on by then.

The minute I opened the door to let her in I knew I'd been lying to myself.

She looked so good, just like she did tonight, except her blonde hair was longer.

"Hey," she said, and I opened the door wider. She had her school bag with her, so I figured we'd be studying. "This is weird, right?"

"Yeah. A little."

"I don't want to put you in an uncomfortable situation with your brother. Maybe I shouldn't have come."

That was the moment I could have avoided the inevitable betrayal. But the truth was, I didn't want her to leave.

"No, we can be friends. We were before him."

She came in and sat on the edge of the couch, her legs pressed together, her hands in her lap. "Does he know?"

I brought her a beer and sat down next to her. "No. With baseball season and the draft coming… I don't want to—"

"No, I get it." She was quick to shut down the topic.

We sipped our beers, and it was so awkward at first that I thought it was never going to work. As much as I still wanted her, anything more than friends wouldn't be possible. We'd never be able to push the Foster-sized boulder from between us.

The awkwardness stopped at some point after dinner and a few beers. But the few beers turned into a few more, and we started to play truth or dare.

"Truth or dare?" she asked me.

"Truth."

"Did you love Aurora?"

We'd moved on from how many people have you slept with and who is your celebrity crush. The questions were getting more intimate, and the anxiety and stress were dissipating the more we drank.

"I think I thought I could. And I think I loved her, but I wasn't *in* love with her if that makes sense."

She nodded as though she understood, but all I could think of was what Aurora had said the day we broke up. "You love her. I can't compete with her. But you might as well bury that crush because she's your brother's, not yours."

Penelope cleared her throat and crossed her legs on the corner of my couch.

"Truth or dare?" I asked.

"Truth."

"Did you love Foster?"

I knew it was stupid and dangerous to bring his name into the room, but I had to know where her feelings for him stood. It was selfish.

She sipped her beer, and I figured she wouldn't even answer. I was ready to take it back and say I'd ask another question before she opened her mouth.

"I'm not sure he wants anyone to fall in love with him."

Her answer only spurred other questions, but she continued.

"He's great. But there was this wall I felt like I would never get through. Does that make sense?"

I nodded because I knew that wall well. Even with me, he'd only lowered it about three-fourths of the way, and I was always afraid that he'd erect it again as fast as he could with one misstep by me.

Hell, just me hanging with Penelope might make him do it.

She leaned against the chair, spreading her legs out in front of her. "He's a hard read."

"I know."

She put her beer down and rubbed her hands together as though she was ready to nail me with a big question. "Truth or dare?"

"Truth."

"One of us needs to take a dare soon, but okay, let me think." She tapped her finger to her lips. Her nails were painted a deep purple. I never saw her without painted nails. "Did you ever think about…" She shook her head, her cheeks turning the cutest shade of pink. "Never mind."

I nudged her foot with mine. "What?"

She took another sip of her beer, and I watched her chest rise and fall. "Did you ever think that we… I mean, back in high school?"

She had to have known. That pull between us never went away.

"No. Not once. You?"

Her mouth fell open, and I laughed. She picked up a bottle cap and threw it at me.

"Yes, Pen, I thought about us a lot. And not only in high school." There, I'd said it.

"Oh." The color on her cheeks deepened, and she picked up her beer.

"That day at your house when I saw you for the first time in college… the minute I saw you, I wished I didn't have a girlfriend."

Her gaze fell to her lap. "It's probably for the best. I mean, we might have destroyed this." She waved her finger between us.

"For sure."

Our words were all the right ones, but it was clear it wasn't how either of us actually felt.

She stood and put her beer on the table. "I have to use the bathroom."

I watched her walk down the hall. And what had started as a fun game had morphed into something else.

Something shifted in that moment. I pushed Foster out of my mind. He had already called me last week from a party and asked me to come join him. I heard the girls in the background. Surely, he'd moved on.

So when Pen came out of the bathroom, I was waiting across the hall for her.

CHAPTER
THIRTY-FOUR

Decker

"Hey." Her voice was small, unsure. "Ask me again."

"What?"

"Ask me."

"Decker." Her shoulders fell, but I was done holding back. "Just ask me, Pen."

She blew out a breath. "Truth or dare?"

"Truth."

"Why are you asking me to ask you?"

"Because I think about us all the time. In high school, after, when you were dating my brother and I had no right to think about us." I stepped forward. "It's always been you, Pen. Aurora broke up with me because she knew what I refused to admit to myself."

Tears filled her eyes, and she pressed her palms to the wall behind her.

I was so sick of wondering what she tasted like, how we

would fit together when I kissed her. All the years apart felt like an eternity. It only took me two steps to cross the hall. Two steps to seal my fate.

I'd thought about it so many times over the years, but when my lips met hers, it was so much better than I'd ever imagined.

The first time we came together that night was rushed, and we were barely unclothed. Years of pent-up feelings and lust exploded out of us. But the second time, we took our time, explored one another's bodies, and I kissed every inch of her skin. I'd never been so happy.

The next morning, I woke up first.

She was asleep in my T-shirt. The gray one from Kingsley with the cracked lettering. Her blonde hair was spread across the pillow, her face relaxed and at rest in a way I'd never seen it when she was awake. I watched her for a minute and thought about all the versions of this I'd imagined over the years and how none of them came close to this moment.

I made coffee, and I was cracking eggs when she came out of the bedroom, rubbing her eyes.

All I thought in that moment was that I could live the rest of my life right there with her, and it would be the best life imaginable.

"Aren't I the cook in our relationship?" She walked in front of me and took over the eggs.

I caged her against the counter, kissing the tops of her shoulders, her neck.

"I'm going to get a shell in it," she said.

"I'd like to ditch the entire egg thing and go back to bed."

She continued to crack the eggs and put them in the bowl, and my hands ran down to the edge of her T-shirt, *my* T-shirt, slowly sliding my palms over her skin.

A knock sounded on the door. I had no idea who would be here so early.

"That better not be another girl." She chuckled.

"I think I proved you're the only one for me last night."

I walked to the door and opened it, thinking it was probably a teammate. A bunch of us lived in the complex and were constantly bothering one another to borrow something or other.

My stomach dropped when I saw Foster standing outside my door. Before I could say anything, he shouldered his way in. I could tell he was already agitated about something. "We gotta talk. Dad—"

Penelope was just coming out of the kitchen with a mug in her hand, her hair down and messy, and wearing my fucking T-shirt. She saw Foster before I could even react. Her face fell. The mug shook in her grasp.

Foster stared at her for a beat as though he thought he was seeing things.

Then he turned to look at me.

Ever since that day, I've tried to find a word for the expression on his face in that moment, and I still don't have one. It wasn't just anger. There wasn't just surprise either, as if he had suspected and hoped he was wrong. There was also betrayal and profound disappointment. Until smugness transformed his expression, and it was like I could see him rebuilding that wall between us, brick by brick.

"Foster…"

He circled around and pointed his finger at Penelope. "Fuck you." Then he turned back my way and pointed the same finger at me. "And fuck you."

He walked out the door, and Penelope stepped forward, but I raised my hand. "Stay here."

I followed him into the hallway, and the door closed behind me.

"It's not—" I started, but what could I say? It was exactly what he thought. I'd done it. I had slept with his ex.

"Don't." His voice was flat, and I knew then that he was going to cut me out. That any progress we'd made over the past few years had been soaked in kerosene, and I'd been the one to set it aflame.

"We were friends before—"

A hollow, sarcastic laugh erupted out of him. "Friends don't wake up in each other's apartments wearing each other's clothes." He practically punched the elevator button with his fist. "Were you fucking her behind my back the entire time?" His jaw was set, and his blue eyes were cold as an iceberg.

"God, no. Just last night, and, Foster…" I couldn't find the words. There were no words that would justify this.

"What kind of brother are you?"

The elevator doors opened, and I was desperate to get him to understand. How much I had always wanted her. How the timing had just never been right for the two of us.

He stood with his back against the elevator wall, all casual as if he was immune to the feelings brewing inside him.

I put both hands on the elevator doors, but he crossed his arms and stared at me until the elevator buzzed.

"Come on, just listen to me."

"Fuck off, Decker. We might be blood, but I never want to talk to you again. We'll never be brothers again."

His words struck me as much as if he'd formed a fist and hit me in the face. I stumbled back, and the doors slid closed.

I stood in the hallway in my bare feet and knew I'd just broken the thing we'd spent three years rebuilding. Broken it beyond repair. I called him six times that day. Twice the next morning. After the third day, I stopped because I knew he wasn't going to answer. I was desperate to make myself feel better, but I was in the wrong. I'd broken the rules with no regard for my brother's feelings.

We were done. I'd committed the ultimate act of betrayal, and Foster would never forgive me. I'd been the one person he could rely on in our family, and I'd turned my back on him too.

That's when Rule Number Three was invented—don't stay somewhere you don't belong. And I didn't belong in Foster's life. I'd chosen pleasure, selfishly put myself before him, and he was right, I was no brother for that.

Kingsley and Hartwell played each other in the conference tournament junior year. Worst fucking time of my life. The draft was a month out. Looking back, I have no idea how we even managed. I was thankful for the different dugouts, different fields, a nod across the diamond when the teams warmed up and nothing else. The unspoken agreement of two brothers who had figured out how to coexist at a careful distance.

In the sixth inning, Foster was on the mound when I stepped up to the plate. The old competitiveness between us was like the tenth player on the field. I fouled one back, and the catcher said something sly under his breath. I said something back, and the home plate umpire warned us both.

The next pitch came in, and I allowed the ball to stay low. I was at the advantage with a one to two count.

I could see my brother brewing after each pitch, fighting himself to stay in control of his emotions, but when the next pitch was a ball, I could tell he was losing his composure.

I should have predicted it. The entire game, both teams were chirping at one another, so when he threw the next pitch, he went for my head. I ducked, and it took less than a second for the benches to clear on both sides.

Foster and I were right in the middle of it all, tearing at one another's jerseys, throwing punches back and forth. At one point, we were down on the ground on the field.

That fucking video played for two weeks on ESPN and followed both of us into the draft.

Before the fight, we were both projected top five picks.

I went twenty-third.

Foster went thirty-first.

I didn't bother calling him after the draft, and he never called me. Our relationship was well and truly severed.

Giving my head a shake, I pull myself out of the memory. I pick up the seating chart from the coffee table and look at Pen's handwriting in the margins.

I set it back down.

It's safer this way, Decker.

Since the night I took something I wanted without considering what I'd be sacrificing, it's been safer to hold the line. Not blow up the things that matter most to me by wanting something that was never supposed to be mine in the first place.

So I sit on my couch and pretend, like always, that she's not worth losing my brother, my niece, my family.

CHAPTER
THIRTY-FIVE

Dr. Nora Bell

I've learned to read the waiting room before I welcome them in.

In the beginning, it was harder. The Davis brothers arrived for every session with the same surface presentation—composed, cooperative, willing to be here in the technical sense of the word. It took me four sessions to really read their body language and understand what they're saying between words.

Today, the space is the same as always.

But something is different in Decker. He arrived two minutes after Foster, which he never does. He's been staring out the window since he sat down. Foster keeps sneaking peeks at Decker, appearing confused.

"Last time," I say, "Foster, you told us that junior year was when you started dating Penelope."

Foster nods.

"Who is Penelope to you both?"

Foster's gaze diverts to Decker, but his brother is definitely not answering, so he does. "Penelope Ripley. Mark Ripley's daughter."

"Oh, your manager's daughter?"

"Yeah."

"So she was with you in college as well?"

"Yeah."

Foster is the only one talking, but Decker's facial expressions say more than I think he realizes.

"Do you want to add anything else?" I ask Decker. "Clearly, her name holds a lot of weight in this room." When Decker doesn't respond, I turn back to Foster. "What's the context of that relationship now?"

"There is no context. I'm engaged and have a daughter with another woman." He glances at Decker, but Decker's attention doesn't shift away from the window.

"Decker, you seem very disengaged right now."

Foster turns his body toward Decker, and he's fighting a smile, which I find odd given Decker's mood.

"I don't want to rehash it all." Decker finally turns to look at me.

"Why?"

"Because me saying sorry will never be enough."

Foster blows out a breath and shakes his head.

"I'm missing something, fellas, fill me in?" I look between the two of them.

Foster waits a minute, but Decker doesn't talk. "Fine, I'll do it. I was dating Penelope, we broke up, and I showed up at Decker's one morning shortly after. Penelope was there, half naked and wearing his T-shirt."

Decker winces.

The room goes quiet.

I lean back in my chair. I should've predicted it all came down to a woman.

"I have no excuse." Decker turns to face his brother. "I'm sorry. I really am."

"I know you are," Foster says, but it's a Band-Aid.

We need to dig deeper.

"Can we start from the breakup, Foster? The relationship ended. Who ended it?"

"I did. I was focused on the season." He blows out a breath. "Draft was coming. I moved on."

"Decker?"

He's back to looking out the window. "I called her."

Foster turns at his confession.

"I waited five days," Decker says. "And then I called her."

I note the precision of it. The waiting. As if five days made the call something other than what it was.

"Did Foster know you were calling her?" I ask.

He shakes his head. "No."

"Why not?"

He swings his gaze away from the window. "Because I knew what I was doing. And I knew if I told him, I'd have to stop."

I let that sit. It's the most honest thing he's said in six sessions, and I don't want to move past it too quickly. It might be the last time Decker Davis crossed a line he shouldn't have.

Foster's jaw tightens, but he doesn't speak.

"What happened from there?" I ask Decker.

He looks at Foster now, directly, in a way he hasn't done inside this room before. "She came to my apartment. And it was just talking at first, but then it wasn't just talking."

The room goes very still.

Foster's hands close over his knees.

"The next morning, you came to my door," Decker says, still looking at his brother. Not at me, not at the window. "You came to tell me something about our dad. And you saw her."

Foster says nothing.

"You walked away," Decker says. "And I followed you, and I tried to explain, and there was nothing I could say because I had done exactly what you thought I had. I'd made that choice. I knew what I was doing, and I did it anyway. I have no excuse."

I watch something move across Foster's face. Old anger. Something underneath it that has the shape of grief.

"It was complicated. There was history between us. I assumed you'd moved on, and I thought—" Decker stops. "Those are excuses. None of that changes what I did. I made the call. I chose what I wanted, and I put it above our relationship, and that's the honest version of what happened."

The room is quiet for a long time.

I remain still.

Foster turns to face forward. His hands don't open. I watch him process this the way he processes everything— internally, quietly, giving nothing away until he's ready.

"I want to name something," I say carefully. "Decker, what you just described—making a unilateral decision about what you wanted and thought was best without bringing Foster into it—that's a pattern we've talked about. Protection that looks like exclusion."

Decker nods.

"But I want to be careful here," I continue, "because naming the pattern doesn't resolve what happened. These are two different things. Understanding why you did it doesn't make it okay that you did it." I look at him directly. "Do you understand the difference?"

"Yes." He nods, then looks down at his lap.

"Foster." I turn to him. "You don't have to respond to any of this today. You're allowed to sit with it."

"I know." There's an edge to his voice.

"Is there anything you want to say to your brother?"

A long pause.

"Deck, you understand that none of this would've

happened had you just admitted what you wanted?" Foster says.

"What are you talking about? What was I supposed to do?"

"Jesus, stop… why do you always think you're the one who has to sacrifice?"

This is what I've been waiting for. Not the confession about Penelope, though that was necessary to get to the root of it. This is the root.

I remain quiet and let them continue.

Decker looks at his brother with the expression of a man who has never been asked that question directly and doesn't have a prepared answer for it.

"Because someone had to keep it all together," he says finally.

"Deck, man, our family is fucked up. You trying to be perfect isn't going to change that."

Decker opens his mouth.

"Let me finish." Foster's voice isn't angry. That's what strikes me most. He's said the words I've been trying to find a sideways path toward for six sessions, and he's saying them without heat, without the old armor. "You decided somewhere along the way that it was your job to hold everything together. Mom, me, the team. You took it all on, and you never once asked if that's what anyone actually needed from you."

"You did need it," Decker says. "When we were kids—"

"When we were kids, yeah. I was a fuck-up." Foster leans forward. "But at some point, we stopped being those kids, and you never adjusted. You kept managing everything like I was still a kid with an attitude problem, and you had to keep things from me."

I watch Decker absorb his brother's words. The way a person looks when something really lands—not defensive, not immediately accepting, just sitting in the revelation.

"The Penelope thing," Foster continues. "I'm not saying what you did was right. It wasn't. But I've rehashed it for years, and what I keep coming back to is that what really got to me isn't that you wanted her... it's that you never told me. Before me, during me, after me. You just kept it locked up and managed it alone and let me walk into that apartment without any warning or context because you decided unilaterally that I couldn't handle the truth."

"I didn't think—"

"That's exactly it. You didn't think I could handle it." Foster sits back. "That's not protecting me. That's deciding for me. And you've been doing it my whole life."

I glance at Decker. Something moves across his face that I don't often see there. Not the managed version of the man, not the careful version. The actual version.

"What was I supposed to do?" he asks, and this time it's a real question. Not defensive. Genuine. Like he actually doesn't know. "You were already dealing with so much. You got the explosive dad, I got the nurturing mom. Everything was in your grasp. I didn't want you to—

"What?" Foster asks. "Blow it all up? It happened anyway. I should've been the number one pick, but none of what you tried to protect me from changed the fact that I did blow up. Sure, I was an immature prick back then, and it took too long for me to figure out who I am and who I want to be. To put all the childhood bullshit on the sidelines and live my life the way I want to. Are you doing the same?"

"I'm not sure what you want me to say. I won't apologize for sacrificing for you."

Foster inhales deeply. "You still don't get it. You kept taking yourself out of the equation. What you wanted, what you felt, who you loved. You just... ignore it." Foster shakes his head slowly. "And then you wonder why I never felt like I fully had you as my brother."

I write nothing. I don't want the scratch of a pen to interrupt this.

Decker is quiet, clearly grappling with something. He swallows a few times before he speaks. "I thought I was easier to be around when I didn't need things."

"That was the problem. You were so easy that *I* never had to show up for *you*. And then one day I found out you'd been carrying something real for Penelope the whole time, and I hadn't even noticed because you made it so easy not to."

Decker drops his head. It's the exhaustion of a person who has been performing a version of himself for so long that the performance became invisible even to him.

"I don't know how to do it differently," he says quietly.

"I know," Foster says. "Neither do I. That's why we're here."

I let the silence settle before I speak.

"What you're both describing," I say carefully, "is an adaptive dynamic. Decker, you learned to need less because needing things felt selfish. Foster, you learned to push through because waiting for someone to show up felt unreliable." I look between them. "Those were survival strategies. They made sense for the children you were and the situation you were in at the time. The problem is that you brought them into adulthood and into your relationship with each other, even though they stopped serving you a long time ago."

Foster nods slowly.

Decker is still looking at his hands.

"The roles you fell into," I continue, "the one who holds everything together and the one who pushes forward—they're opposite ends of the same wound. And you've been reinforcing each other's patterns for decades without realizing it."

"So, what do we do about it?" Foster asks.

"You're already doing it," I say. "This conversation. Right now. This is what doing it differently looks like."

Foster looks at Decker.

Decker looks up and at his brother.

Something passes between them that I don't try to name. I've learned that some things in this room don't need a clinical category. They just need to be witnessed.

When our session is over, they leave together, which is a good sign.

I sit in my chair after the door closes behind them and think about the architecture of two people who were handed a broken blueprint and spent almost thirty years building from it anyway and are only now, in this room, starting to draw something new.

I write some notes in my book.

The real therapy starts now.

CHAPTER
THIRTY-SIX

Decker

The Langham does events right, I'll give them that.

The ballroom has been transformed into what Penelope envisioned—from round tables with low centerpieces so guests can actually see each other across the table, to the stage lit in warm lights instead of harsh white ones, and the sponsors' signage tastefully dotted throughout the space so that it doesn't look like a trade show.

She's good at this.

As I look at her across the space, a selfish part of me hopes that when she slid her gorgeous body into the black dress she's wearing, it was with a big fuck you to me in mind. If so, it's working.

We've been cordial for two weeks. Ever since the night she walked out of my condo. Cordial is what she asked for, and that's what I've given her. Our texts are professional, and other than one brief conversation full of pleasantries at Hayes and Leighton's place when I didn't leave fast enough after Hazel's hula hoop lesson, there's been nothing else.

Being cordial with her is more exhausting than last week's back-to-back away series. Add on the latest therapy session with Foster and my mind is a jumble even the most genius psychologist couldn't unravel.

At my table are sponsors, two season ticket holders and their wives, Easton, and the woman he brought as his date. I didn't bother with a plus one because there's no one I'd rather bring than Penelope.

I already checked, and she's at a table across the way, so I figure I'll eat my dinner and stick around for a half hour before I sneak out.

"Penelope," Easton says, looking up at her standing at the table's edge.

I'm talking to one of the season ticket holders, who is being polite and telling me how stupid the Colts will be if they don't sign me for next year.

"Do you guys mind if I join you? Someone didn't RSVP for their spouse at my table, and I know this table had an opening."

"Course not, come on over here." Martin Caulfield, a commercial real estate guy, stands and pulls out the chair for her.

"Thank you."

Pen taking the seat next to Martin puts her right across the table from me.

Now that I think about it, I wish she'd chosen higher centerpieces.

"Goldie, you good?" Easton has one arm swung over the back of his date's chair and the other holding his glass.

"Fine." I pick up my drink, looking over the rim of my glass, but Penelope looks everywhere but at me.

Martin Caulfield is in his mid-fifties and conveys the confidence of someone who has written enough checks to the

Colts that he thinks he pays our salaries when, in reality, he probably pays for our snacks in the dugout. But he thinks he's entitled to every perk they're willing to give him.

Needless to say, I dislike him.

A lot.

He turns his body toward Penelope, not paying attention to anyone else at the table.

She smiles graciously and stays professionally polite, while he keeps leaning in a little closer.

Out of your league, man.

"Goldie, you're looking a little red there." Easton's smirk is prominent.

"I'm fine."

Now Pen's angled slightly away from Martin without making it obvious. Good girl.

I struggle through the salad, the soup, and finally the meal, watching her from across the table. When a season ticket holder tries to engage me in a conversation about my new Noir Cologne ad and how his wife was very excited when she found out they'd be sitting with us, I find it hard to look away from Pen to converse with the couple. The wife's cheeks are flushed, and they share a laugh. Even through all that, I kept taking sneak peeks at Pen as Foster's words from therapy ring through my head.

Finally, the speeches start.

Whitaker addresses the group, but I'm not really interested. I know he's the one behind me not getting my contract renewed. It's obvious when we're all together. Ripley says something about community and how we're all on the same mission—to win the World Series.

Martin leans over to say something to Penelope after her dad's speech.

She smiles politely, then turns back toward the table.

He says something else to her, leaning in too close.

I pick up my water glass, and my fist tightens around it.

"Goldie." Easton says my name like a warning.

"I'm fine."

"You keep saying that."

What does he want from me? I am not actually fine.

By some saving grace, dinner clears shortly after, and people start moving between tables.

I abruptly stand but get stopped at the next table over. Again, someone comments about my contract.

Right now, I don't care about my fucking contract.

I shake hands and talk baseball and say all the right things to all the right people, tracking Pen's movements the entire time. When she moves. Where she stops. How Martin follows her toward the balcony doors with a fresh drink in his hand.

I wait a few minutes, and when neither of them returns, I follow.

The balcony overlooks the river. This evening showcases Chicago at its best. Everything surrounding us is lit up, and a soft warm breeze brushes over my face. I love this city. Penelope is at the railing with her arms crossed, looking as if her patience is running low. Martin is beside her, gesturing at something on the skyline.

I cross the balcony toward them.

"Sorry to interrupt." I don't sound sorry, and I don't care. "Penelope, can I borrow you for a minute?" I nod at Martin. "Event question."

Martin glances in my direction, looking as if he wants to throw down until he sees it's me. "Decker Davis, of course." He smiles at her. "Come find me when you're done."

He touches her arm, and my hands fist at my sides, my knuckles white.

We both wait to speak until he goes inside.

Penelope turns to me with her arms still crossed. "Event question?"

"Can we talk?" I approach, half expecting her to throw her drink in my face.

Her feet stay planted. "What's the event question, Decker?"

I look at the door Martin just walked through and back at her. "He's been following you around for an hour."

"He's a sponsor."

"He's interested."

"He's a sponsor," she says again firmly, as though that settles it. "And I was handling it. I don't need you to swoop in like some savior."

"I know you don't need me to."

"Then why—"

"Because I'm done." The words tumble out of my mouth. "I'm done with this cordial bullshit between us. God, Pen, it killed me to watch him chatting you up tonight. To have all your attention on him."

Her arms don't uncross. "Good." I deserve that. "Might I remind you that you said that the other night too? But then Easton knocked on the door, and you pushed me away again."

"I know." I push a hand through my hair.

"So what's different now?" Her defenses are up and for good reason.

"I've been fighting this since I was eleven years old, and I'm thirty-four, and I'm so damn tired, Pen. I'm done fighting it."

Something shifts in her face. The composed professional version flickers for a moment to a woman filled with hope. "And Foster?"

"I have to talk to him, but I couldn't let another man take you home."

"He didn't have a chance of taking me home."

"I know, but I just… wait right here?"

She huffs and her eyes narrow. "What are you doing?"

"I want us to have a fresh start, and to do that, I have to talk to Foster."

She's quiet. All I hear is the city noise around us. She could say no, and I wouldn't blame her.

"Go." Her voice is quiet.

I hold her gaze for one more second. "You'll wait here?"

She nods. "You have ten minutes."

I step forward, but she retracts. Of course she doesn't want to kiss me right now. Not until she feels more secure. She needs to know that she's not going to give me all of her just for me to break her heart.

I turn and steadily walk back into the venue, searching for Foster.

The question I haven't asked until right now is what do I do if he says no?

CHAPTER
THIRTY-SEVEN

Decker

Foster, a water in hand, is standing at the bar with Hayes. I weave through the clusters of people, nodding polite hellos and putting up my finger, telling them I'll be right back, for those who want to talk to me.

"Hey, I haven't seen you all night," Hayes says when I approach.

"I need to grab Foster for a second."

Hayes's eyebrows lift. "I won't be a whiny Easton." He pats me on the shoulder and walks away.

"You feeling okay? You have beads of sweat along your forehead." Foster sips his water and looks over my shoulder, probably looking for Callie.

"I'm fine. Can we go to the hallway quick?"

His eyes narrow. "What is going on with you?" But he leads me out of the venue into the hallway.

We stand there for a moment, the sound of the event muffled behind the doors, and I look at my brother in his suit and can't help but think about those elevator doors closing between us and the two of us not talking for years. But he opened a door during our therapy session, and I intend to walk through it.

I don't want to ruin what we've built, but I can't live without Penelope anymore.

"I need to ask you something," I say.

He sips his water and doesn't say a word.

"Penelope." Her name alone should tell him what I'm asking.

He's not an idiot, he sees it, as does everyone in our friend group, and he has much more history to go on.

Foster glances over my shoulder again, then back at me, and I wait for his response. His smile shines first and relief seeps in a little, but I keep my armor handy, afraid to hope.

"I wondered how long this was going to take," he says.

"Foster—"

"The only thing I care about with regard to you getting together with Penelope is that I just lost a bet to my soon-to-be wife." He shakes his head. "In all seriousness, Deck, I can't believe it took you this long. Talk about waiting a damn lifetime."

"But do I have your permission?" I glance at my watch to see how close I am to the ten minutes.

"And if I don't give it to you?" He leans his back against the wall, and his shit-eating grin annoys the fuck out of me.

"I'm not gonna lie, I can't do it anymore. I love her. I've always loved her, and I love you too and everything we're building, but Foster, to live without her—"

He puts his hand on my chest. "Go get your girl." He waves, and Callie saunters over, sliding up to his side. He wraps his arms around her waist and kisses her temple.

"What am I missing?" Callie looks between us.

"Deck got his head out of his ass and is finally going to go after Penelope," Foster says while looking at me. His smile still wide, the casual stance still not rigid.

"Really?" She pushes away from my brother and wraps her arms around my neck. "Congratulations. Where is she?"

Foster tugs her back. "I'll fight to the death for this one," he says, wrapping both arms around his fiancée. "What are you waiting for? Go."

He nods toward the doors.

Something loosens in my chest that has been tight for a near decade.

"We're good?" I ask one more final time.

"Go!" Callie says, her eyes wide.

She swivels in Foster's arms, and he looks down at her. The love in his eyes is so transparent that I'm envious of his happiness.

I break away and go back to the ballroom, weaving back through the guests.

Pushing the balcony doors open, my heart sinks when I find it empty.

CHAPTER
THIRTY-EIGHT

Penelope

Eleven minutes.

I gave him one extra minute, and I counted every one of them while standing at that railing, watching the Chicago River do its beautiful thing below me. When ten minutes became eleven, I picked up my clutch and went inside, found my dad, said good night, and called an Uber.

I'm not trying to punish Decker. I told him to go to Foster if that's what he needs, but I'm not going to embarrass myself again. So many of the most embarrassing moments in my life were because of him. I'm not standing out front in a black dress at ten-fifteen making a point. I'm just done waiting for him to come back to me.

The Uber pulls up, and the doorman opens the back passenger door for me.

"Pen!"

It's Decker's voice, and I take note of the desperation in

the way he says my name. I can't deny that my body wants to turn around and run to him.

"Ma'am?" The doorman waves for me to get into the Uber.

I pull out a tip and hand it to him, sliding into the back seat. "Thank you."

I make the mistake of looking out the window. The Uber driver honks at a party van that has stopped in front of him, trying to park. The doorman gets involved, and while everyone's attention is on the commotion in front of us, I lock eyes with Decker, running out of the doors.

His jacket is open, his tie a little askew, and he looks as if he's run through the entire venue.

Do not just lie down for him, Penelope.

"Pen." His hand grabs the door handle, and I can't react fast enough to lock it. He heaves for a breath. "Why are you leaving?"

The Uber driver continues to honk his horn.

"Because." I have no words. I wouldn't want to say them in front of all these people anyway.

"Let me come with you." He doesn't step in. He waits for me to decide.

Such a Decker thing to do.

"I can't do this with you again just to end up—"

"No, Pen. I just… I want us to start on the right foot, and in order to do that, I had to give Foster a heads-up. But now, all that bullshit is behind us, and we can start with a clean slate."

"Hey, man, in or out?" the Uber driver asks now that the party bus has had no choice but to go around the block, after all his patrons have staggered to the bar on the corner.

Decker looks at me.

"You realize I make my money on how many rides I take?" the driver says.

"You can see me home." I slide over, and Decker climbs in, shutting the door after him.

His big body takes up the majority of the back seat, but there's still a little room between us. The problem is that space feels like live barbed wire.

The Uber driver pulls away from the corner, and I stare at the busy street. All the couples with linked hands walking down the sidewalk pull that feeling out of me of how I want that so badly. But not with just anyone. Sure, Elias was nice, but if I'm being truly honest with myself, it's Decker I want. And if I can't have it with him, I don't want it at all.

"Foster said go." Decker's voice is soft. "He doesn't care."

I fidget with my hands in my lap.

"Pen?"

"I heard you."

"I need you to know something." He turns in the seat to face me. "It's always been you. Since I was eleven, I think I knew on a subconscious level that you were meant for me... and I fucked it all up, wasted our time. First because your dad was my coach, and then we got close. Like, really fucking close and you were my person, Pen. The one I told everything. When I went to Kingsley, it killed me to say goodbye to you, but..."

Tears well in my eyes. I don't want to do this in front of an Uber driver, but I've also waited so long for him to tell me all this.

"I was leaving, and I didn't want to do that to you. I knew the time I'd have with you would be limited, and you deserved better, even if it was without me. Who would have thought your dad would get a coaching job at Hartwell and in just one year you'd be so close to me again? Had I known, I never would have..."

He doesn't say her name, and I'd rather not hear it anyway.

"That night you walked out with Foster, it nearly killed me."

I put my hand over his mouth. "I don't want to rehash it."

He gently takes my hand and lowers it between us, keeping it clasped in his. "I don't either. I want all that behind us. I don't care why you never came back to the hotel three years ago after we reconnected."

"Oh… um…"

"No, I don't care. I just want to be with you. Every girlfriend I had. Every rule I made. Every time I wouldn't cross that imaginary line." His voice is steady, but something underneath it isn't. "It was always because of you. Because the alternative was wanting something I was convinced I wasn't allowed to have."

The Uber moves through the city. The driver says nothing, pretending he's minding his own business.

I look at Decker for a long moment. Twenty years of baggage we're trying to sort through in the back seat of an Uber. All the versions of us that almost happened but never did.

"I'm really scared."

He looks down at our hands, lacing his fingers through mine, and doesn't let go. "I know, and I promise you, I'm never going anywhere unless you want me to. I want to be with both of you, but I understand you might not want that. That building your trust that I'm not going anywhere takes time. We can do this however you want. I can go home tonight and maybe we plan a date. Go slow. Whatever pace you feel comfortable with."

We pull up along the curb outside my house, and since I live on a one-way street, my door is along the curb. I release his hand, as much as it pains me to do it. I thank the Uber driver, open my door, and step onto the sidewalk.

Decker says something to the driver about where to go

next, but I never shut the door, leaving it open as I walk to the front steps of my house.

"Buddy, she's inviting you in," I hear the Uber driver say.

I glance over my shoulder, and Decker's staring at me. I smile and shake my head, reaching my front door.

Decker tosses some money at the Uber driver and gets out of the car. "You are inviting me, right?"

I don't look back, setting my clutch on the entry table and slipping out of my heels. I hear the door close softly behind me and his footsteps on the hardwood, then his hand is on my waist, turning me around.

He looks at me in the dark entry the way he looked at me on the balcony. With more sureness than I've ever seen.

"Hi," he says.

"Hi."

CHAPTER
THIRTY-NINE

Penelope

Decker brings his hand to my face, his thumb dragging slowly across my cheekbone, and since there's no one around, this time there're no interruptions, no reason to rush. Thank God Leighton's mom and aunt agreed to keep Hazel overnight with the other three kids.

He kisses me.

It's not tentative. And definitely not careful.

He takes my mouth as though he's done waiting, and I feel it everywhere at once—the pull of his hand in my hair, the hard press of his body crowding me back against the wall, the cool plaster at my spine, and the heat of him along every inch of me. I catch his lapels in both fists and drag him closer because I don't want even an inch of space between us. I've waited too long for this.

"God, Pen," he says against my mouth, the words rough and unsteady. "You have no idea."

"Tell me," I whisper, already breathless, wanting to hear that he's been thinking about this moment as much as I have.

His mouth slides from mine to my jaw, slower now, but somehow no less devastating. He kisses along the sensitive line beneath my ear, and I shiver.

"Every time you walked into a room," he murmurs.

Another kiss, just an inch lower.

"Every time you laughed."

His hand tightens at my waist.

"Every time I caught you watching me."

My fingers flex in his shirt. "I never watched you."

He doesn't lift his head, but I can feel his smile against my skin.

"Oh, Pen." His voice drops, rough with want. "You were always watching me."

His hand slides down my back, deliberate, possessive, until his fingers find the zipper of my dress. He hovers there.

"But I was watching you too. There wasn't a room I entered that I didn't seek you out."

My whole body goes taut with desire, blood rushing, every nerve fixed on the feel of his hand at my spine.

"You wore this for me." Not a question, but rather a statement.

I should have known he'd know. "Yes."

His mouth grazes my neck, and he groans.

It sends another pulse of heat through me.

"The second you walked in tonight, I stopped hearing half the conversation around me. All I could think about was getting you alone. Getting my hands on you. Getting this dress off your body."

My breath catches.

His fingers brush the zipper again, slow enough to make me ache. "Do you know how hard it was sitting across from you?"

I tilt my head back against the wall, offering him more of my throat. "Probably not as hard as it was for me."

That gets a low sound out of him—half laugh, half groan—and then his mouth is on mine again, deeper this time, his hand finally pulling the zipper down in one slow, maddening drag.

The dress loosens around me, the fabric slipping, his knuckles grazing bare skin as he opens me up to him. He doesn't rush. And that's what undoes me. The way he takes his time as though this matters. As though he's wanted this for so long, he refuses to miss a second of it.

"Decker." It comes out softer than I mean it to.

"I know." His forehead presses to mine for one brief second before his mouth moves to my throat again. "I know."

The dress slips from my shoulders.

He helps it down my body, his hands following the path of the falling fabric, palms warm and reverent over my bare skin until it pools at my feet.

The air feels cooler, sharper, and every place he touches is suddenly alive.

He steps back, and his gaze falls down my body, his thumb running over his lips. For a second, Decker just looks at me. The hunger in his eyes undoes most of my patience.

I'm standing in a black bra and panty set while he's still fully dressed in his suit. Need settles low in my stomach and spreads.

His hand slides over my waist, then higher, slowly enough to make me tremble. "Tell me this is real."

I lift my hands to his face and hold him there, make him look at me. "It's real."

His shoulders fall, softer than moments ago.

Decker kisses me again, and there's nothing careful left in it. His hands move with purpose—down my back, over my hips, pulling me into him until I feel exactly how much he wants me. My head tips back against the wall, a breath leaving me when his mouth drags down my throat.

"Decker." His name sounds wrecked coming from my mouth, and he answers it immediately, his hands tightening.

"I've got you." The words are low and hot against my skin. "I've got you."

I believe him.

That might be the most dangerous part, putting myself one hundred percent into us. But I'm doing it.

My fingers go to his shirt, suddenly impatient. I don't want layers. I don't want barriers. I want skin on skin and all the years between us burned down to nothing. I start at the buttons, but he catches my hand gently, planting the sweetest kiss inside my wrists.

"Upstairs." The word is barely more than a breath off his lips but sounds like a command.

He takes my hand and leads me up the stairs, and even that feels intimate somehow—my bare feet against the floor, his hand snug in mine, both of us knowing this has gone beyond teasing, beyond flirting, beyond all the almosts of the past. This is finally happening.

When we reach the bedroom, he turns back to me, and for a beat, he only stares.

"You're very quiet," I say, though I'm no steadier than he is.

"I'm trying not to lose my mind."

I laugh softly, but it breaks when he steps in close again.

His fingers skim my collarbone, grazing over to my shoulder. "I waited three years to have you again. I don't want to rush through a single second of tonight."

The tenderness in his voice almost undoes me more than the hunger.

Then his mouth is back on mine, and the patience he was trying so hard to keep starts slipping. His hands roam more urgently, the kiss turning deeper, hungrier. He pushes me backward until the backs of my knees hit the bed.

He stops only long enough to search my face. "Still good?"

I slide my hands into his hair, pulling him down. "You don't even have to ask."

His eyes close for half a second as though he's been waiting a lifetime for me to say that. But his restraint only lasts so long, breaking quickly.

He kisses me as if he wants to make up for lost time, and I gladly let him. His mouth is hot and demanding, and his hands are everywhere now—my waist, my thigh, my back—touching me as if I might disappear. A ragged breath tears out of me when he lowers me onto the bed and follows, braced over me, his mouth trailing down my throat again.

"Do you know," he says, voice rough, "how many times I've thought about this?" His hand slides along my side, dragging another shiver out of me. "How many nights I've laid awake imagining what it would be like to have you under me again?"

My pulse kicks harder than a bass drum.

"You have too many clothes on." I push at his suit jacket, and this time, he allows me to undress him.

He doesn't rush to help the way most men might. Doesn't try to take control. We get off the bed, and he stands there, tall and solid in front of me, watching and waiting to see what I'll do next.

I slide the jacket off his shoulders. The heavy fabric slips down his arms and drops to the floor.

"You're very patient all of a sudden," I murmur.

His mouth curves faintly. "You seem determined."

"That's because I want to see you."

"I get it. Believe me, I fucking get it." His hungry eyes take me in one more time, and he nestles his hand along my hip.

I reach for his tie, loosening the knot slowly. My fingers

brush the warm skin of his throat, and his breath hitches. Something about this man on the verge of losing control because of me is the most potent aphrodisiac.

"You could help."

"I could," he agrees.

He doesn't move.

The tie slides free, and I toss it over the chair before moving to the buttons of his shirt. One by one, I work them open, my knuckles grazing his chest as the fabric parts.

He stays still through all of it, shoulders relaxed, arms loose at his sides, as though this—standing here while I undress him—is something he's been waiting to see happen.

When I reach the last button, I push the shirt open and slide my hands across his chest. "Still not helping?"

His voice drops lower. "You told me to let you do it."

I push the shirt off his shoulders, and this time, he lifts his arms slightly so I can pull it free from his waistband. My fingers manipulate the button on his pants, and his stomach indents with a big breath. I slowly lower the zipper over his bulge, and the groan that escapes him pulls a smile from my lips.

"Something funny?"

"Nothing." I slide my hands around the inside of his waistband to his ass and push the pants down.

I'm so hot and horny for this man, I have no idea how I've waited this long.

He steps out of his pants and takes off his socks as I sit on the edge of the bed and admire him in only his black boxer briefs. Once he's done, he steps closer, hovering over me. I run my hand over his dick trying to free itself from his boxers. His fingers unhook my bra, and I slip my arms free of it.

Staring down at me, his eyes turn molten, and he bites into his bottom lip. "Take off your panties."

I hurriedly shed them.

His hands dive into my hair, his eyes roaming along every bare inch of my skin. "Get farther up on the bed, Pen."

I do as he says while he takes off his boxers, his thick length bouncing out and up from the fabric.

He climbs onto the bed, and I almost smile, but it dissolves when he kisses me again and his weight settles fully over me. I can feel how tightly wound he is, how close he is to the edge of his control, and it only makes my desire stronger.

"I'm yours," I whisper.

His reaction is immediate.

A low sound leaves him, and his forehead drops briefly to mine, as if he's gathering whatever frayed pieces of control he can scrape up.

"Oh Pen, I'm yours too. Always have been." He says it with so much heart that tears fill my eyes.

His mouth moves down me again, his hands learning me in long, unhurried passes that feel anything but innocent. Every touch is more intimate than the last, every kiss drawing me tighter and tighter until I'm arching into him without thinking, wanting more, needing more.

"I'm on the pill, and I haven't…"

"I haven't been with anyone in a long time, Pen. I've been tested."

The tip of him teases my opening, and I arch, needing him to fill me completely.

"Okay."

He lifts his head just enough to look at me. "You want me bare?"

I nod. "Yes."

His expression changes—something hotter, darker, fiercely satisfied transforming it. He slides into me, every inch earning another guttural groan from him. "Shit, you're wet."

"Don't stop."

"I have no intention of it."

And he doesn't. He gives me everything slowly at first, as

if he wants to feel every reaction, hear every breath, learn every sound I make when I'm falling apart under his hands and mouth. Then the pace shifts. His control thins. The desperation we've been holding back for years finally shows, and it turns the whole thing wilder, needier.

It isn't sweet, though there's tenderness threaded through every movement. It's want. Longing. Relief. It's over a decade of unfinished business finally given somewhere to go.

At one point he stills just enough to brush my hair back from my face, his chest rising hard, his gaze locked on mine. "You okay?"

I nod, barely able to catch a full breath. "More than okay."

He slides his hand along my jaw. "Tell me if you need anything."

I pull him back down by the back of his neck and kiss him until the question disappears.

Then there's no talking—only broken sounds, the rasps of breath, the soft creak of the mattress, him whispering my name as if it's the only word left in the world.

I hold on to him just as tightly, my nails in his shoulders, his back, anywhere I can anchor myself, because suddenly the distance of all those lost years feels too vast.

He buries his face against my neck, breath hot and uneven, his grip tightening around me as the rhythm between us falters, rebuilds, then finally breaks.

"Pen—" he breathes, the rest of my name dissolving into a rough exhale.

The sound of his desperation sends something sharp and bright through me, and I cling to him as the moment crashes over me. I come on a whimper, and before I even recover, he's there too, as if he was holding it at bay for me.

For a second, neither of us moves.

He remains braced over me, chest rising and falling hard, his forehead pressed against mine. Our breaths mix in the small space between us.

My hands loosen their grip on his shoulders.

"Jesus," he murmurs.

I'm still catching my breath myself, my fingers tracing down his back.

Years of almosts and maybes and what-ifs, and somehow it all led here—to this quiet moment when neither of us has the energy to pretend we don't belong exactly where we are.

He lowers himself beside me, pulling me against his chest as though this is our new normal.

And maybe it is. I hope to hell it is. I hope that we can get it right this time around.

CHAPTER
FORTY

Decker

I keep waiting to wake up. Tonight was a dream, and I'll wake up in my own bed, alone.

I run my hand down Pen's arm, reminding myself that we're here, together, and we are only going to move forward —together.

She's asleep on my shoulder, and her hand is on my chest, and for the first time in as long as I can remember, the thing I want most is to be exactly where I am.

I press my lips to the top of her head.

She doesn't stir, exhausted after our night of rediscovering each other.

I close my eyes and pull her closer, and for the first time in a long time, I don't make a single rule.

Well, maybe one—Once you get her, don't ever let her go.

CHAPTER
FORTY-ONE

Decker

I can't help but watch her. In a T-shirt and cotton shorts, padding barefoot around the kitchen, preparing breakfast.

She places eggs and a bowl in front of me. "Do something useful and beat these."

I grab her around the waist before she can escape. She laughs, and I kiss the hollow of her neck. My bare chest pressed to the soft cotton of her shirt makes me want to strip her down again. But we both need to eat before we pass out.

"Sure you want to eat?"

She wiggles out of my grip, and even though she's only just across the kitchen, I miss being right next to her. How will I sleep at my condo alone? If she asked, I'd move in tonight. Might not even go home to get my stuff, just order new shit.

"We should probably talk." She looks at me with a pensive expression.

Guess I shouldn't be surprised she wants to get it all out in the open—how we move forward.

I nod. "All right. You go first."

She places bacon on a cookie sheet and puts it in the oven. "I'm not ready to broadcast our relationship to the world yet."

I concentrate on breaking the eggs and avoid eye contact. I understand her concern. I'm not exactly someone to bet on yet. There's a lot more I need to prove. "Okay."

"I mean, our friends…"

The word *our* hits me square in the chest. I love the word our when it comes out of her mouth.

"I'm fine with them knowing," she continues. "But." She comes over to me, and I prepare myself for whatever has that concerned expression on her face. She slides between me and the counter and wraps her arms around my neck, tilting my head to look right into her eyes. "I know this is real, Deck. But I have to put Hazel first."

"Of course."

"So that means we can't tell her yet."

I lower my head and kiss her. "It's your decision. Whenever you think it's right."

She smiles and kisses me once more, but I slide my tongue into her mouth. It gets a little out of control before she slides out under my arm. "Thank you. That means a lot."

I finish the eggs, scrambling them. She throws some bread in the toaster and refills her coffee again.

"We don't have to worry about our friends," I say. "They'll never tell anyone. They know the score."

"I know. That's why I'm okay with it. We have a lot of other things to deal with. My dad being your manager. Me handling the Dugout Social Club. There might be non-fraternization rules we don't know about, and I won't jeopardize your career. This is your contract year."

"I don't really care anymore." I wrap my arms around her

as she puts butter in the pan and starts cooking the eggs. "I have everything I want in my arms right now."

"I'm serious."

"I am too. Right now, baseball doesn't matter."

She tilts her head, offering me her neck, and I take the opportunity to prove to her she's all that matters in my life right now.

"I'll never finish a meal if I let you help me in the kitchen all the time."

My hands skate under the hem of her T-shirt and run up her ribcage. "I'm not doing anything."

"You know exactly what you're doing." She laughs.

"Okay then." I step back, and she glances over her shoulder seeing me leaning against the opposite counter, watching her. "What are your thoughts about cooking naked?"

"I think I like my skin too much."

I laugh, but we're interrupted by the oven buzzer for the bacon. I grab the hot pad and pull the tray out of the oven before putting the strips on the paper-towel-covered plate she already set out.

Then I butter the toast as she finishes the eggs. This is exactly what I want every day for the rest of my life. Just her and me conquering simple tasks together.

I plate our meals while she puts all the dirty dishes in the sink, then I take the plates to the table.

Her breakfast nook is tucked into the corner of the kitchen and is the only part of the house that feels like her. Built-in benches wrap the walls, the cushions covered in some soft, pretty fabric I never would've chosen. It shows the promise of what this house could become with some time and attention.

Pen slides in next to me, her knee hitting mine. "There's just one more thing."

"And here I thought I was the list-maker out of the two of us." I pick up my fork and dig into my eggs. I barely ate my meal last night, and although we raided her kitchen in between shower sex and me discovering how much she loves my mouth on her pussy, I'm still starving.

"These are important issues." She sits back and brings her coffee mug to her lips. "And you'll come to learn we're on a time crunch. Hazel is supposed to be home at noon."

"I'll be leaving at 11:59 then."

She laughs, and I bump my knee to hers. There's a lot of stuff ahead of us that we have to deal with, but I know we'll do this together.

"It's about Hazel's dad, Deck."

I stop eating when I hear her tone. The worry there raises my antenna. I wipe my mouth and sit back to give her my full attention.

"I can't tell you who he is. I signed an NDA while I was still pregnant with her. He pretty much…" She puts her mug down and inhales a deep breath.

I take her hand, squeezing so she knows she can tell me whatever it is, and I'll still be here. That there's nothing she could tell me that would ever make me leave.

"He paid me off to go away. It's the reason I don't have to work and have had the luxury of being a stay-at-home single mom. But if I tell anyone who he is, including her, I have to pay restitution plus a large percentage."

The fuck? Who the hell is Hazel's father? That's my first thought. I'm not even sure how much money we're talking about. This house wasn't cheap, and I assumed it all came from her mom's family. Her mom's side is well off. The wealthiest family I knew of in Philly. So I assumed she got some kind of trust when she turned a certain age.

I squeeze her hand again. "Okay."

"You're okay not knowing? It's a secret between us, and I don't want anything between us." A tear slips down her cheek.

I push her table back and urge her to straddle me on the

bench. She does, and I take her face in my palms, brushing away the tears.

"It's okay. I get it. Whatever the two of you decided is your business. We're good."

"Really?" She says it as though she can't believe I would be good with this news.

"Whatever happened in between all of our almosts stays there. Hazel is wonderful, and I feel bad that her dad didn't want a relationship with her, but I'm glad she has a mom who didn't back down. You fought for what you want."

"You don't think I'm weak for just taking the money?"

My thumb catches more tears. "God, no. You did what was best for you and Hazel, and your future."

She falls into my arms, and I run my hands down her back. "I wish I could tell you. I really do."

"It's fine, Pen. I mean that. It doesn't matter to me. I want to get to know Hazel even more and figure out where my relationship can stand with her."

She draws back. "She loves you. And when she finds out about us, she'll be so happy, but I just want to make sure this is good before we involve her. You understand that, right?"

I laugh. "Yes, you're worrying like I usually do."

And that's the truth. All I want is to be with her now. All the other bullshit is nothing we can't handle together.

"Thank you. I'm not betting against us, I just need to be sure."

I kiss her. "Don't thank me. I'm not doing you a favor. Now… how do you feel about breakfast table sex?"

She laughs, but I push our plates to the side, lift her up to sit on the table, raise her shirt, and take one of her nipples into my mouth with no plans to stop there.

And the best part is we have three more hours before I have to leave. Hopefully no one rings the damn doorbell because this time, we're not answering.

CHAPTER
FORTY-TWO

Penelope

Decker is adamant that he doesn't want their week of away games to happen before we tell our friends that we're together. I argued it might be fun to keep it to ourselves and sneak around for a while, but he said he wishes we could tell everyone, so he at least wanted to tell them.

Who am I to argue with a man who is so proud to tell everyone I'm his?

Peeper's Alley isn't very busy. Which is good. Thankfully, our friends were able to get babysitters when we asked for a no-kids night. Decker sent the group message, and I feel as if they probably all know what's coming.

He already talked to Foster. The girls know about my feelings for Decker. I'm not really worried about telling them, although I'd prefer the news not to be broadcast anywhere else until Decker's contract is secure.

Decker's hand is snug in mine as we enter the bar. There are no Colts fans except the regulars at the bar who don't pay us any attention. I wonder how much Ruby makes on nights like this. She must make up for it when the Colts are playing, and it's wall to wall people in here.

I let him guide me through the empty pub tables, but instead of going into the backroom, he stops at the edge of the bar.

"Ruby, you know Penelope."

She looks at us over the rim of her reading glasses since she's doing the crossword puzzle in *The Chicago Tribune*. "No, I just hit my head. Who is she?" She shakes her head and tosses her reading glasses and pen on the paper, pointing at the guys at the bar. "Anyone fills in one box and you're out." She makes her way to the end of the bar.

I like Ruby. She's nice in her own little mean girl way. But she's sweet to Hazel every time she's here, though she's protective of the guys. I know Decker's brought me over here to tell her we're a couple. Suddenly, I feel as though I'm meeting his mother for the first time and not just his barkeep. Then again, Ruby is so much more to these guys than just a bar owner.

She glances at our linked hands. "What do you want, a ribbon for getting your head out of your ass?"

"I just wanted you to know, she's the reason… my mood the other day."

He doesn't have to elaborate. I've had so many days and nights when I thought this day might never come. He glances at me.

"I know. We all know. You're the last one to figure it out." She looks at me. "It's same story, different player. It's like they took too many balls to the head or something."

I smile, but she doesn't. Then again, I've never seen her smile when I think about it.

She cracks open my favorite lime seltzer and places in front of me.

"Well, it took—"

She pours a beer while Decker tries to explain. "I don't care to hear it. But way to go, you finally stepped out of your own way." She puts the beer down in front of Decker. "And those aren't on the house." She walks back to where she left the paper but stops halfway. "The rest of your group is ready for your declaration ceremony."

Decker and I share a look, and both laugh.

She has a point. This does feel a little like a declaration ceremony, but it's been such a long road for us, I don't really care. I love that I'm able to walk into that room holding Decker's hand. That I can sit in his lap, kiss him, touch him, and just be.

We take our drinks, and Decker releases my hand to open the door. Once the door is open, he links our fingers again.

The whole group is clustered around the large round table, all arguing about something on the television, I think.

Callie is in Foster's lap.

Hayes's arm is swung over the back of Leighton's chair.

Easton is leaning halfway across the table as he tries to prove some point that Callie is arguing with him.

I love this group and feel so honored to be welcomed in.

Hayes sees us first. His gaze drops to our linked hands. Back up. A slow smile forms on his lips. He pats Leighton's shoulder and nods toward us.

Then Leighton turns and catches our hands, her smile big with an almost *I told you so* expression.

Callie's eyes snag on us mid-argument with Easton, and she nods, her smile emerging as well. Foster leans back in his chair, not surprised, but not showing much of a reaction.

Easton is the last one to see us. He looks at our hands, then at Decker, at me, and says, "Finally, Goldie! Ruby, we need a round of shots. He's finally walked into the light."

"Fuck you." Decker walks us into the room. He pulls out my chair, and I sit down.

Both of the girls are looking at me as if they're going to ask me to see the ring. This moment feels a lot like an engagement with so much leading up to us being together.

Then everyone grabs cash from their pockets and purses and tosses it on the table, arguing about who won.

Easton grabs the fist of money. "I told you all, I was right."

Ruby comes in with a tray of shots. "Good, you can pay for the shots. These three are water for anyone who might not be able to drink." Her eyebrows raise as if she knows something we don't.

Leighton and Callie look at one another, but they both turn away. They know each other so well, I feel as if they'd know if each other were pregnant just from looking.

"What were the terms?" Decker asks.

"Everyone picked an event when they thought it would happen."

"I had the river cleanup, and I was so close." Leighton raises her thumb and forefinger with a little bit of space in between. "I saw that almost kiss."

Decker and I look at one another.

"I had after the game when you were going to his place," Callie says. "And if it wasn't for Easton..." She narrows her eyes at him.

"If you and Foster used condoms, I would've banged on your door. Desperate times." Easton counts out his money.

Hayes raises his hand. "I had after the BBQ at our place."

"I thought it'd be season's end," Foster says.

Man, they were all so invested—it's oddly endearing.

Callie pulls her phone out of her purse. "Which one will I choose?" She taps her lip with her finger, and Foster narrows his eyes at Decker.

"What did you lose?" Decker asks Foster, then turns to me. "Callie and Foster had their own private bet about us."

I turn to Callie, remembering her mentioning it at the Colts game. I can finally hear the terms now.

"My dear fiancé thought that Penelope would have to

make the move. That Decker wouldn't. So now, my nice parents get to spend some quality time with Ellis while I go to an away game series." She points at Leighton and me. "And you two are coming. Find yourself some babysitters."

"You just took mine." Leighton laughs.

"And mine," I say. "Let's remember my dad is away when all the guys are."

Decker's hand runs along my shoulder, and he slides a little closer.

Easton cracks up laughing watching it.

"What about Mom?" Foster says to Decker.

Decker looks from him to me. "I'd like you to meet her."

I chuckle. "I've met her. She taught me how to make your favorite brownies, remember?"

"Yeah, but you haven't met her as my girlfriend."

I put my hand on his knee. "That is true."

"She's coming next week for a home game," Foster says.

Decker leans in. "I'm not saying meet her so she can watch Hazel and you come to an away series. That's too soon, but—"

"I'd love to." I kiss his cheek.

"Oh, it's so cute." Leighton wipes her eyes. Hayes grabs a napkin and hands it to her. "Sorry, I'm really emotional."

"Are you gonna get your period or something?" Callie asks.

Leighton doesn't answer.

Easton throws a twenty on the table. "New Year's Eve baby!"

"No way, Christmas." Callie grabs her wallet and tosses cash on the table.

"Let's all just hope she doesn't go into labor during the playoffs," Decker says.

Callie and Foster look at one another and smile.

"No one said she's pregnant," Hayes says.

"Okay." Callie holds up two shots, one with water and one with alcohol. "Pick one."

Leighton looks at Hayes, and he shrugs. She does an eenie meenie miney mo, then takes the water one and downs the shot.

Everyone shouts and gets up to congratulate them.

"Apparently, we have to fill every bedroom in our house," Hayes says and kisses Leighton's temple.

We all hug and congratulate them, taking shots to celebrate.

At the end of the night, I go upstairs with Decker to his condo, and we don't make it past the foyer before he's inside me and I'm screaming his name. Best night ever.

CHAPTER
FORTY-THREE

Decker

With us trying to keep our relationship a secret, we don't have a lot of choices for me to take Pen out. If I picked a restaurant, especially one with a reservation and a wine list and dim lighting, we might have our picture taken. And then keeping it between us is over and done.

So, I used my connections and arranged what I hope is a romantic dinner, just us, where we can be alone.

I open my building's door that leads to the rooftop and lead her through the bar that serves the patrons on Colts game days, finding her hand and leading her out to the open area.

"You guys get access to this? I always wondered what it's like to watch a game from here."

"Me too." We both laugh. "Although I might be able to find out soon."

She squeezes my hand. "I just know Shane Whitaker will come to his senses."

"I hope so."

I open the doors to the small concrete platform before you can take the stairs to go up to the bleachers.

"Deck," she says, stepping to my side. "It's beautiful."

"Just so we're clear, my idea, not my execution."

She lays her cheek on my shoulder. "I love it."

I lead her to the table for two with a black tablecloth, candles lit under hurricanes, and our meals already waiting. "We're alone, just so you know."

"I feel like you might be thinking something dirty to tell me that."

I slide out the chair, and she smooths out her dress and sits.

"You are teasing me with that dress."

"It's practically a sundress." She tilts her head. "And what about you? Slacks, a V-neck shirt?"

"Maybe it doesn't matter what the other wears, we just want to tear the other one's clothes off."

She laughs, knowing it's probably true. These past few weeks with the away games, we definitely mastered our sexting, and I thanked God baseball players get their own rooms.

"Well, you look very sexy tonight, Decker." She says it in a polite voice like she's complimenting the chicken.

"And you look stunning."

She smiles, her face glowing in the candlelight.

I take the silver cover off her dish. "I can't cook like you, but if memory serves, this was your favorite."

"Spinach and garlic?" she asks, perusing the heart-shaped deep-dish pizza.

"Yes. Your own personal pan."

She peers over at mine. "And what do you have?"

I lift my lid to see my usual thin-crust onion and green pepper shaped in a heart, which I didn't ask for. Nice of the pizza place to make it special.

"I never understood why you don't like deep-dish."

"Too much cheese."

We both pick up a piece. "And just so you know, you're outnumbered. Hazel likes everything I like. I've already brainwashed her." She smiles right before she takes a bite.

"I can convert her." I take a bite of my thin crust and then realize I never even poured our wine, so I put my pizza down and open the bottle before pouring us both a glass.

"No, it's ingrained now. Sorry." She shrugs. "Maybe the next one." She hurries and takes another bite, concentrating on her plate.

"And all the ones after that."

She peeks up. "You don't have to say that. It's probably too soon for me to have said that."

"Pen, I want an entire house full of kids with you."

Her smile emerges again, and the tension around us dissipates. Thank god.

"Me too."

Our eyes lock and hold over the flickering candles, and I place my hand over hers.

"It's weird, right? I mean, that it feels so natural already?" She wipes her mouth and takes a sip of her wine.

"Yeah, but I love it. It's what I always wanted. And I don't want to go slow just because someone said you have to, or society dictates what makes a relationship successful and long-term. I love you, Penelope, and I want to become a father figure to Hazel, but on her terms. I want to marry you, I want to have more kids with you. And I'm done being scared to admit that. And I don't want to wait when we've already waited so long."

"You're going to ruin my makeup." She swipes a finger under her eyes.

"Is that you avoiding a response because you don't feel the same?"

"No!" She shakes her head. "I do… I want all of that. It was always you, but there's a lot still to consider."

"Like?"

"Like my dad is your manager, and how it will look if that comes out. Your contract and what that means. Relocation?"

I've been playing great lately and feel back to my old self. Every good game I have, I gain more confidence. "I hope I get to stay in Chicago."

"Me, too."

"I'm not sure what I did to piss that guy off. Or why he wants Harkins to take my spot. My only saving grace is that I have your dad on my side."

She smiles, slides her chair out, and walks around the table to me. "And he'll always be on your side. He loves you more than he loves me."

I open my legs and she slides between them, sitting on my lap and putting her arms around my neck. Nothing feels better than when she comes to me.

"No, you're his baby."

"Ah, Hazel took that spot, which I'm thankful for." She leans her head to mine. "Whatever happens with your contract, we'll get through it."

"I can commute. There's no need for you and Hazel to move. She's settled here."

She doesn't move, allowing me to hold her. "Let's just give it some time, but Decker." She pulls back and looks me in the eye. "If this is going to work, we are united. It will be hard for Hazel, but having you in our lives trumps that."

God, she's killing me. A small part of me still feels like I don't deserve this. To have everything I've wanted so fast is making it hard to really believe that I'm here, living the life I want. That it won't be snatched away.

"Oh." She gets up off my lap, and I reach for her, but she swats my hands away, grabbing her clutch from the table and pulling out her phone. "Did you see this?"

She returns to my lap. I stare at Webber Field across from us while she searches on her phone. I can't imagine playing for anyone else. Sure, I want to stay here for the family I've built with my teammates, and I don't want Hazel or Penelope to upend their life, least of all for me. I love this city, I love this team, and I love the fans. It would break my heart to leave. But what I don't tell Penelope is that I'm almost positive I'm already out. I don't think my performance is the problem. I think it's my salary.

"Look." She puts her screen in front of my face, and it takes a second for my eyes to focus.

"HandsOffDeck." My forehead wrinkles.

I take the phone from her, scrolling down the Instagram account and looking at the posts. It looks like an account dedicated to keeping me here in Chicago. Everyone on here is talking about the fact that my contract is up this year, and Chicago hasn't said anything about re-signing me.

"Look at all the comments. I mean, it just started, but it's gaining a following. Chicago loves you."

I scan a few comments about people saying Whitaker is stupid for even playing around with me. That another team is going to snag me. All their comments hit me right in the heart. Maybe this city loves me as much as I love them.

I hand the phone back to Penelope. "Not sure any of that will matter, but it's nice."

She clicks Follow. "I'm a fan."

"Well, I'm a fan of you." I push all the bullshit any player has to face at some point from my mind. "Straddle me?"

The rooftops aren't exactly private, so there's no way I'm going to strip her down here, but I think I'll tease her a little bit for what's to come when we get back to my condo.

"What's your plan?" She stands between my legs.

"Hike up the skirt, Pen." I pat my lap.

"So far I like where this is going." She hooks one leg, then the other around my waist, and I shift us until her back is braced against the table, giving her something solid to rest against.

"This is only the appetizer." I drag my mouth along the line of her jaw. "My full meal will be downstairs."

Her laugh catches, turning into a shuddered breath when I slide my hand up her thigh beneath the hem of her skirt.

"Deck," she whispers, but it comes out less like a warning and more like a plea.

I kiss her before she can say anything else, swallowing the little gasp that leaves her mouth her when my fingers find the inside of her thigh. She's already warm, already shifting against me, her hands on my shoulders for balance.

"Stay still," I tell her, though I like the fact she can't.

My thumb strokes a little higher, along her wet panties. She breaks the kiss with a shaky exhale and tips her head back, exposing her throat. I take advantage, pressing my mouth there, tasting her skin while my hand keeps moving beneath her skirt.

"You like making me wait?" Her voice is thin and breathless.

"I like watching you fall apart."

Her fingers dig into my shoulders, and I slide the edge of her panties over, my finger running along exactly where she's aching.

She jolts against me, her forehead dropping to my shoulder. "God," she breathes.

"Thanks for the praise."

She rocks against my hand, and I laugh softly under my breath, tightening my hold on her hip with my free hand to keep her where I want her. My fingers slide through her wetness, my thumb applying a little pressure on her clit.

"Look at me, Pen."

She lifts her head. Her eyes are glassy, and her mouth is parted. I take a moment to memorize this version of her. The one where all her pleasure comes from me. I slip a finger inside her, and she jolts up off my lap before settling again.

"That's it," I murmur.

Her body softens and tightens at the same time, a war between satisfaction and desperation. I kiss her hard as I add another finger and arc them inside her. Her breaths turn sharp and uneven, and she clutches my shoulders as though she's afraid I might stop.

"Deck—" My name breaks off into a moan.

I press my forehead to hers. "Come for me. Let me watch you come on my hand."

I thrust my hand again, my thumb adding more pressure. She rides my hand, her arousal dripping down my hand. Anyone could see us and know what we're doing even though we're clothed. But I don't care.

A shudder runs through her, her mouth falling open against mine, her fingers biting into my shoulders as she rides out her orgasm in my lap. I keep my hand on her, coaxing her through every pulse until she falls boneless against me, spent and catching her breath.

For a second, neither of us says anything.

Then I brush my lips over hers and murmur, "That was still just the appetizer."

Her laugh is weak and sexy as hell. "You are entirely too pleased with yourself."

"Not yet." I slide my hand out from between her legs before placing my fingers in my mouth and tasting her. Her eyes go molten as if she's already primed and ready for round two. "But give me five more of those, and I will be."

CHAPTER
FORTY-FOUR

Decker

"Okay, today is just to make sure you remember it." I sit on the porch steps of Pen's backyard. She's one step up, and my fingers graze along her smooth legs as Hazel gets set up. "Ready?"

She nods, and I play the music on my phone.

Hazel runs through the routine from the top. Waist, chest, then the neck roll hits, and the hoop wobbles and drops. She groans. One thing I've discovered is that Hazel isn't a crier. I waited for the tears many times during all these practices, but she'll just grunt and groan and make frustrated noises that make me laugh.

I climb off the stairs and crouch down to her level. "Relax. It's okay, we have all night."

She nods, her determination similar to her mom's, and picks up the hoop.

I feel Penelope's eyes on me from the steps behind me. She's been staying out of it, which I appreciate. I started this as someone else in Hazel's life, and now I want to be a helluva lot more to her. I'll never get there without Penelope giving us space, which I'm sure is difficult for her. But I'll never let her regret trusting me with the most precious person in her life.

Hazel tries again. Gets the hoop to her neck and does two full rotations before it drops.

"Better," I tell her. "But you're fighting it. When it gets to your neck, you tense up, expecting it to drop. Let's close our eyes."

She tips her chin down and glares.

"Come on, humor me."

Penelope laughs lightly behind us.

Hazel reluctantly closes her eyes.

"Visualize the routine all the way through to the very end. Do you see it? All the moves you've mastered, how well you're doing. Do you see how great you finish? The neck roll four times and then everyone claps."

She nods, and her small chest rises and falls. "I do."

"Okay, then let's do it again."

I step back, not going back to the stairs since the temptation is too much with Penelope there.

Hazel runs through the routine again, but it's her worst yet.

"Okay, here." I pick up the other hula hoop.

"I feel like I should take a video of you doing it." Penelope stands and takes out her phone.

"No video evidence, thank you."

"Hazel, would it help later to watch the video of Decker?" Penelope ignores me, her smile so wide and teasing that I know she's going to use this against me someday.

"Yes, Mommy."

Penelope sits down in the grass, and Hazel sits next to her. The two of them watch me with rapt attention, Penelope's phone raised.

Now it's me grunting. This is the part I've been dreading. I start the hoop at my waist, which goes fine, and work it up to my chest, which goes less fine, and by the time I get it to my neck, I'm sure I look like a grown man having a medical emergency. But I do what I told Hazel. I stop fighting it, and it holds.

Hazel and Penelope both clap.

"You're better than me," Hazel says.

"I've had a lot of years practicing things I'm not naturally good at." I put the hoop down before I embarrass myself further. Then I sit across from her. "Can I tell you something?"

She nods.

"This season I had a problem. With baseball. The thing I'm supposed to be the best at. I started thinking too hard about every play. Worrying about whether I was going to mess up. And you know what happened?"

She shakes her head. "What?"

"I messed up every time. Because I was fighting my natural instincts instead of trusting myself. Does that make sense?"

Hazel picks at the grass. "I think you're a real good baseball player."

I catch Penelope smiling at me. "I do too, just like you're a really good hula hooper."

"So, what did you do?"

I glance to her side at Penelope. "I found something that was more important, and it stopped my mind from fixating on making a mistake. Is there anything you care about more than this hula hoop talent show?"

Hazel processes this the way she processes most things, which is quietly. Then she gets up and grabs the hoop.

She starts the routine. Waist to chest to neck, and this time she looks as if she feels different doing it—the release, the trust—and it spins around her neck for four full rotations before she rolls it back down and catches it at her hip.

She stares at the hoop as though she can't believe she actually did it. "I got it!"

"You got it." I'm not surprised, instead more relieved and proud that she saw it through.

Penelope's eyes widen. "Haze, honey."

Hazel drops the hoop and throws herself at me. She hits me like a small freight train, and I hold her, swinging her up and around. She shrieks, and I hold her for a few seconds before setting her down.

She grabs the hoop immediately. "Again, Decker."

She runs through the routine. Waist, chest, neck roll, catch.

"It worked." She still looks amazed by herself.

"What did you think about? Actually, you don't have to tell me. Just think about it at the talent show, okay?"

She nods and turns to Penelope and back to me, picking up the hula hoop. After the fourth time she does it all perfectly, she stops and holds it at her waist. "Decker?"

"Yes?"

"Are you going to sit with Mommy at the talent show?"

A soft noise falls out of Penelope.

Hazel looks at me with big serious eyes that don't miss anything and probably never have. This doesn't feel like a casual question. She wants to make sure I'll be there because I'm someone important to her. And she's important to me too.

"Yeah," I say. "I'll sit with Mommy."

She nods once, seemingly satisfied.

"And after, right?" She circles the hula hoop around her waist.

Man, she's come so far.

"After?"

"Cookies and juice." She says it as if I should know this. "In the gym. All the families stay. Leighton's bringing the black-and-white cookies from Steingold's. Mommy is bringing ones from Levain." Leave it to a seven-year-old to name the best cookie places in Chicago. "You have to come to that too."

Some emotion moves through my chest that I can't describe.

I crouch back down to her level. "Like I would miss cookies and juice."

She studies me for a moment the way she does, as if she's trying to figure out if I mean it. Then she nods and lifts her hoop.

"Okay," she says. "I'm going to do it ten more times."

"Ten more times?"

"Yes, you said no reward comes without hard work."

She starts the routine, and I sit down next to Penelope to watch. Her shoulder is warm against mine. Neither of us says anything. We just watch Hazel run the routine over and over until she's satisfied.

On the sixth pass, she adds a bow at the end that I did not teach her.

"She made up a bow." Penelope's voice is almost wistful.

My throat is doing something I'm not going to look too hard into right now.

I lay my hand over Penelope's on the step between us. She doesn't move it. Then I turn my attention back to the backyard.

Hazel runs it again. The bow gets more dramatic, like a curtsy. By the tenth pass, she's holding it for a full count before she drops the hoop on the grass.

"Can we get Portillo's now?" Hazel asks.

"Sure." Penelope smiles at her daughter.

Hazel looks at me. "You're coming, right?"

"Where else would I be?"

"Go get your shoes." Penelope watches her go inside for her shoes.

Then we turn to each other, and we're just sitting on the

back steps with two hula hoops on the grass and an empty backyard.

"I think she might know," Penelope says.

I nod. "Yeah, I think so too."

"You know she's going to tell Monroe."

"Monroe probably already knows. They might be in cahoots with each other, who knows?"

Penelope laughs. Actually laughs. The real one she doesn't always let out, and I think about the letter I wrote when I was seventeen and how I said she had the best laugh of anyone I'd ever met. All these years later, it's still the truth.

I stand and hold out my hand.

She takes it, and I pull her up off the step.

I want to hold her and kiss her and tell her how much I love her and her daughter. Every morning since we got together, I've wanted to pinch myself to make sure I'm living in the here and now.

The back door swings open.

"Let's go." Hazel scurries down the stairs and jumps off the last two. She takes Penelope's hand, and they walk along the side of the house to the sidewalk.

I follow, but once we're on the sidewalk, Hazel's small hand slips into mine. I look over her head at Penelope, and we both smile.

Yeah, I think Hazel knows.

Penelope

I lead the way to our seats for the end-of-the-year talent show. Most know Decker is part of our friend group, but they don't know the secret we've been keeping. As much as I want to hold his hand or have him place his hand on the small of my back, that isn't our reality yet.

We settle into our seats and are the annoying people who throw my purse and our coats across the seats around us, claiming spaces for everyone. Decker sits two seats away from me to help claim our row.

I'm still not sure if Hazel knows about Decker and me, but she held both our hands the entire time on the way to and from Portillo's the other night. And when we got there, she wouldn't let me sit on her side of the booth, saying she wanted it all to herself. Decker took full advantage, sliding his hand under the table and running it up and down my thigh throughout dinner.

By the time Hazel went to bed, I was a needy mess, and I

had to have him even though it had to be fast and with limited clothing removal. It was still hot as hell.

"We're here!" Easton waves, coming down the row holding Ellis's baby carrier.

"You let him hold the baby?" Decker asks Callie. He takes the carrier and talks in a baby voice to his niece, telling her how much he missed her.

"He's looking for single moms. Thought the baby would endear them to him." Callie rolls her eyes as she comes down the row. We all slide over to make room.

Decker puts Ellis on the seat next to him, sitting next to me.

Callie slides past Easton.

"Hey, I'll take care of her," Easton says.

"Go find someone else's baby to bait women with."

Foster moves in next to Callie. "I don't understand why we have to be here. We'll have to endure these things with Ellis for years."

"Because they're our nieces and nephew." Callie bats her eyes at him.

"I can understand a recital, but I've seen Monroe's dance routine. I've seen the hula hoop routine. I've seen Lincoln do his magic trick or whatever he's doing."

Callie pats him on the leg. "Well, just think how many times someone might say, 'I've seen Foster Davis pitch, it's not all that impressive.'"

"Point made." He turns to Decker. "She ready?"

How fast he shifts his stance these days still amazes me. Back in college, it was near impossible to change his mind on anything. Must be the Callie effect.

Hayes and Leighton join us with Lake, who sits at the end of the aisle, scrolling through her phone.

"Hi, Lake, such a pleasure to have you join us this evening." Easton embarks on conversing first.

She's a typical teenager now, so you never know what

you're gonna get. Where we all handle her with kid gloves since she can snap like a hungry bear, Easton seems to go with "How fast can I piss her off?"

"Not today," Hayes says before whispering something in Lake's ear.

Lake dramatically leans forward. "Hi, Easton, how are you this evening? I hope you're well." She smacks on the fakest smile I've ever seen.

Leighton sighs. "Good luck, all."

"I'm only having boys," Easton says, and we all stare at him.

Decker takes the bait. "You can't control that."

"The sex is determined by the dad. I'm only giving the Y chromosome."

Leighton rolls her eyes. Hayes is still talking to Lake in a quiet voice, but she doesn't seem to be having any of it.

"Good luck, buddy." Foster pulls out his wallet. "I've got twenty on him having five girls."

"I'm in. But I bet one boy sneaks in there," Decker says.

Hayes passes a twenty down to Foster. "I bet he's got nine kids like his dad's family and all girls just because he kept trying for that boy."

Everyone laughs except Easton. "You guys are assholes."

The lights dim a bit, signaling that the talent show is about to start, and we all quiet down. But when the lights go down completely and the spotlight hits the stage, my anxiety ramps up.

"You're strangling your program," Decker whispers in my ear.

"I am not." I look at the program crinkled in my hands.

His light laugh reaches my ears.

The seat next to me is still empty. It's not like my dad to ever say he can come and not show up, especially when it involves Hazel. He's always reliable where she's concerned.

Decker sits the way he does all the time—shoulders back,

no indication of discomfort, perfectly at peace. He's wearing a navy Henley and jeans. Nothing special, but still my body yearns to be touched by him.

"Stop stressing. She's ready," he says softly.

"I know she's ready."

"Then why are you—"

"Because I'm her mother, and she's seven, and she wants this, and I want this for her." I stop and look at him. "What if…"

"She did it perfectly twelve times yesterday."

"She did it twelve times in my backyard. Not on a stage with all her peers and parents watching her."

"She's gonna be fine either way."

I widen my eyes at him.

"I'm just saying." He shrugs.

The principal makes an announcement about the hard work all the kids have put in, then the show starts.

We watch two piano pieces, a magic act that involves a suspicious amount of parental assistance, two sisters do a dance routine, and Lincoln's friend Micah plays the harmonica. His other friend, Bodhi, does a jump rope routine that's truly impressive. I clap for all of them. Our row goes crazy for Monroe's dance routine and Lincoln's juggling with baseballs using his glove.

As the acts move on, my heart rate climbs.

When the principal announces Hazel, I nearly stop breathing. Decker's hand slides into mine, and he squeezes.

The curtain at the side of the stage parts, and she walks onto the stage in the outfit we picked together—white shorts, the pink top I had to change from the sequined one she originally wanted after she decided the sequins interfered too much with the spinning hoop. Her hair is in the two braids Decker complimented when he came to walk us to the school, and she was pleased he noticed. She's carrying the hoop at her side, and she surveys the audience with those serious eyes, I know she's looking for us.

I raise my hand with the hopes she sees, and it sets her at ease.

She finds me in the crowd. Her eyes shift to Decker, and the anxiety slides off her face. Can I really be surprised he has the same effect on my daughter as he does on me?

The song she picked plays, the one I have heard approximately 473 times. As she starts the hoop, my breathing stops. I can hold it for the two minutes of her routine, I'm sure of it.

She's good. I know this, I've watched it every night for weeks, but she's good in a way that is different with the lights on her and music filling the auditorium. The waist rotation is clean, fluid. She looks like a natural. I'm already relaxing and ready to clap and whistle and jump up on that stage and hug her. Okay, I won't do that, but I want to.

Then the hoop gets to her neck.

And it drops.

My hand goes limp in Decker's. "No," I whisper.

"It's okay, she's good."

I want to turn to him and say no she isn't. She's embarrassed, and I'm going to go get her and hold her and let her cry and tell her she never has to do anything like this again.

Hazel stands with the hoop on the stage floor, and the music keeps going. For one very long second, she stares at it. I could very well see her tossing it into the audience and saying she's done.

Instead, she steps into it again, looks to the side stage, and the music stops and restarts.

She gets it to her chest. And I watch her do the thing—the release, the trust, the getting out of her own way—and the hoop spins around her neck for the full four rotations. Decker cups his mouth and whoops for her.

"Goldie, calm down there," Easton says.

Decker doesn't respond, and I glance at him and the look

in his eyes. As if he already considers her his. It undoes something in me.

I don't try to stop what's happening in my chest. I gave up managing that somewhere around the night he walked through my front door.

Hazel finishes her routine. She catches the hoop at her neck, pulls it down to her hip and holds her bow—the full three-second dramatic curtsy she added herself—and claps ring through the auditorium.

She walks off stage, and Decker leans in. "Our girl did good. I'm so proud of her."

I want to kiss him, to hug him, but all I say is, "Me too."

Someone turns around and says how great it was that she didn't give up and just tried again, and Decker sings her praises like a proud dad.

I guess in a way, he's on his way there.

I really need to send that email tomorrow.

CHAPTER
FORTY-SIX

Decker

"Hey, daddy of the year?"

I turn around after getting the cookie that Hazel told me to take. I think she really wants to get mine since Penelope told her she's only allowed one because they're so big. At some point I might have to stop being the fun uncle type and be on the same side as Penelope. But tonight is not that night. It's a night to celebrate.

"Tedi." I hug her, unable to get my arms fully around her because of her swollen belly.

"So… the manager's daughter?" Her dark eyebrows shoot up to her hairline, and she runs her hand over her stomach.

"I don't know what you're talking about." I put the cookie in a napkin and hold it. "Congrats. I saw your announcement online."

"God, you're even blushing." She ignores me and pushes me with her hand. I lose my balance for a second because I forgot what Tedi was like. She's the older sister of my two best friends back in Philly. A few years ago, she bribed me into having a fake relationship with her to help keep her away from her ex-boyfriend, and now husband, Tweetie.

"Where's the kid?" I ask, changing the subject.

"The kid? You mean Addison?" She points to the corner of the room where Tweetie has Addison propped up on the ledge of a window and is feeding her a cookie.

"All the Falcons are here?"

"Yeah. You're stuck with us. This was technically our school first."

"I don't know about that. Leighton's kids were coming here way before any of your kids."

The Falcons and Colts rivalry to own this city will probably never die.

"Jade and Henry went here as kids. So sorry." Her shoulders lift. "You lose."

I catch sight of Penelope across the room, talking to Leighton and another mom. "I didn't lose."

"Oh my, you're a goner already." She leans in. "Is she the one? The one you were talking about that time we had donuts and hot chocolate?"

I nod.

"Ah, Deck." She punches me in the chest. "I'm so happy for you. But the manager's daughter." She cringes. "Oh, hey!" She pulls her phone out of her back pocket and thumbs around before lifting it to show me something. "I'm a follower."

She shows me that @HandsOffDeck Insta account that has made it their job to try to save my spot on the team. It's truly a waste of their time, but I appreciate the sentiment.

"Thanks."

"You'll be fine. Want to take up hockey again?" She laughs, knowing I sucked at hockey as a kid when I played with her brothers. "Tweetie's retiring this year."

"I heard something about that."

"This one is all his." She runs her hands down her belly again. "And it's a boy, so be on the lookout. I have a feeling he won't be as guarded as my little girl." She glances back and smiles.

The few times I've met Addison, she doesn't seem like the hellion you might expect would come from Tweetie and Tedi. More cautious, like Hazel.

"Anyway." She hugs me again. "Congrats on finally stepping out of your own way. Don't be a stranger." Then she walks away and shouts across the gym, "Babe, Decker's here."

Tweetie nods at me but doesn't smile. Not sure he ever got over me pretending to be Tedi's boyfriend to keep him at arm's length.

"Thanks." A hand grips my shoulder, and I look to my right, seeing Ripley.

"For what?"

"For making my granddaughter the best hula hooper in the world."

I chuckle and stuff my hands in my pockets. I don't like feeling as if I'm keeping things from Mark, but at the same time, if we tell him, it puts him in a bad position we don't want to put him in. I'm probably not going to be a Colt next year, so we can hold off and tell him after the season ends.

"She's a natural," I say. "I didn't see you come in."

"I slid in the back. Chicago traffic." The way he's looking at me, I have to wonder if he's telling the complete truth. "Anyway, I gotta go and prepare for tomorrow. Keep this up, Deck, and you'll be buying the stuffed animals at the airport gift shops soon, not me." He raises his eyebrows and claps me on the shoulder again before walking toward Hazel.

I watch him say goodbye, hug her, then Penelope. There's no way he knows. He's just suspicious.

"I say we just take them right here," Easton says, as my

three teammates huddle around me with juice cups and cookies in their hands.

What world have we morphed into?

"What are you talking about?" I frown.

"The Falcons. Do you see everyone eyeing them and trying to ask them questions? I mean, we're the Colts. We're just as good."

"Technically, they have how many Cups, and how many series have we won?" I raise my eyebrows.

Foster and Hayes look at the Falcons in the corner of the room.

"Tweetie's retiring," I say. "We all have our golden years left and they're retiring soon. They'll start having more babies."

"They've got the Chipmunks ready to take their places," Foster says.

"I'm gonna have four by year's end," Hayes says, "That's more than any of them."

"Yeah, but that's because you inherited three of them. You've got plenty of years left." Easton sips his juice.

All the Falcons look over and wave, nodding at us.

"One day this city will be ours," Foster says, stepping toward them.

"This could be our year," Hayes chimes in, following Foster.

"Definitely, we're gonna have a fucking parade." Easton falls in line with me. "And you're going to be on that fucking bus. With Penelope and Hazel and all of us. This is your town, Goldie, don't forget it."

I nod, unable to say anything past the lump forming in my throat. But the further we get into the season, the more I'm pretty sure my name is being scratched off the roster.

So I say nothing, and Easton doesn't push me.

We huddle with the Falcons and their families. We complain about them all the time, but they're a great team and even better guys. At least if we have to share a city, it's with them.

Mid-conversation, Hazel comes over, and I slyly give her the cookie I've been holding. I watch her run over to Monroe, and they share it.

"What's up with that, Decker?" Henry asks, pushing a stroller back and forth.

"That's Penelope Riley's daughter, Hazel," I say.

"Yeah, I've heard about her. Bodhi told me she doesn't have a dad in her life?"

I tilt my head.

"We'll apologize ahead of time. Bodhi has a tendency to… interfere." He smiles as though he's telling me I've been interfered with.

"Did he do it again?" Conor asks, then laughs.

"For sure! He just gave her a cookie, and did you see him look like a proud daddy when she did her routine?" Henry laughs, and they all join in. "He's never done it when it wasn't meant to be though." Henry pats me on the back. "If you want to thank him, he's right over there."

I glance in the opposite corner where a brown-haired boy stands with Lincoln and another boy, talking to Hazel and Monroe. They're all staring at us.

Shit, did I get swindled by a bunch of grade schoolers?

Guess I should thank them.

CHAPTER
FORTY-SEVEN

Decker

"I love when you return from an away series." Penelope's legs tighten around my waist.

"I can't believe you sent those pictures. I was in the dugout for one of them. I almost had to go to the plate with a fucking hard-on." I drill into her, pressing her back into the wall.

"All the Decker fan girls would have loved that."

"I only care about one of my fans." My head falls to her neck. I love kissing her there, but mostly because of the noises she makes when I do. It's definitely an erogenous zone for her.

She laughs and uses her hand on my shoulders to push up a little more, and my hands dig into her ass to push deeper inside her. "I would hope so."

The more we have sex, the better it gets. It's only been a little more than a month. I can't imagine what our sex life will be like a decade from now.

"God, I missed your pussy so fucking much." I punctuate each word with a thrust.

"Just my pussy?" Her words come out as a pant.

"Your tits too." I smirk into her neck, kissing her shoulder. "Every damn inch of your body."

"You complain about all those women seeing you as a sex symbol, yet you say the only thing you miss about me is my body."

"Fuck no, I miss your massages too."

She smacks my back, but I plunge into her, and her head rocks against the wall. "No more talking, just fuck me, Deck."

"Gladly."

And I do. I thrust and whisper only praise for her body. The way her pussy is meant to take my cock. How wet she gets for me. How many times I beat off during this away series was probably a record.

"I'm gonna come." Her body tightens in my hands. Pen's feet dig into my ass, and I push her harder against the wall, needing the leverage. "Deck, right there. I can't... I need... oh damn... you're too good at this..."

She has this adorable tendency to go on and on as she comes, and it only makes me grow harder inside her.

A strangled moan erupts out of her, her fingernails digging into my shoulder blades.

Once I'm positive she's come, I push into her again. She doesn't slow, clenching around my length, and I come right after her with a mumbled curse.

I hold her weight, leaning into her as we come down and catch our breath.

Eventually, I lower her to the floor and make sure she's steady on her feet. She heads to the bathroom, and I follow her. We're already over the whole "let me clean up and then you clean up" thing. We clean up at the same time, and I fucking love the normalcy of that.

"You know if you take Hazel to this Dugout Social Club

pet adoption thing, you're coming home with a dog, right?" I tell her as she pees. I use my towel from earlier when we fucked in the shower to clean up.

Hazel is at camp now that school's been over for a month, so as soon as she left, I came over. I'm kind of done with sneaking around behind Hazel's back. We do so much stuff as a threesome, but we've yet to tell her we're officially together.

"No. She'll just love to pet and play with them." She comes over and washes her hands.

I lean along the counter and soak her in. I love her naked. My dick twitches, but we don't have time for another round. We've been at each other all day. Got one errand crossed off before we came home and fucked again. This is what happens after an away series, and I'm starved for her. Now we're done for the day because Hazel is due home.

"Have you not seen the fridge?"

She laughs and goes into her bedroom so she can put on her clothes. "She knows we can't get a dog until we get this place fixed up. It wouldn't be fair to the dog."

I follow her into the bedroom and grab my boxers and shorts. "If you say so."

"I do, and I'm her mother, so I have the final say."

"Says the woman who was ready to jump on stage at the talent show and swarm her in a hug. Big talker."

She laughs, knowing I'm right.

I grab my shirt and throw it over my head. I'm about to tell her how I hate when she's covered in clothes and sweet-talk her into letting me stay here tonight—so I can sneak into her bed after Hazel goes to sleep—when my phone vibrates in my pocket.

I pull it out, seeing Jagger's name. I show her the screen, and she rises on her tiptoes, giving me a quick kiss. "You take it. I'll go get her."

I open my mouth to argue, but we're past mid-season now and still the Colts haven't made a move, despite my performance being great and the groundswell of support that Instagram account has gained to try to save me.

The businesses around town are all making up different sandwiches and drinks with punny names to try to keep me. It's great, and I've never been more honored, but it's a blaring red flag every time I see something that reminds me I'm probably not staying here.

"Hey," I answer.

"How's my favorite client?"

"I don't know. I'm not with any of the Falcons right now."

He laughs. "Ah… you boys have to stop. I love you all, I just love them a little more. Win me a series or two, and you guys might get the jump on them."

"That will be hard to do when I play for another team."

"Nah, don't be talking like that. It's not over 'til it's over. We've got time, but I am calling with some good news."

I sit on the edge of Penelope's bed. "I can't imagine what."

"Money. You like money, right?"

"Who doesn't love money?"

The truth is that as arrogant as it sounds, I have enough money. I've been single since I came into the league, scored some great signing bonuses and contracts, invested well. I could retire this season and still want for nothing, mostly because I don't live a lavish lifestyle. I want to play because I love baseball, but I'm not going to play for less than I'm worth.

"Good. Graham Sutter called and threw his hat in the ring."

"New York?" They have the biggest bank roll for players. Which means I have a chance of making even more there than I do in Chicago. And they win a lot of titles.

"Who's your daddy? Ah… don't answer that until you sign on the dotted line. But this is big, and it means options. So, get ready to sublet that condo to Harkins or someone."

My eyes scan Penelope's room. "I don't know about moving. I really don't want to leave Chicago."

Sure, the walls here need to be painted, and things need to be updated, but it's Penelope's space with her things. I want to be here with her and Hazel.

I've never had to think about anyone but myself in all the times I've played in other cities.

"Well, if you want to play baseball, you better start getting used to the idea. Maybe we'll see if the Trojans bite, but that new GM, Bianca Banks, is a real trip. I don't think she likes me."

"I can't imagine why," I say dryly.

"Okay, gotta go. I'll be in touch. You score a big contract with New York, and it's a big fuck you to Shane Whitaker. Talk soon."

He hangs up, and I hold my phone in my hands.

I stuck to all three of my rules, but I'm not sure it will matter.

I didn't take what wasn't mine—Penelope was mine.

I didn't stay where I didn't belong—this is where I belong.

If I take an offer in a different city, I did promise what I can't keep. A life here in Chicago with Penelope and Hazel.

"We're back!" Penelope yells extra loud.

I scramble to my feet and walk down the stairs.

"Hi, Deck." Hazel flies by the bottom of the stairs into the kitchen with a drawing in her hand.

Penelope looks at me. "You might be right."

"What is it?"

"Another dog drawing."

I laugh and hug her quickly, but I don't pull away fast enough. I hear Hazel's footsteps stop. We both look at her and find her mouth is hanging open.

I start to move away, but Penelope clings to me tighter. "Haze, honey, we gotta talk."

CHAPTER
FORTY-EIGHT

Penelope

"Are you sure?" Decker whispers.

"It's time." I step away, keeping my hand in his. "Hazel, let's sit."

"Is this about Decker being my daddy?" Hazel runs into the living room and throws herself onto a chair.

I pause for a second but sit on the couch and tug Decker down next to me. I think he's thrown. I probably should've given him a heads-up, but this is having kids. You do things on the fly sometimes.

"It's not about Decker being your daddy."

"It's not?" Her face distorts with displeasure, and I rear back, surprised by her reaction. "They said it would work. That all I had to do was get you guys to spend time together, and he'd be my daddy."

I glance at Decker. He told me about Henry Hensley's son, Bodhi, and how he likes to interfere in couples' relationships.

He alluded that Bodhi might have had something to do with us.

"Hazel, who is *they*?"

She sinks into the chair, looking anywhere but us.

"Hazel." I use my stern voice, and she peeks up, seeing that this conversation will not end until she tells us.

"The boys… Lincoln, Bodhi, and Micah. Bodhi and Micah said they got his parents together. That they just had to push them together. So…"

Decker hasn't said anything yet, and I feel as if I'm in a dark room and feeling my way to the exit with this one. I definitely didn't think this was what she was planning the entire time.

"How did you push us together?" I ask.

She glances at the door.

"Hazel."

She blows out a big breath. "The hula hoop talent show. They all saw how good Decker was at the field day, and Monroe said how she overheard Hayes and Leighton talking about you and Decker. I like Decker. I want him to be my daddy."

I turn to Decker, whose eyes are wide open.

"Would you excuse us for a minute?" I ask him. He doesn't need to be here when I tell her she can't just appoint someone to be her daddy.

"I'd rather stay if it's okay with you."

My eyebrows crinkle. "You would?"

"Yeah." He nods.

"Okay…" I slide my hand from his and go over to Hazel, kneeling by her chair. "Listen, honey, I know you've been wondering a lot of things about having a daddy. And you like Decker, but you can't just pick someone, then trick them—"

"There wasn't any tricking on my part," Decker says.

I tilt my head and give him a look like *I got this, just stay over there.* "You lied and did things to have Decker take the time out of his schedule to teach you the hula hoop. And…"

I draw a blank, unsure how to even approach this the right way. It's honestly brilliant that a group of elementary kids are such good matchmakers.

"May I?" Decker asks, getting off the couch and coming over to the chair. When I nod, he turns his attention to Hazel. "First of all, I'm honored, kiddo. That out of everyone, you'd want me to be your daddy. But I think what your mom is trying to ask is why?"

Oh yeah, that's a good question. Shit, I have seniority here, and he's trumping me.

"You love Mommy."

Decker smiles at me. "What made you think that?"

"You always stare at her. You do nice things for her. You do nice things for me. Do you not love Mommy?" She frowns.

"Honey," I say, realizing this is going the opposite direction of what I'd like.

"Yes, I love your mommy."

"Then why can't you be my daddy? Daddies love mommies, and mommies love daddies."

Not all the time, but that's a conversation for another time.

"It's not really up to me to be your daddy. It's actually up to your mommy and then you."

I fall a little more in love with him.

Hazel turns to me. "Mommy, can he?"

I smile at my daughter. "Okay, listen, Hazel, I appreciate the effort you put into this, but I need to talk to Decker alone. We will revisit the daddy thing again. What we wanted to tell you"—I sit on the coffee table and take her hands—"is that I do love Decker, and he loves me, and we are dating."

A big smile lights up her face. "So it worked? You're together?"

"We are." Decker nods and returns her smile.

"But that doesn't make him your daddy. It might happen at some point, but not right now, honey."

Her smile falls, and she glances at Decker, her little eyebrows drawn together.

"Listen, Hazel." He stands. "Your mom and I just have to get some things figured out. Right now, we're telling you about us, but it has to be kept a secret because there are some adult things we have to deal with first."

"But you might be my daddy, right?"

"Hazel, I promise you—and you can ask your mom, I do not make promises I cannot keep, so believe me when I say— that one day I will be your daddy."

"Yay!" She jumps off the couch and into his arms. He holds her as she buries her head into the nook of his neck.

He looks at me over her shoulder, and I nod because yes, one day he will be. Of that I have no doubt. We just have to tackle one problem at a time. The first problem being the asshole who isn't returning my phone calls or emails, which I guess is his right. But I don't want any secrets between Decker and me when we get married, and there's an urgency to get this handled. Which is why I want to handle another problem right now.

Hazel draws back. "Can we go get ice cream tonight?"

"Sure," Decker says.

And he thinks I'm the softie.

She gives me a hug, then runs upstairs, saying she has to change her clothes.

"She's so you." Decker gets up off the floor and sits on the couch.

I swivel around on the coffee table. "We need to talk."

"I think I did pretty good there. And you know I don't make promises I can't keep."

"Yeah, yeah, I know. But, Decker, now that we've told Hazel, and we're committed to this going the distance, I don't want any secrets between us—except the obvious one I'm still working on being able to tell you. I want to explain why I never came back to your hotel room three years ago."

We'd run into each other at the All-Star game and made plans to grab a drink together since it had been so long since we'd seen each other. One thing led to another, and our evening ended in his hotel room.

I see the old him wanting to emerge, wanting to close the gate between us. But instead, he says, "Okay…"

I run my palms down my legs and sit up straighter. "It was an amazing night, and I only slipped out while you were sleeping to get us some food. But as soon as I shut the hotel room door, Foster was coming out of his room."

"I forgot he was there," Decker says, probably recalling that they were on the same team. He told me that night it was the most uncomfortable game he'd ever played. "Did he say something?"

I shake my head. "He just stared at me, then your door, and made a sound and shook his head. It wasn't a good sound."

He frowns. "I didn't think it would be."

"I got all up in my head, started spiraling. I didn't want to get between you guys. A video showed the two of you talking during the game, and I thought, 'There's no way I can get in between them again.' I thought he'd always be between us—whether you had a relationship with him or not. And what if we did try to make it work, and I introduced you to Hazel? What if she fell in love with you and then you left? Seeing Foster scared me. Because I felt that if it came down to it, you wouldn't pick me. You'd have to choose, and I would be the one left behind like all the times before."

Decker takes my hands and pulls me over to him, positioning me on his lap. "You don't have to tell me any of this. I put that shit aside the minute we started this."

"I know, but now with Hazel…"

He tucks a strand of my hair behind my ear. "It's okay. It's only been a few months. It was a long hard road to get here. I understand that it will take some time for me to earn your trust."

I shake my head. "That's just it… when you told Hazel you'd be her daddy someday, I didn't feel any fear. I knew it was the truth. I'm not scared anymore, so I want you to know something else."

"Okay." He waits patiently for me to finish.

"I know you may get offers from other teams, that the Colts aren't promising anything. What I'm saying is that wherever you go… we go."

"Pen."

"Yes, Decker. We're not going to do this cross country. So, don't worry about any of that when you're talking to other teams. Make the best choice for you, and we'll be by your side."

He nods, although I know it will be one of many times I have to reinforce my point.

Hazel runs down the stairs in a new outfit and digs into her backpack from camp. "I forgot. Look what Bodhi gave me today." She rummages through and comes over, handing something to Decker. "One of the bakeries is making these."

Decker looks at the All Hands on Deck #HandsOffDecker cookie in the shape of a hand and shakes his head.

"Everyone wants Decker, Hazel, but guess what?" I pat Decker's other leg, and she crawls up on it.

"What?"

"He's all ours."

She smiles at Decker and wraps her arms around his neck. "Yeah, he is."

I kiss his temple, and we all share a hug.

No matter where we land, we'll be together.

CHAPTER
FORTY-NINE

August

Penelope: [link to the Noir Cologne ad]

Decker: I know. Easton keeps playing it.

It's everywhere

And?

And nothing.

Pen.

I may have watched it more than once.

How many times?

That is privileged information.

More than five?

Goodnight, Decker.

More than ten?

I said goodnight.

I'll be home in two days.

I know.

Wear the blue thing.

What blue thing?

You know what blue thing.

CHAPTER
FIFTY

September

Decker: Tell me why hotel beds are the worst when you're not in them.

Penelope: Because I'm not there making a mess of it?

Exactly.

Bold of you to assume I'd let you sleep.

Baby, I haven't stopped thinking about you since I got on the plane.

That so?

Mm-hmm. You in one of my shirts.

I have one on now.

Are you teasing me, Miss Ripley?

Maybe a little. Sounds like you miss me.

> That's putting it mildly.

Good. Suffer a little.

> I am. And then I'm coming home and making you very, very sorry for it.

Promise?

> Count on it.

CHAPTER
FIFTY-ONE

October

Penelope: [screenshot of HandsOffDeck follower count: 75,003]

Decker: How does someone get that many followers so fast?

Dedicated fan base.

I want to send them something. A signed jersey or something.

That would be nice of you.

I miss you.

Me too.

Show me how much.

Goodnight.

C'mon. I'm dying over here.

(picture of lifting her shirt)

CHAPTER
FIFTY-TWO

Decker

Maybe the Colts have a good reason not to re-sign me.

We won our division but fell short in the league.

So, here we are in the press room, our last one for a while. Hopefully not my last one ever. Regardless, I couldn't be happier to have some dedicated time with Penelope and Hazel coming up. Except it more than likely means we're moving, if I get to continue playing ball. It'll be sad to say goodbye to the house. It's where we fell in love.

We all enter the media room—Foster, Easton, Hayes, and me. Ripley stands off to the side, knowing he's next and wanting to make sure we appear as a united front.

I try not to think about how it will be my last time standing on this podium with these three guys. Foster is my biological brother, but Easton and Hayes are my brothers too, and I hate that I won't be with them next year.

I'm gonna have some major fucking FOMO.

The reporters settle, cameras up and notepads open.

Here we go.

The first few questions are standard. What happened in the final series. What does the team build look like going forward. What would you like to say to the fans. Hayes takes the majority of questions as our leader. Foster fields some about his pitching and whether the pitching was the problem.

No one can fault him for his sour attitude. Who wants to do a press conference after a loss? No one.

I answer what questions come my way. My numbers were good this season. Better than good honestly—the second half of the year, I played the best baseball of my career, and I know it regardless of what anyone thinks, including Shane Whitaker. Even though everyone in this room knows it, how well I played doesn't change anything. Whitaker made his decision back in June.

The questions rotate. Someone asks about Harkins, and Hayes cuts in and answers diplomatically before I have to. Good. I would not have been diplomatic in my response.

Then a reporter in the third row stands.

We've figured out that her name is Jordan Blake. She's the one who's been calling us out the last two seasons. She outed Hayes and Leighton's relationship. And last year, she outed that Foster and Callie were expecting a baby. So I'm wise to have my guard up when she makes her presence known.

Penelope and I have kept our relationship private. We've sacrificed a lot of time we'd like to be out in public with Hazel. If we go somewhere, it's usually the entire squad of us. I've grown tired of the subterfuge, but we did it for Ripley. We didn't want him to be in a situation where everyone knew one of his players was dating his daughter. But the season is over and Whitaker doesn't want me, so I don't give a shit anymore.

"Decker," Jordan says.

"Here we go," I mumble.

"There's been a lot of speculation this season about your contract situation with the Colts. Do you think it's a result of your rusty start this season?"

I lean toward the microphone, my body taut. "I can't speculate what the front office thinks. Wish I could, maybe I would've tried to please them."

A few chuckles ring out from some of the media, and Jordan sits. Thank God.

We field a few more questions about specific plays and whether they were the ones that lost the game for us. They call out Easton for an error in the fifth when he bobbled the ball.

"You have to be kidding me. That play should earn me a Gold Glove." Easton shakes his head and settles back in his chair.

Another reporter stands. "Hayes, rumor is you're up for the Gold Glove this year. It would be your first. How does it feel?"

Hayes leans in. "It would be great. I have an entire life outside of baseball that I cherish, but of course it's nice to be recognized. Even this late in my career."

Light laughter rings out in the room.

Jordan raises her hand again, and I groan when she says, "This one is for Decker."

"I figured," I answer.

Everyone laughs, knowing she always picks one of us to put in the hot seat.

"Do you think you're not getting a contract renewal because you're dating the manager's daughter?" She stands there with a smug look, waiting for my response.

The room goes silent.

I glance at Ripley, but he has no expression on his face.

Here goes. If I admit to the relationship, I'm kissing my

chance of playing in Chicago goodbye. But if I deny it, it's completely disregarding what Penelope and Hazel mean in my life. I'd never sacrifice them for anything, including who I play for. I'll retire before my job affects them and their feeling of worth in my life.

I pull the microphone closer. "Well, you sure do your research."

Hayes shifts beside me. Just slightly. Only someone who knows him would catch it.

"Since my contract situation has nothing to do with my performance this season—and I think anyone who watched me play knows that—that's between me and the organization. I'll leave it there." I pause. "As for Penelope…"

I feel like every reporter straightens in their chairs, holding their microphones a little closer.

"Yeah, we're together."

Cameras start snapping immediately. I continue because why the hell not?

"I'm not going to get into when or how, because that's our business. What I will say—" I look directly at the reporter— "is that the suggestion that a relationship with the manager's daughter is somehow responsible for a contract decision is the kind of question that assumes the worst about both of us. Penelope Ripley is one of the most professional people I have ever worked alongside. She has never once—not once—used her relationship with her father or her position with this organization for anything other than doing her job exceptionally well. The idea that my contract situation is her fault is not only wrong, it's insulting to her."

The reporter opens her mouth to form a rebuttal, but I'm not done.

"And for the record, if anyone in this organization made a decision about my contract based on who I'm in a relationship with rather than what I did on that field this year, that says a great deal more about them than it does about me or Penelope."

Complete silence blankets the room.

Foster pats me on the back, and I look over to see a wide grin on his lips.

Then everyone is talking at once.

"Is it serious?" someone calls.

"Yes." I don't elaborate.

"Are you in contract discussions with other teams?"

"That's a question for my agent."

The questions shift. Someone asks Foster about the season. Someone asks Hayes about the defense going into next year. The media scrum moves on as it usually does.

When it wraps, I stand and shake the hands I'm supposed to shake and nod at the cameras I'm supposed to nod at, then Ripley's hand finds my shoulder.

Not grabbing me. Not stopping me. Just his hand on my shoulder the way it's been since I was a kid standing on the field, not knowing what to do with myself.

I turn.

"My office," he says. "These guys can wait."

"Yes, sir."

I follow him to his office. When we get inside, he sits behind his desk, and I sit across from it the way I have a hundred times.

He looks at me.

I look at him.

I'm not even scared.

"How long?" He leans back in his chair.

"Since the VIP dinner." I pause. "We've been working up to it longer than that."

Something moves across his face. "I know."

"I should have come to you first. Before the press conference. Before any of it. That was wrong, and I'm sorry."

He leans back in his chair and blows out a breath. "You going to New York?" His mouth is a thin line.

"I don't know yet."

His nostrils flare. "I have ears, Decker."

"I don't know," I say again. "I want to stay here. I want to figure out a way to stay. But if I go—" I stop. "Pen said they'd come with me."

His eyebrows lift. Telling your boss that you've not only been dating his daughter behind his back, but now you're taking her and his granddaughter thousands of miles away isn't easy. And I might not have the guts if I didn't have an inkling that it wasn't only Hazel playing matchmaker this season.

"It's her decision to make," I say. "Not mine. I'm not asking her to upend anything. But she said it, and I'm telling you because you should know."

He's quiet for a long moment. "She's been through a lot. Things you don't know about and things I can't tell you. What I can tell you is that she hasn't let anyone in for a long time and the last person she let in didn't deserve her."

"I know," I say, assuming he's talking about Hazel's father.

"Do you?" He arches an eyebrow, leans in a bit.

"I know enough to know I'm not him. And I know enough to know that I'm going to spend the rest of my life making sure she doesn't regret this." I hold his gaze. "I should've said this to you a long time ago. I've wanted to be with Pen since I was seventeen years old, but I was too scared of losing you as a mentor to say it. But I love your daughter, which I understand is complicated, and I understand if you need time to—"

"Deck."

I stop.

He leans forward on his desk. "I know you know."

I stare at him, trying to appear shocked by what he's going

to tell me. I'd never tell him he wasn't as smooth as he thought he was.

"The Dugout Social Club." A smile forms on his lips. "Penelope needed something to do with her time and her skills. That was true. But I also thought that if I put the two of you on the same task long enough, the rest would sort itself out." He pauses. "It took longer than I expected, to be honest. I hope Hazel doesn't get her mother's stubbornness."

"I assure you, she did."

He groans and rubs his hand down his face. "I know."

I look at him. The man who has been in my corner the better part of my life. Who came to every game of my career that he could and pushed me when I needed it and left me alone when I needed that too. The man who was more of a father to me than my own.

He set this up.

"Thank you for engineering this."

Ripley shakes his head. "I only created an opportunity. What you did with it was up to you."

I relax back into my chair.

"You're the only person I would trust with both of them," he says. "Don't make me wrong about that… no matter where you end up."

"No, sir. I won't."

He nods once.

"Now I have to go into that press conference." He stands, and I do as well. "I'm still rooting for Whitaker to change his mind. I'm doing my best to keep you here, and not just because I don't want to lose my daughter and granddaughter. But whoever gets you is a lucky team, Deck." He holds out his hand, and I shake it.

"Thank you for everything, but most of all for trusting me with both of them."

He smiles, and we release hands.

"Just don't give me a reason to show up on your doorstep one day for anything other than a visit."

"Never." My phone rings in my pocket, and I pull it out. "It's Pen."

He pats me on the shoulder. "Good luck. She's gonna give you hell."

And he leaves the room as my thumb slides across the screen.

CHAPTER
FIFTY-THREE

Penelope

> Leighton: OMG…what a guy!!!

> Callie: GO DECKER!!!

> Leighton: Pen, you must be swooning hard.

> Are you kidding? I'm pissed.

> Callie: 😔

> Leighton: He just confessed his love for you in a press conference.

> When he doesn't have a damn contract for next year. This is not a good look for him.

> Callie: I guess, but you guys deserve to be out in the open.

She's not wrong. I've been going stir crazy, and lying to my dad wasn't great. Although he's been oddly busy lately, even asking Decker to pick the last stuffed animal and bring it home to Hazel.

Leighton: Callie's got a point, but I really hope Whitaker sees all the love he's getting on socials and at all the local businesses. I was at a small café, and they had The Decker Defender drink.

Callie: I was at the deli in Lincoln Park, and they had Goldie's Grinder. The entire city wants him to play here.

And I think he just blew it all up.

Callie: I don't think so.

I'm the manager's daughter.

Leighton: Love is love, there no actual rule, right?

I think it's an ethics thing.

Leighton: Gotcha. Oh…they're done.

I check my television and send them a quick text.

I'm calling him.

Callie: Be nice, he just loves you.

Leighton: I cried, that means something.

Callie: You cry at everything these days.

I leave the group text chain.

I give Decker fifteen minutes, knowing he's probably with the team, and they just lost. All of us were going to fly out there tomorrow since we thought for sure they'd make it to the next game, but I guess we'll be waiting for them to come home instead.

"Hey, Pen," he says when he answers.

"Are you crazy?"

"Hello to you too."

"Decker. Jordan Blake is going to run that on every platform she has by tonight, and my dad is going to—"

"I already talked to your dad."

My head rocks back. "You talked to my dad?"

"Yeah, turns out he's been Team Pecker all along."

"Did you just make a couple name for us?"

"I did. Well, I didn't. Technically Easton did."

My eyes squeeze shut for a second. "Then tell him to figure out another one. We are not going to be known as Pecker."

"I thought it was okay. And there really aren't any other options. I mean… Denelope sounds like a species of deer. Declope sounds like a drug. Pecker is really the only option."

"Decker…stop saying it, or it's going to stick."

"Okay." His warm chuckle echoes in my ear.

"I wish you wouldn't have let that Jordan get it out of you."

I hear his sigh through the phone. "It was time."

I get it. I do. I want to be out too, but not at his expense.

"Hey, we all want to get the hell out of here and get home. Can you take it out on me in bed, preferably naked?" There's a calmness in his voice.

"Decker!"

"It's starting to turn me on when you call me by my full name. Does it turn you on when I call you Penelope?"

"Actually, it doesn't."

"I'll stick to Pen. I'm by the locker room. Call you when we take off, and we can discuss all this when I get home. Okay?"

I blow out a breath, but I can't have him missing the bus or the plane. "Fine."

"I love you, Pen."

"I love you."

"Say it."

"Say what?" I ask.

"You know what."

"No, *Decker*, I do not know."

He just laughs. "Love you so much, and I can't wait to kiss you on the streets of Chicago in front of everyone."

Oh boy, he's too good. I have no response to that.

"And carry Hazel when she gets sleepy at the zoo."

"You're too smooth for your own good."

"And just think, I'm all yours. Pecker forever."

"Decker!"

He laughs and hangs up.

I grab my laptop, sending another email with the hopes that the asshole answers this time. Especially since he's going to hear about my relationship with Decker. Then again, maybe he'll actually respond to me now. Bastard.

CHAPTER
FIFTY-FOUR

Decker

I get out of bed before Penelope.

She wasn't as mad at my outing us by the time I got home, understanding that we couldn't—and I wouldn't—live in the dark anymore. Our life together comes before my contract, and she agreed—eventually. It might have taken a few orgasms to make her see the light.

Her dad called her and asked to have brunch next week, so we're all going out, me as the new member in their crew.

Although it's not official yet.

Which is why I'm grabbing my sweats and T-shirt and tiptoeing out of the room, trying not to wake her.

I head downstairs and go to my bag I left at the bottom of the stairs, digging out the box. Then I head back up the stairs just as quietly.

I twist the doorknob of Hazel's bedroom door so the click is barely heard, and slip into her room. She's asleep on her stomach, sprawled out as always. One of her legs is out of the blanket, her arms tucked under her pillow, and her hair a messy ball of blonde.

I kneel next to the bed, keeping the box in my free hand as I tuck her blonde hair away from her face. She looks so angelic and sweet, and I love her so much it hurts. She's mine in every way that counts.

"Sweetie," I whisper.

She doesn't stir, which I figured would be an issue when I came up with this plan.

"Sweetie, it's time to get up." I nudge her a little.

One hand comes out from under the pillow, swatting at me. I draw back and laugh. She peeks one eye open, then the other, before getting up in bed and crossing her legs. She pushes her hair out of her face, and she looks awake. It's always surprising how she can go from dead asleep to fully awake. The energy is amazing.

"You're home!" She leans forward and wraps her arms around my neck. "I'm sorry you didn't win."

"Thanks." I hug her tightly, my hands running down her back.

I missed her so much. Sometimes I think retirement is the way to go, but I still want to play, and I have a few years left. I just wish they could always be with me. But I'm not going to dwell on that now because I'm off for the moment.

"Season's over, so you're stuck with me."

She giggles and sits back up in bed.

"I have a question for you."

Her eyebrows rise, and she looks so much like Penelope it's almost jarring. I hope our other kids take after their mom too.

"What's the question?" She pushes her unruly hair out of her face again.

I pick up the box and open it. "Will you be my daughter?"

She looks at the small flower ring, then up at me.

Her small hand reaches out to take the ring, but I shut the box before she can. "You have to answer first."

She laughs. "Of course. I asked you first, remember?"

I shake my head, taking out the ring. "Very true. Now give me your right ring finger so I can put it on."

I slide the ring on, and she lifts her hand to examine it just like I hope her mom will later this morning. "I love it."

"I hoped you would."

She throws herself at me, wrapping her legs around my waist and attaching herself to me like a koala bear. "I love you."

"I love you… so much, Hazel."

She squeezes me then draws back. "Does Mommy have one too?"

I shake my head, and she frowns.

"I was hoping you'd help me with that part."

Her eyes widen with excitement.

So I tell her my plan, and I carry her downstairs to the kitchen to put our plan into motion.

CHAPTER
FIFTY-FIVE

Penelope

I hear them before I'm fully awake.

Whispering outside my door. Although I wouldn't consider it whispering. It's louder than regular talking and proof that Hazel has not yet mastered the concept of volume control.

"You have to let me carry the tray," she says.

"Better if I do. You'll drop it."

"I will not drop it."

"I'll carry the tray," Decker says. "You can open the door."

"Fine. I carry the tray next time."

"I'm hoping there isn't a next time," Decker says.

I lie in bed and stare at the ceiling, listening to Decker and Hazel negotiate tray logistics outside my bedroom door at eight in the morning, and I feel something so large and warm in my chest I don't have a word for it that is sufficient.

The door creaks open, and I pretend to be asleep, peeking through one eye as they file in with the focused energy of people executing a plan. Hazel first, both hands wrapped around a glass of orange juice, tongue pressed between her teeth in concentration. Decker is behind her with the tray.

Hazel makes it to the nightstand without spilling, and her expression when she sets down the glass is the specific triumph of someone who has been doubted and proved a point.

"Breakfast in bed," she whispers.

I pretend to just wake up, but I'm pretty sure Decker knows I wasn't asleep.

"There was a disagreement about the tray," he says.

I sit up. Decker sets the tray across my lap, and I look at the eggs slightly overdone, the toast cut diagonally, the coffee in the right mug. "This is wonderful. Thank you both."

"It was Decker's idea," Hazel says, sliding up and over my legs to the other side of me.

"It was a team effort," he says, sitting on the edge of the bed.

They look at one another, and I'm definitely not missing anything.

"Is this about the dog thing?" I ask. "Trying to butter me up?"

"Would it work?" Hazel asks. "If I make you breakfast in bed, we can get a dog finally?"

"No." I run my hand over her knotted hair. There will be whining when I brush through that mess later. "Not yet."

She groans, rolls her eyes, and flops into the pillow.

I pick up my coffee.

Decker is watching me. Hazel straightens and tucks her hands in her lap, watching me.

Something is absolutely going on.

"Okay," I say. "What's happening?"

"Nothing," Hazel says immediately.

I look at her.

She stops bouncing.

"Nothing is happening," she says, slower this time, with the exaggerated calm of someone who was briefed on this question and prepared an answer.

I give Decker an accusatory glare.

He looks at the ceiling.

"Hazel," I say.

"Decker has something to—"

"Hazel," Decker says.

She claps both hands over her mouth.

I set down the coffee.

Hazel is vibrating, both hands still pressed to her mouth, eyes enormous, looking between Decker and me.

Decker sighs.

"Sorry," Hazel says.

"Don't be." He pulls a box from his pocket, opens it, and places it on the breakfast tray.

Simple. Classic. A round solitaire. Perfect and so very me.

Hazel makes a sound behind her hands that isn't quite a word.

"I've loved you since I was eleven years old," he says. "I have been careful and managed and controlled about it for far too many years, and I am completely done." He holds up the ring. "I want to marry you. I want to live in this house and go to Portillo's and sit in school auditoriums and find out what the dog's name is going to be because we both know it's happening."

Hazel laughs, and I roll my eyes. He's probably right about the dog, but I'm putting up a good fight.

"I want every ordinary thing with you. Just you. For the rest of my life." He steadily looks at me. "Marry me, Pen."

"What do you think I should say, Hazel?"

Hazel gets up on her feet, and the tray wobbles.

Decker quickly takes it and moves it to the dresser. "Just in case. We don't need you wearing the breakfast, although it's probably not that good. Part of the proposal is cooking lessons by the way."

"Say yes, Mommy. I did." She holds her hand out to me.

I look at Decker. I love his blush. "You asked her?"

"Pen, I'm still waiting over here," Decker says, holding the ring between his two fingers.

"Yes, of course." I hold out my hand, and he slides the ring on my finger.

Hazel plops down on my lap, holding her hand over mine, my diamond and her flower shining under the sunlight pouring through the windows.

"We match," she says.

"We match," I say.

Then she throws herself at Decker, and he catches her the way he always does, and I can't hold back the tears.

"Can we call Monroe?" Hazel asks into his shoulder.

"After breakfast," I say.

"Can we call Grandpa?"

"After breakfast," Decker says.

"Can we—"

"Hazel. After breakfast."

She sighs dramatically and disentangles herself, climbing off the bed. "Eat fast. I have a lot of people to call."

She leaves. We listen to her footsteps down the hall and her door closing.

Decker slides into bed next to me. "I love you."

"I love you."

I lean into him, and he puts his arm around me, and we lie in the morning light of a house that needs painting and probably an entire gut job.

None of that matters because the one thing we have an abundance of in this house is love.

It might have taken decades, but we got here, and that's what matters.

CHAPTER
FIFTY-SIX

@deckerDavis43
[image: three hands stacked. A man's hand on the bottom, a woman's hand in the middle, a small child's hand on top. Three rings. A plain band on his. A round solitaire on hers. A small flower ring on the littlest hand.]
Chicago, IL 📍
Took me too long.
@peneloperipley ∞
🤍 847,203 likes

@easton_bailey2 TEAM PECKER FOREVER!

@leightonluvshayes_ 😭😭😭 I KNEW IT I KNEW IT I KNEW IT

@fosterdavis14 Finally. (Callie owes me nothing, I owe Callie everything.)

@callie_carlisle I won!! Welcome to the family Pen 🤍

@hayescarlisle77 Couldn't be happier for you three. 🤍

@markripley_colts Don't make me wrong about this. 🤍

@tweetiebird_falcons Congrats man. About time someone on the Colts did something right 😂

@alvin_chipmunk_ GOLDIE!!!!!

@simon_chipmunk_ THE GOAT 🐐

@theodore_chipmunk_ we are NOT worthy

@HandsOffDeck someone tell Shane Whitaker what he did

@RubyPeepersAlley Good. 🍺 Drinks are still not on the house.

@BodhiHensley_ you're welcome

View all 94,847 comments

CHAPTER
FIFTY-SEVEN

Decker

The Colts aren't signing me.

Jagger says the market is strong.

I say the market can take its time because I'm newly married and my daughter just started second grade and I'd like to be present to celebrate both of those things, but Jagger says that's not how free agency works, and I say I know, and so we do the meetings.

BOSTON

Pellegrino has the handshake of someone who wants you to know he lifts. He slides a folder across the table with numbers that are genuinely impressive and talks about legacy and championships and the history of the franchise for twenty-two minutes without asking me a single question about what I want.

I eat the steak they ordered for me.

I think about Hazel's second-grade teacher sending an email about the holiday play last week and asking if both parents would be available to help.

When Pellegrino finally asks if I have any questions, I say no and thank him for his time. Jagger tells me to get my shit together.

I buy a Boston sticker with a clover on it for Hazel.

Houston

The warmer climate is a plus. The GM here is a woman named Dana Chu who has done her homework. She knows my fielding percentages for the last four years, my numbers against left-handed pitching, my range factor. She asks good questions and listens to the answers, and the conversation is the best one I've had since this process started.

I almost mean it when I tell her I'll think about it.

On the flight back, I text Penelope a photo of the Houston skyline and she texts back a photo of Hazel's second-grade art project, which appears to be a self-portrait of a girl with a hula hoop and a large dog.

The dog is not subtle.

Hazel wants to name the dog Goldie, she texts.

I buy a Houston magnet with an astronaut on it for Hazel.

Seattle

It rains the entire time I'm there, which feels appropriate. The organization is rebuilding, which means they want my veteran presence in the clubhouse. That's a polite way of saying they want me to mentor the twenty-two-year-olds who will eventually take over my position. Hernandez is a good GM who is honest about where they are and what they're offering, and I respect his honesty even while knowing my answer.

I walk back to the hotel in the rain and call Penelope. She answers on the second ring and I say nothing for a second, and she says *that bad*, and I say *it's fine, it's just Seattle*, and she says *come home*, and I say *tomorrow*, and she says *Hazel wants to know if you're bringing her something*, and I say *obviously*, and she says *she wants a snow globe*, and I say *it's not snowing*, and she says *she doesn't care*, and I find a snow globe of the Space Needle in the hotel gift shop.

ATLANTA

The money is the best offer I've seen. The GM knows it and leans on it the way people lean on a thing when it's the strongest thing they have. The weather is good. The team is young and talented and hungry, and they'd use me well.

I sit across the table and do the math.

The flight home from Atlanta is two hours and twenty minutes. Chicago to Atlanta. I could manage that. During the season, it wouldn't matter. I'd be traveling, regardless. In the offseason, I'd be home.

Penelope said wherever you go, we go, and I know she meant it, but I also know what that means. The house. Hazel's school. Ripley. The life she built there.

Two hours and twenty minutes.

I eat the bread they bring to the table and tell them I'll be in touch.

I buy a stuffed Coca-Cola bear for Hazel.

NEW YORK

I was already in the city to shoot another ad campaign for Noir Cologne, so Jagger set up a meeting between Graham Sutter and me. The restaurant Sutter picks is the kind of place where the menu has no prices, and everybody acts as though money isn't a thing.

I arrive exactly on time because I'm not in the business of power moves with men I haven't decided if I even like yet. Sutter is already there, which is its own kind of power move —arriving first so I walk to him instead of the other way around. He stands when he sees me coming, hand already extended, smile already in place.

"Decker." The handshake is firm without being a contest. "Glad you made the trip."

"Thanks for the invitation."

He's in his late fifties, the kind of man who wears money like a second skin. Good suit, no tie, the specific casualness of someone who stopped needing to prove themselves a long time ago. He pours the wine himself when it arrives—an Italian red that probably costs more than my first car—and he does it the way you do things when you want them to feel intimate. Personal. As if he's a regular guy and this is just two people having dinner.

I've sat across from a lot of men in this business. I know the move.

"I'll be direct," he says, settling back in his chair. "I've wanted you on this roster for two years. The timing wasn't right before. It's right now."

"I appreciate the directness."

"Your numbers speak for themselves. Four Gold Gloves. Fielding percentage in the top two percent of the league for the last six seasons. You read the game better than anyone I've seen at that position in twenty years." He picks up his glass. "And the second half of this season was the best baseball you've played in your career. Which tells me you've got something to prove. I want to be the one who gives you the field to prove Shane Whitaker wrong."

I wonder which one of his lackeys gave him my stats.

The conversation moves on through the appetizers and into the main course. He's sharper than his presentation suggests, and the vision he has for the team is real and thought through. He talks about the roster, the gaps, where he sees them in two years. He doesn't oversell. He lets the facts do the heavy lifting, and they're genuinely good. It's New York, of course they're good. More than good.

The offer comes out with the main course, slid across the table on a single card.

Jagger was right. It's significant.

I look at it. Look up and at him.

"Three years," Sutter says. "With a player option on the fourth. We want you long-term, not as a bridge. The team around you is real. You're not walking into a rebuild."

I put the card face down. "What happened to Ferrara?"

"Retiring. Knee." He says it without sentiment. "Which is why the timing is right. I need someone who can step in day one. No adjustment period."

The waiter refills our glasses without being asked. Everything in this room runs on that frequency—smooth, anticipatory, no friction. Sutter has built himself an environment where things happen before he has to ask for them. He must be a regular.

I'm cutting my steak when he leans back and says, almost as an aside, "Heard you married Ripley's daughter?"

My knife slides along the plate and squeaks.

For the first time tonight, his smile doesn't seem genuine. "News travels."

"Yes, we got married a month ago."

"I give Ripley credit. Not sure I could handle if one of my players was seeing my daughter behind my back."

"Oh, I wasn't aware you had kids?" I just want to detour this conversation away from my personal life.

"I don't, but if I did." He winks and finishes off his glass of wine.

"I've known the Ripley family a long time."

His eyebrows lift, and he pours himself another glass.

"Good family. Ripley's one of the best managers in the

league." He swirls his glass. "Must be an interesting dynamic. Dating within the organization. I imagine that complicated your contract situation."

He says it lightly. Conversationally. As if he's making an observation about the weather. But I hear it in his tone.

I look at him across the table. Take a sip of my wine. "She had nothing to do with my contract situation. The Colts made their decision based on factors that had nothing to do with my wife."

"Of course." He nods, backing off the way people do when they've said the thing they wanted to say. "I just meant —it's a lot to navigate. New relationship, engagement, marriage, free agency all at once."

"It has been," I say, but I don't bother telling him I wouldn't change anything.

"Well." He raises his glass. "Congratulations."

I raise mine. We clink. We drink.

The conversation moves back to baseball, and he's smooth enough that we're halfway through dessert before I've finished deciding whether I like him. He hasn't done anything wrong exactly. Nothing I can specifically point to. He's professional and prepared, and the offer is real, and the position sounds as though it's mine.

I shake his hand at the end of the night and tell him I'll be in touch and walk out of the restaurant into the New York night.

I stand on the sidewalk.

Jagger is going to tell me this is the best offer I'll see. He's probably right.

I take out my phone and call Penelope.

She answers on the first ring.

"How was it?" Her voice is clipped, stressed.

"It's a good offer."

"You okay?"

"Yeah." I put my hand in my pocket. "I just need to get

home. I need to see you and Hazel and think about all of this at home."

"We're waiting."

"Tomorrow," I say. "I'll be home tomorrow."

I stand on the sidewalk a little longer after we hang up.

The number on that card is real and worth considering.

But so is the drawing of a little girl with a hula hoop and a dog on a refrigerator in Chicago.

So is *both parents* in a forwarded email.

So is a flower ring on a seven-year-old's right hand.

They are everything to me, but baseball is my career, my way to support them, give them a good life. And Graham Sutter made a serious offer that I'm not sure I can say no to.

I buy an I Love New York keychain for Hazel, although there is a chance she'll be able to buy any souvenir she wants because New York will be her home next year.

CHAPTER
FIFTY-EIGHT

Decker

The minute I step off the plane, Jagger's calling me.

"Hello?"

"Trojans want a meeting. Sooner the better. I told them this morning. I'll send you the address."

"I just want to go home." My voice holds a slight whine, but I don't care. I miss my family.

"This might enable you to stay in Chicago. Bianca Banks is the new GM after her daddy bought the team. She's got deep pockets. I know it's not the Colts, but you won't have relocate your family."

I walk toward baggage claim. "Do you really think they can beat New York's offer?"

I walk by a display of shirts in the gift shop and stop.

DeckCantGo

DeckorNothing

There are a bunch of others. Unreal. I wish I could thank the person responsible for this campaign to keep me with the

Colts. They put so much work into it, and it didn't help. On some level, I feel as though I've let them down.

"It's worth hearing her out. And Sutter called me this morning. He loves you. Wants you. He had to fly into Chicago today last minute for something, so if you want to shake hands and accept, he gave me his hotel info."

I wait by the baggage claim and lean on a pole away from everyone else. "Why do you think he wants me? I mean, not my worth. But what he's offering… it's more than anyone."

Jagger groans. "Only you, Davis. Only you would question the reason a guy wants to pay you the money he does. New York has the deepest pockets, and they pay for their players. It's the reason they win so often—they have the most talent on their team. You're hot right now. Between the way you played the second half of the season and the fact Chicago is running a Save Decker campaign, it says that you're the it player. The it players get the money. So just enjoy it."

I nod although he can't see me. "Okay. Send me the address for the Trojans meeting."

"Good boy, I'll be in touch."

He sends me the address, and I blow out a breath. At least if I play for the Trojans, we can stay in Chicago. I'm just not sure they can offer me what New York is.

Guess I'll find out.

Bianca Banks is already at the corner table when I walk in.

She's younger than I expected. Sharp eyes, the posture of someone who feels she needs to prove her worth. She has a black coffee in front of her and a tablet open, and when I sit down, she doesn't do the thing people do where they pretend they weren't watching the door.

"You're two minutes late," she says to her computer screen.

"Chicago traffic, and I just got off a plane."

"I walked." She slides the tablet toward me. My stats, same as everyone else, but annotated differently. Margin notes. Questions. Things she actually wants to talk about rather than things designed to impress me. "I'm not going to tell you the Trojans are a better organization than the Colts. You know this city, and you know the rivalry between us, so I won't insult your intelligence."

I like her immediately. I don't want to, but I do. "Then why am I here?"

"I need a third baseman who can play defense in his sleep and mentor two kids in my infield who are talented, but twenty-three years old and making every mistake talented twenty-three-year-olds make." She picks up her coffee. "I'm going to tell you the South Side is different from the North Side, but it's still Chicago. Congratulations on your new marriage. If you play for me, your family remains in the town they love and the town that seemingly loves you. All you do is change the color of your jersey."

"You say that like it's a small thing."

"It's a practical thing." She looks at me evenly. "Is it a dealbreaker?"

I look at the tablet.

Thirty-four years old, and I'm sitting in a coffee shop considering playing for the rival team I hate. Foster will lose his mind. Easton might actually disown me as his best friend. Hayes will be diplomatic about it for approximately four minutes before he says see you in the cross-town classic.

"What's the offer?"

She tells me.

It's not New York money, but it's decent. It doesn't have the flash of Sutter's card across a white tablecloth. It's just a number that respects the conversation.

I'm thinking about how to respond when the door opens. Ripley saunters in.

He sees me at the same moment I see him. His eyes move from me to the woman across the table, and something shifts in his expression that I have never seen on Mark Ripley's face before.

Something that looks a lot like dislike. Which I guess makes sense. The Colts and Trojans are rivals.

Bianca Banks sees him at the same moment.

She picks up her coffee and looks almost bored.

He breaks the distance.

"Mark," she says first.

"Bianca." His voice is even. Which for Ripley is its own kind of temperature. His gaze shifts to me. "Decker."

"Mark." I pause. "Just coffee."

"Of course." He holds my gaze for one second longer than necessary, then looks back at her. "How's the South Side treating you?"

"Better every year," she says pleasantly. "You should stop by sometime. See how the other half lives."

"I've seen it. Not as nice as the North Side. Have a good meeting." He nods once—at her, at me, at the table in general—and moves over to the counter.

I watch him order.

Bianca watches me watch him and doesn't comment, which tells me she has excellent instincts. A good thing for a GM.

"Old friends?" I arch an eyebrow.

"Something like that." She sets down her coffee. "He has a problem with how I run my organization. I have a problem with how he handles competition." She says it without heat, as though they're just facts. "We've disagreed for a long time."

"About what specifically?"

"Ask him." She looks back at the tablet. "It won't affect

my offer, and it won't affect how I manage you if you sign. I don't bring personal history into the field."

I glance back at the counter. Ripley has his coffee and is on his phone, his back to us, but he hasn't left yet.

"He thinks I poached two of his scouts last year," Bianca admits without looking up. "He's not entirely wrong."

I look at her.

The corner of her mouth moves. Not quite a smile, but she's definitely enjoying this.

Ripley passes our table on his way out. He puts his hand briefly on my shoulder without stopping—the same gesture he uses to say something without words—and walks out the door.

She bundles up all her stuff. "Take your time. But not too much." She stands and picks up her jacket. "The offer's real, Decker."

I sit for a moment with my coffee.

The Trojans.

God help me.

I pick up my phone to text Jagger.

> Still processing.

Process faster.

> I'll talk to Penelope and circle back.

Good.

I dial up Penelope on my way back home.

As always, she answers on the first ring. "How did it go?"

"I think it's between two offers, but one is significantly better." I have to be honest with her. The money, the position, the chance at championships are all waiting for me in New York, but the Trojans would keep us here.

I hate Shane Whitaker a little more for putting me in this position.

"Which two?" she asks.

"Trojans and New York."

"I figured… we need to talk, Decker."

I hate when she uses my full name outside of when she wants to have sex.

"Yeah, I'm on my way home. See you soon."

"I'll be here."

I really hope she's not about to tell me she's changed her mind about coming with me, but if so, decision made—I'll be a Trojan.

CHAPTER
FIFTY-NINE

Penelope

I'm officially out of time. I've tried to make contact, but of course he has to be a stubborn bastard.

Decker's Uber pulls up along the curb, and I open the front door, waiting for him to get his suitcase and walk up the stairs. As soon as he steps in, he drops it and wraps his arms around me, pulling me into him.

I relish the safety of his arms, but if I don't do this right away, I might lose my nerve. I take his hand and lead him into the family room.

"Have I been a good boy?" He waggles his eyebrows.

"Yeah, I'm not into that kind of role play." I sit on the couch and pat the spot next to me.

He takes a seat and lies back, closing his eyes. "I sleep like shit when you're not next to me." His forearm goes over his eyes, and he tries to get me to snuggle with him.

"Decker."

His eyes peek open, probably hearing something in my tone. "What's up?"

"I have to tell you something."

"Is Hazel okay?" He sits up straight. "She's at school, right?"

"Yeah."

His face softens. "Are you pregnant? Did something happen with your birth control? I gotta say, I was going to bring up trying. I mean, Hazel is only getting older, and I don't want them to be too far apart in age."

"Deck!"

He rears back and holds up both hands. "Okay, not pregnant. Got it."

I take his hands and inhale deeply. "Hazel's dad... I've tried to get a hold of him. I was trying to get his okay for me to tell you who her father is. I've emailed, called his office, and he won't take my calls or return any of my emails. He's definitely sticking to the part of the NDA that says there is to be no contact. Essentially, he made it like Hazel, and I, never existed."

His jaw flexes, but he lets me continue.

"Things have changed though, so... I'm going to tell you who it is."

"Okay." He stares at me.

"It has to stay between us. By breaking the NDA, I take the chance of having to pay back everything plus more. That money is for Hazel's future. And I could see him suing me."

"You can trust me. And you know I'll always look out for Hazel regardless of whatever this asshole does or doesn't do."

I nod, but he doesn't understand the severity of what I'm about to tell him. "Hazel's dad is..."

"Hey, Pen... you can trust me."

I nod, but tears fill my eyes. "I know I can. It's just... I'm going to crush your dreams at the same time, and that's what is the hardest for me."

He frowns, a confused look on his face.

"Hazel's dad is Graham Sutter."

His hands go limp in mine, and his Adam's apple bobs. "Graham Sutter, general manager of the New York team, or some other random Graham Sutter?"

I tilt my head and give him a look.

He bolts up off the couch.

"I'm sorry, Deck. If you want to take the offer, I understand. I know it's the best one you've gotten, and I don't know what that means for us—"

"Fuck that, I'm not taking anything he has to offer." He whirls around. "I'm not playing for a man like that."

I sit back on the couch and cross my legs, letting him process the news I've known this entire time and was unable to share with him. Graham left me no choice. I have no idea why he even wants Decker, knowing he's my husband now and the stepfather of his biological daughter.

"How can he sit across from me at dinner?" He paces. "He even brought you up, how we just got married. Something felt off, but I couldn't figure it out. God, he's good." He turns to me. "Why does he want me? It would bring you and Hazel right to him, and if—"

"I have no idea," I answer. "Our relationship was brief. We were only together a few times. He was friends with my dad, and it just kind of happened. After I found out I was pregnant, he denied it, then the paternity test results came in, and he had the papers sent to me. I never even talked to him after our one brief conversation when I told him I was pregnant. His lawyer served me with an NDA and a check to make Hazel and me go away. I took it."

"And your dad?"

"He knows only because I told him I was pregnant before talking to Graham."

He nods and swallows, then nods again. "Well, I'm not going to play for him. He's gotta be fucking delusional." He sits next to me and puts his hands on mine. "Thank you for telling me, for trusting me with this."

I nod, nervous that he seems so calm. But that's Decker for you, it's always brewing just under the surface.

"How the fuck could he sit across from me at that dinner. At one point he literally told me he didn't have any kids." His jaw tightens, and I run my palm over it.

"That's just the kind of man he is."

"It makes me want to tell him that I know and that he can take whatever fucking games he's playing and fuck off."

"You can't. I'll lose everything." Unshed tears rest in the corners of my eyes.

He places his hand on my cheek. "I would never say anything unless you said it was okay, Pen. But damn it, I want to stand up for you and Hazel. Tell him what a piece of shit he is for treating you and Hazel the way he did."

I wrote Graham off a long time ago, but I can see how heated Decker is. The idea of letting him have a go at Hazel's absent father does hold some appeal.

Decker turns his head and kisses the center of my palm. "Pen, you know if he came after you that I'd pay. Without question."

"Do it." The words are out of my mouth in a rush.

Decker arches a dark eyebrow.

"Do it." I nod. I trust this man implicitly.

"Thank you. I'll make sure he doesn't bother you after our conversation though." He leans forward and kisses me, then takes out his phone.

He types out a text and pockets it.

"I'm gonna shower, then I'll be gone for a little bit, but I'll be back before it's time to pick Hazel up from school." He kisses me again and gets up, picks up his suitcase, and goes upstairs.

I blow out a breath and fall back onto the couch. Why

can't Shane Whitaker just be a stand-up man and re-sign the best third baseman in the league?

My phone dings on the table with an Instagram notification, and I pick it up. It's worth one last attempt to get Decker signed to the Colts. This man is going to put his entire career on the line to protect Hazel and me. The least I can do is try to save his job until he's actually signed with another team.

CHAPTER
SIXTY

Decker

Penelope was worried. I saw it on her face after I showered and told her I'd be back before pick-up.

Nothing will stop me from giving a piece of my mind to that prick. I probably should calm down more, but I'm thinking retirement looks good right about now.

Sutter is staying at the Langham. Not surprising. It's the best hotel in Chicago.

I text him from the lobby.

I'm downstairs. Coming up.

Graham Sutter: (thumbs up emoji).

He probably thinks I'm here to shake hands and agree to his offer.

I ride the elevator up, trying to cage my rage so I can manage to have a conversation with him.

The hallway is quiet the way expensive hotel hallways

always are. Thick carpet, low lighting, expensive paintings on the walls. I find his room number and knock twice.

He opens it, wearing an expensive dress shirt, jacket off, the ease of a man settling in for a celebration. His smile is already in place. It looks a little more practiced now.

"Decker." He steps back to let me in. "Champagne is on the way."

"Why do you want me?" The heat already present in my tone tells me there's no way this will be a calm conversation.

I step inside, but I don't sit. I stand in the middle of his hotel room with my hands in my pockets so I won't get arrested for assault.

He turns from the door. The smile stays in place but the quality of it changes, the way lighting changes when a cloud moves past the sun. Same light, different temperature.

"Let's talk through whatever concerns you have," he says. "The offer is strong. I heard the Trojans are pulling at you, but New York—"

"It's not about New York. It's not about the offer or the money or the position." I look at him steadily. "Why me?"

His face goes very still for a beat, then he smiles again and raises his hands. "You got me. I have a little competition with Shane Whitaker. He's an idiot for not re-signing you. I'd like to prove to him how wrong he was." He smiles as though that would satisfy me.

"No. I mean, why would you want me when *they'd* be coming with me?"

"Who?" Still playing stupid, I see.

"I know who you are to her," I say. "I know what you did. So I'm not here to sign with you because I will never play for a man who wrote a check to make his daughter go away."

He sets down his drink and still has the nerve to hold the same arrogance he did at the restaurant. "I see Penelope broke her NDA. That's serious legal exposure. I'd think carefully about—"

"Don't." I step toward him. Not threatening. Just removing the comfortable distance he's used to operating from. "Don't finish that sentence. Don't call a lawyer. Don't send her a letter." I hold his gaze. "Because if you try to enforce that NDA, I will make sure every person in this league knows exactly who you are. Think about that story, Graham. You were probably, what? In your late forties at the time? A woman barely out of college. A child you denied and paid off to make disappear." I give him time to really think about it. "Imagine what the media would do with that story. Imagine how New York would feel."

His jaw tightens.

"It wouldn't be good," I say. "For you."

He's quiet for a long moment. The only sound is the hum of the hotel heater.

"You're making a mistake," he says finally. "The offer is genuine. Whatever you think of me personally—"

"Personally? You have to be joking. She's mine. *They* are mine. And I will never regret not playing for you."

Something flickers behind his eyes, and I'm certain he knows how serious I am.

"This is done. Don't test me, because if you go after her, I go after you. Stay the fuck away from my wife and my daughter." I turn and stalk toward the door.

Once the door closes behind me, I draw in a deep breath in an attempt to calm the adrenaline coursing through me and demanding an outlet.

As soon as I'm outside the hotel and my anger has dissipated, I call Penelope.

"Done," I say when she answers.

A rush of breath. "Are you okay? Did you hit him?"

I look up at the Langham once, still tempted to go back up there and knock him out. Then I look away from it because he doesn't deserve any more of my attention.

"Unfortunately, no," I say. "But I'm good. I'll be home in twenty minutes."

"Do you mind getting Hazel? I had to run out to do an errand."

I frown. "Where? I'll meet you."

"No, I'll be home soon."

"Okay." Something sounds off. "I love you."

"I love you. See you soon."

I put my phone in my pocket and slip into an Uber, determined to put this all behind me, but very aware I still don't know where I'm playing next year.

CHAPTER
SIXTY-ONE

Penelope

I'm desperate for a miracle, so I'm going to play every card I have. Especially since Decker just turned down the offer of a lifetime for me.

I can't remember the last time I was this nervous though.

Derek, Shane's assistant, tells me I can get fifteen minutes with Shane. I'll take what I can, so I sit in the waiting area of the Colts' front office. I look at my rings, and I think about Decker and how he shouldn't have to sacrifice anything.

Derek waves me in, so I gather my courage.

Shane is on the phone when I walk in, clearly talking to another GM, negotiating players as if they're sports bets in Vegas. His laugh makes me want to cringe. Talk about not trusting someone. Makes me think that maybe Decker should go play for Bianca Banks.

He gestures to the chair across from his desk and ends his call.

I sit.

"Miss Ripley." He folds his hands. "What can I do for you?"

"Mrs. Davis," I correct him.

Something moves across his face. Quickly. Gone before I can name it. "That's right. Cute post by Decker. Congratulations."

"Thank you." I set my folder on the desk. Not opening it yet, just placing it on the edge. "I'll be direct. I'm here about Decker's contract."

He leans back slightly. "Not the Dugout Social Club?"

"No."

"Decker's contract, or lack thereof, is a matter between the organization and his representation."

I hate that he talks so matter-of-factly about a player. They're people.

"I understand that. I'm not here to negotiate." I keep my voice even and professional. "I'm here because I think there's information that might be useful to you before you lose your chance to snag him."

I can tell he's not particularly interested in anything I have to say.

I open the folder. "Have you heard of the #HandsOffDeck Campaign?"

"Is this the Instagram girl who loves his ad for Noir?"

"So, you haven't noticed the entire city pulling for Decker? Wanting you to sign him?"

"When something is thrown in your face so much, it's hard to miss," he says.

"And you're not afraid of pissing off the fans?"

He laughs and opens a drawer, grabs a jerky stick, and takes a big bite.

"As of this morning, that account has more than a hundred thousand followers. It's been covered by three sports blogs, two local news segments, and was mentioned in the *Tribune* last week." I turn to the next page. "Thirty-one businesses within a two-mile radius of Webber Field have created Decker-themed products since the campaign launched. The Decker Defender at the café on Clark. Goldie's Grinder at the Lincoln Park deli. The Save Decker cookie that a bakery one block down from here is selling out of every week." I turn the page. "Here's the social media engagement numbers for the Colts' account on posts featuring Decker versus posts without him. The difference is significant."

I'll give Whitaker one thing. He looks at the papers. Not picking them up. Just looking.

"The city is paying attention," I say. "And when a player leaves—especially one with this kind of community investment—people remember who made that decision."

He nods slowly. It's the nod of a man acknowledging that words are being said, but who's not moved by them.

"There's one more thing you should know." I lean back in my chair, linking my fingers together. "Graham Sutter made Decker a significant offer and wanted him badly enough to fly to Chicago to seal the deal."

That one lands. I see a small recalibration behind his eyes.

"Decker hasn't made a decision… yet. He wants to stay here. He has built his life here, and he wants to keep building it here. He's committed to bringing this team home a championship. I don't think that's a small thing when you're deciding what this organization looks like going forward."

Whitaker relaxes back into his chair. His expression hasn't really changed since I walked in. He's made his decision and is not moved by the woman in love with the man.

"Mrs. Davis, I appreciate you coming in. I understand you have a personal stake in this situation, and I respect that. The organization's decisions about the roster are based on a number of factors that I'm not in a position to discuss with you." He folds his hands again, giving away nothing. "I'll take what you've shared under consideration."

He won't. We both know he won't.

His voice is courteous, and now he's waiting for me to leave so he can get on with his day.

I gather my folder and stand. "He's the best third baseman in this league." I try to keep my voice from being too emotional. "You know that. Everyone in this building knows that. I hope your decision reflects it."

"Thank you for coming in." He doesn't bother standing to see me out.

Derek is already at the door.

I walk out through the waiting area, down the hallway, and out of the front office. The cold November air hits my face as I stand on the sidewalk outside Webber Field and look up at the stadium.

I did what I could.

I take out my phone and do not call Decker because there's nothing to tell him yet. He doesn't need to know I'm here.

Instead, I go to my @HandsOffDeck Instagram account and make a post as a last attempt at saving my husband's job.

@HandsOffDeck
⏰ THE CLOCK IS TICKING ⏰
Free agency decisions are coming, and we are NOT going quietly!!!
Decker Davis turned down New York to stay in Chicago.
He chose this city.
Now it's time for this city to choose him back.
Here's what you can do RIGHT NOW:
📧 Email the Colts front office. Let them know how you feel.
📱 Tag @ChicagoColts in every post. Every. Single. One.
📍 Show up. Wear your Goldie gear. Make some noise.

🍪 Buy a Save Decker cookie. Support the businesses that support our guy.

Shane Whitaker—we see you. Chicago sees you.

Don't let the best third baseman in the league leave this city.

#HandsOffDeck #SaveDecker #GoldieStays #ChicagoColts #DeckerDavis #OurCity #NotDoneYet

CHAPTER
SIXTY-TWO

Decker Davis Re-Signs with Chicago Colts on Four-Year, $72 Million Deal

Written By Bryce Cavanaugh | The Breakout

CHICAGO —The Chicago Colts have officially re-signed third baseman Decker Davis to a four-year contract worth $72 million, with a mutual option for a fifth year. The deal, confirmed Tuesday morning by both the organization and Davis's agent, keeps the four-time Gold Glove winner in Chicago.

Davis, 34, spent the offseason as one of the most closely watched names in free agency after the Colts initially declined to extend a qualifying offer. Multiple teams were reported to have made significant runs at the veteran infielder, including at least one major market club whose offer was described by sources as "substantial." Davis declined them all.

The signing ends what became as much a civic conversation

as a baseball one. The @HandsOffDeck account, which appeared in September and amassed more than a hundred thousand followers by November, became a rallying point for fans frustrated by the organization's apparent willingness to let one of its most decorated players walk. Businesses in the Webber Field area ran Decker-themed specials for the better part of two months. The Save Decker cookie, sold at a bakery one block from Webber Field, was reported to have sold out for six consecutive weeks.

Whether any of that moved the needle inside the front office remains a matter of speculation. What isn't speculation is the result.

Davis posted the best defensive numbers of his career this past season, with a fielding percentage that ranked first among National League third basemen and a second-half offensive surge that silenced early questions about his trajectory. He remains one of the most competent players at his position in the game.

The Colts did not make any additional comments beyond a brief organizational statement: *"Decker Davis is a Chicago Colt."*

 # GoldieStays

EPILOGUE

Easton

Love. It's fucking everywhere. I always had my teammates and Peeper's to count on, but one by one, love has slipped through the cracks here too.

I grew up with parents who loved one another. Hell, they were the couple everyone talked about in our small Alaskan town. Their story is probably written somewhere in the Lake Starlight archives.

I'm a Bailey, and in Lake Starlight, that means something. The problem is I'm now the problem child of my family. I moved away, which is fine with them, but I have no interest in settling down, which none of my family understands. Jesus, even my sister is settled with a kid. If someone had bet on which of us would have been married with a kid first, most would have bet on me.

I'm not stupid like my teammates. I'm not saying love isn't for me. I'm just saying it's not for me *right now*. I only have a few more good years to play ball before some hot new shortstop comes for my spot. And I don't plan on going down without a fight.

I can't say love doesn't look nice though.

I glance around the back room at Peeper's.

First there was Hayes. He didn't stand a chance. It was his first full year with us, so I don't know who he was before coming to the Colts, but the rumors would suggest that he wasn't looking for love. Now, he's sitting here with four kids and a wife. What the hell?

Lake and Lincoln are arguing at the pinball game about whose turn it is.

"You two break it, and they're paying." Ruby points at Hayes and Leighton.

They both mumble sorrys. Everyone is a little afraid of Ruby.

"I told you two." Leighton gets up to talk to them both while Hayes holds their new baby girl, Flora, named after the Flora Conservatory. She had to be named after a Chicago landmark.

The name thing is a long story, all of us were vying for the naming rights. I personally liked River for the Chicago River.

After them, the one man I thought would be my ride or die in bachelorhood fell. Who the hell saw Foster Davis settling down?

He used to walk into a room and make it smaller just by being in it. Now, he's walking over to Callie as she places a dart in their eighteen-month-old Ellis's hand.

"You can't give her a dart," he says.

"She wants to throw at the dartboard." Callie tips her head to the side.

"And she'll poke her eye out." He takes the dart out of Ellis's hand, and she cries.

Callie snickers at Leighton and Penelope.

"Fine." He gives it back to Ellis.

Callie walks her up to the dartboard and presses it into the board with Foster's help.

I remember Foster Davis in college. I remember him in the minors. I remember the younger version of him who would have made fun of the man he is today.

And last, my best friend on the team, Decker. I'm still not over the fact that we almost lost him as a teammate. The Colts wouldn't have been the same without him.

Deep down, I always knew he was a believer in love. But he masked it well.

Decker and Penelope couldn't get their shit together for so many years. Now look at him, sitting there with Penelope on one side and Hazel on the other, sneaking french fries to a golden retriever in a sports bar.

"Gentle, Sparkles," he says, feeding the dog a fry from the Portillo's they brought with them.

Did he even get a say in what they named their dog?

Love. Ugh.

They're all happy. Even Decker and Foster have squashed whatever shit was coming between them. From what Decker told me, therapy got them to where they are today. It's nice that we can all be in the same room without tension rising every time one of them says something to the other. The other day, I overhead Foster talking about their mom moving to Chicago to be closer to Ellis and Hazel.

So, I'm alone on the single train now. And that's fine because I have the Chipmunks, although I wish their offseason coincided with mine.

"Another round of chocolate milks?" Ruby comes in with a tray for the kids.

Is this really my life now?

Sadly, it is. I love my friends, but I feel a little left out.

That doesn't mean I'm going to try to find someone to settle down with though.

I check my phone.

There's a text.

I read it.

I put my phone in my pocket, and I look around the table one more time. Decker with his family. Foster with his. Hayes with his. The dog on the floor who's already won Ruby over. Just look at the dog treat on the tray of chocolate milks.

I finish my beer and stand. "All right." I grab my jacket off the back of the chair. "I'm out."

Everyone looks at me, then at each other.

"Where are you going?" Decker asks.

"Out."

"It's eight thirty." Foster frowns.

"I'm aware."

"You never leave before eleven," Hayes says.

"New chapter." I slide my arms into the sleeves of my jacket, then walk over to the door.

The whole table is still watching me. They never mind their own business. I can't fault them—I don't either.

I stop right before I open the door and hear Ruby talking on the other side. "What the hell? This is a bar, not the safe haven baby box at the fire department." A few seconds later she walks in with a baby carrier.

"Now they're just being delivered by the stork? Slow down, guys. I'll never catch up." I laugh and look back at my friends.

They all have confused expressions on their faces— eyebrows drawn, downturned smiles, widened eyes.

"It was a joke. Excuse me, Rubes, I got somewhere to be." I try to slide past her, but she thrusts the carrier at me. "Rubes?"

I peek my head in the carrier. The baby is cute. Dark hair with a slight auburn tint. From the blue clothes, I assume it's a boy, but who really knows. "He's cute." I twist my body to get past her and through the door.

"This was just delivered for you." She leaves me no choice but to grab the carrier in my arms.

"Funny, Rubes. Last thing I ordered from Uber Eats was Thai food, not a baby."

The sound of chairs scraping across the floor echoes through the room, and suddenly all the women are huddled at my side.

"Oh, he is cute," Leighton says.

"He has the most adorable little nose." Callie taps it lightly with her index finger.

"And looks at his little lips moving as he sleeps." Penelope reaches in and runs her finger down his arm.

"What's going on, Rubes?" I look after her, but she's already half out the door.

"A guy came in and said there was a delivery for someone here. Your name is on the letter."

"Letter?" Callie reaches in and finds it sandwiched between the baby's arm and the side of the carrier.

Sure enough, my name is on the envelope. And so there could be no mistake that it was meant for some other Easton, my jersey number is scribbled right next to my name.

"Holy shit," Decker mumbles behind me.

I turn and place the baby carrier on the table, and everyone surrounds the little one.

"Can I hold it?" Monroe asks.

"Not now, sweetie," Leighton says.

"What is this? A joke?" I look around, hoping someone else is connecting the dots differently than I am.

"I don't think it's a joke, Kodiak, I think you're a dad." Hayes reaches the same conclusion I have.

"Hey," Callie says quickly, grabbing my arm. "Breathe."

I try.

My ears start ringing.

The edges of my vision go fuzzy.

And I'm vaguely aware of more chairs skidding along the floor right before everything goes black.

The End

COCKAMAMIE
UNICORN RAMBLINGS

If you read the Cockamamie Unicorn Ramblings from *The Wild Card*, you know that we really wrote ourselves into a corner with Decker's book.

When we first put him in *Mr. Charming* (*The Nest* #4), we didn't really know he'd even be in this series. We hadn't decided if we were even going to go to baseball after *The Nest* when he first appeared on the page. But we put him in as a Colts player just in case. And then we did what we always do and added one line about him still pining away for a girl from his past. It was one of those things that just came out while writing. And so, we had to make good on that.

We can't even remember when we decided that Foster and Decker wouldn't have a present-day relationship. You'd think we would learn by now, but half the fun is trying to find our way out of the corner. Although we will admit sometimes it's like we're both blindfolded, sitting on Zoom in silence as we try to think of something to start the snowball rolling downhill during a brainstorming session.

And… Decker's story was originally going to be book one, but when it was solidified that his story was a second-chance romance, we knew that it moved him down the order.

So, needless to say, going into *The Hotshot*, all we knew was that he would be given a second chance with a woman from his past. Then Penelope just popped up on the page with her daughter and the new coach. Foster addressed her, she made that comment about the Davis brothers… and suddenly we saw their story. Although it did change slightly.

All in all, we love how Decker and Penelope's story turned out, but this might be the one book that changed the most—especially during the writing phase. It seemed like we were constantly on Zoom trying to reconfigure their journey.

So what specifically changed?

• It was going to be Foster who cheated with Penelope and not Decker. She was never going to know that Foster opened the door one morning to Decker on her doorstep. We flipped that right before Foster's book.

• Penelope was going to be a widower. Her husband would have died a year before she came to the team.

• The baby daddy had passed, and his parents wanted custody because he didn't take responsibility for Hazel, and they never knew about her. At one point, they were going to kidnap Hazel (yes, there are no limits in our brainstorming sessions).

• Hazel's dad was going to be involved, but would cause problems.

• Penelope's mom was going to have just died.

• And yes, we did throw multiple scenarios around where Hazel was Decker's child.

We're telling you, we were everywhere on this one! BUT we always believe that, however the story turns out, it was the right path. And bonus—we got to see our wonderful unshowered, no-makeup selves over Zoom more than we would otherwise!

As always, we have a lot of people to thank for getting this book into your hands…

Nina and the entire Valentine PR team. We appreciate you SO much!

Cassie from Joy Editing for the line edits and for always graciously working with our chaotic schedules. Asking you a week before for a rush, and you always deliver for us!

Ellie from My Brother's Editor for line edits and proofreading. We love you!

Olivia Winston for giving our manuscript one final look over before we hit publish. We love your notes!

Simone and Angela at Buerosued for our illustrated cover. Your work is amazing as always, and we're so happy to be working with you on another series. Decker, Penelope and Hazel couldn't be more perfect!

All the bloggers and influencers who choose to read us when you have so many options out there. We're appreciative and honored to be on your list of must-reads and love reading all your reviews, edits, and more. The support you've thrown behind this series has been tremendous and we are extremely grateful!

All the Piper Rayne Unicorns who support us all day, every day. We'd be lost without you answering our polls and telling us what you love and hate. We strive to listen to you and give you what you love about our books—with a twist every time. Sorry to all of you who probably did want Hazel to be Decker's. LOL

You, the reader, who has an abundance of books to choose from—thank you for picking up one of ours. Word of mouth is always the best form of advertising, and we appreciate you sharing your love for this series with the romance community!

Finally, we're on to Easton—the one most of you Bailey fans have been waiting patiently for since he first popped into *Mr. Heartbreaker*. And let us tell you, you know you're in for a ride when we change the storyline and tropes in the middle of writing the book prior. At least this time we didn't write ourselves into a corner. Maybe we are learning from our mistakes!

See you soon!

xo,

Piper & Rayne

ALSO BY PIPER RAYNE

The Dugout

The Hotshot

The Wild Card

The Rulebreaker

The Troublemaker

The Nest

Mr. Heartbreaker

Mr. Broody

Mr. Swoony

Mr. Charming

The Nest Before Christmas

Hockey Hotties

Countdown to a Kiss

My Lucky #13

The Trouble with #9

Faking it with #41

Tropical Hat Trick (Novella)

Sneaking around with #34

Second Shot with #76

Offside with #55

Chicago Grizzlies

On the Defense

Something like Hate

Something like Lust

Something like Love

Kingsmen Football Stars

False Start

You Had Your Chance, Lee Burrows

You Can't Kiss the Nanny, Brady Banks

Over My Brother's Dead Body, Chase Andrews

Modern Love

Charmed by the Bartender

Hooked by the Boxer

Mad about the Banker

Single Dads Club

Real Deal

Dirty Talker

Sexy Beast

Hollywood Hearts

Mister Mom

Animal Attraction

Domestic Bliss

Bedroom Games

Cold as Ice

On Thin Ice

Break the Ice

Chicago Law

Smitten with the Best Man

Tempted by my Ex-Husband

Seduced by my Ex's Divorce Attorney

Blue Collar Brothers

Flirting with Fire

Crushing on the Cop

Engaged to the EMT

White Collar Brothers

Sexy Filthy Boss

Dirty Flirty Enemy

Wild Steamy Hook-up

The Rooftop Crew

My Bestie's Ex

A Royal Mistake

The Rival Roomies

Our Star-Crossed Kiss

The Do-Over

A Co-Workers Crush

Holiday Romances

Single and Ready to Jingle

Claus and Effect

Merry Kissmas

Yule Be Mine

The Baileys

Lessons from a One-Night Stand

Advice from a Jilted Bride

Birth of a Baby Daddy

Operation Bailey Wedding (Novella)

Falling for My Brother's Best Friend

Demise of a Self-Centered Playboy

Confessions of a Naughty Nanny

Operation Bailey Babies (Novella)

Secrets of the World's Worst Matchmaker

Winning my Best Friend's Girl

Rules for Dating Your Ex

Operation Bailey Birthday (Novella)

The Greene Family

My Twist of Fortune

My Beautiful Neighbor

My Almost Ex

My Vegas Groom

A Greene Family Summer Bash (Novella)

My Sister's Flirty Friend

My Unexpected Surprise

My Famous Frenemy

A Greene Family Vacation (Novella)

My Scorned Best Friend

My Fake Fiancé

My Brother's Forbidden Friend

A Greene Family Christmas (Novella)

Lake Starlight

The Problem with Second Chances

The Issue with Bad Boy Roommates

The Trouble with Runaway Brides

The Drawback of Single Dads

The Complication with the Best Man

Plain Daisy Ranch

One Last Summer

The One I Left Behind

The One I Stood Beside

The One I Didn't See Coming

Chasing Forever

Chasing Love

Chasing Home

Love in Apartment 3B

Hit or Miss

Three's A Crowd

Good on Paper

The Abbott Brothers

Rent a Husband

Buy a Boyfriend

Standalones

Don't Mind if "I Do"